# The Godhead Spot

A Neurotheological Thriller

M. St. Croix

*for Jeff*

"Dazzling and tremendous,
how quick the sun-rise would kill me,
If I could not now and always send sun-rise out of me."

Walt Whitman

# 1

# The Book of Judd

When he was growing up in Baxter, North Dakota, the deep timbre of Judd Russell's voice was a common conversation starter. But no one regarded it as a gift from God until he turned fourteen. After hearing him sing in the church choir, Reverend Hocklund took Judd's father, George, aside, "Your son sings like a strangled frog, but his vocal cords rattle stained glass. How would you feel about him reading a passage from the Bible this Sunday?"

Without asking for his son's approval, George said, "We'd be honored"—three words that charted the teenager's course like a fixed star.

Trinity of Christ Church stood on a glacial moraine in the center of town. It was built in 1928 with stone blocks cut from a local quarry. It's high copper spire shone like a lighthouse to farmers plowing their fields a mile away. The church's acoustics amplified Judd Russell's readings from Ecclesiastes, Proverbs, Psalms and John, enlivening the words so much they resonated in the bones of the faithful.

Initially nervous, in time Judd let his voice own the hallowed space. He added emphasis to the scripture, batting and fisting the air, his right hand a conductor's wand. Within only a few months he became a prominent feature of every service—the opening act for Reverend Hocklund's sermon. And his dad felt honored. Surely Jesus must have anointed his troublesome, good-for-nothing son.

It didn't take long for Judd to revel in the narcotic of attention. Standing tall at the pulpit above the locked eyes of worshippers, he felt full of purpose and potency. And they wanted more. Much more. After repeated requests, the young man's one-minute readings of scripture inflated to five, six, and seven minutes.

Word spread. Attendance jumped, the pews often filled to capacity. The parking lot had to be expanded. Many hailed the young man as "Christianity's Orator of the Future." Some even asked why his name was not on the church's marquee.

Behind closed doors the elders plotted Judd's life in timely increments— seminary college, cross-country tours, mass assemblies, an evangelical TV show. He was unaware the church was grooming him to be the next Billy Graham. But he knew full well his weekly presence boosted the Sunday till. After four years, he wanted in on the action. Money, yes, money. Pots of it. Gushy praise and pats on the back can't buy a reliable car. Nor did his father's pride satisfy Judd's high-and-mighty sense of self-worth. Not by a country mile. No more secretly pocketing a twenty from the offering plate. No, he wanted stacks of righteous cash. Call it an endowment, call it a token of gratitude, whatever. He felt beyond entitled and it was time to collect.

Then came an unseasonably hot and humid Sunday in early June. The stifling air inside the church felt like breathing fur. Judd, now eighteen, was days from graduating from Baxter

High. After the congregation sluggishly sang "How Firm a Foundation," he ascended the pulpit with a bold new message.

He'd been keeping a journal of his thoughts under the title, *The Book of Judd*, and felt it was time for a sermon of his own. And why not? If he was the "emergent" voice of the Holy Spirit, he needed to deliver something true to his spirit. Something that would shake the floor, ring the bell, inspire cheers, roaring applause, and prevail upon the church to deposit 50 percent of its proceeds into his measly bank account.

As hymnals closed, he set his Bible on the oak podium. A token of appreciation from Reverend Hocklund, the holy text was big as a cinderblock with a lavishly embossed cover and thick parchment pages edged in gold.

Judd scanned the faces of family and friends, of merchants, farmers, nurses— working-class folks and students who called him "the giraffe" because of his gangly, six-foot-seven-inch height. No, he may not have been valedictorian for his high school graduation, but he would be a mouthpiece for the Lord.

"It is time ..." Judd nodded at the life-size crucifix on the back wall—the white figure of Jesus hand-carved in fine detail, head bowed, fingers curled, square-headed spikes protruding from both palms.

He turned back to the assembly. "Time to save our Savior." He opened the bible to an inserted piece of paper with words he'd written and memorized.

"Time his suffering comes to an end. He's been up there too long, impaled, alone, stranded for two ...thousand ... years ... hanging over our heads, woeful and wronged." There were muffled coughs, a baby's cry. A nervous leg drummed the floor.

"It's time we release Christ our Lord from his misery! Time we pried out the spikes, bandaged his bleeding wounds, and made kindling of that horrid cross. Let's stop perpetuating the persecution and give the Son of God his peaceful due." Parishioners squirmed. One whispered: "Is he saying what I think he's saying?"

"He may have died for our sins, but let us each bear witness to the sin of reenacting his suffering with this grotesque mannikin of torture! Let us free his likeness from an eternity of pain!"

It took a while for the congregation to stop fanning their flushed faces, for jaws to slacken, lips to part.

Judd swelled to crescendo.

"It's time to save our Savior! Time to take him down from the cross! Take him down, down, down off every altar in the land!"

Instead of amens and hallelujahs, a tide of gasps rippled to the rear wall. To the surprise of some, two worshippers booed.

The Reverend laid his oven mitt of a hand on Judd's shoulder. He nudged him from the podium and growled, "Nuff of that."

# 2
# Judd and Jury

After his "down from the cross" catastrophe, Judd thought he lost everything—his purpose, his identity, his popularity. But losing everything came years later, after an ice fisherman reeled a woman's body out of Lake Minnetonka.

She'd gone missing for three days before a jigging lure hooked her diamond wedding ring. Up through the augured ice hole a blue, wrinkled hand surfaced and, according to the fisherman, "waved a howdy at me."

The middle-aged woman's death created a stir in the community. His fellow actors told Judd she championed the under-privileged and was a major Guthrie Theater donor. Not that he followed any of it. Not until the next winter when he sat in a jury box as her husband stood on trial for her murder.

It was late December. An arctic freeze clamped Minneapolis between icicle teeth. Even the halls of the courthouse felt cold enough to hang meat. The chill intensified Judd's bitterness. Jury duty robbed him of the daylight hours he needed to audition for the Guthrie's upcoming season. At twenty-six, Judd had landed his first union role in the theater's annual *A Christmas Carol.* He played "The Ghost of the Future Yet to

Come." Typecast, some claimed, because of his skyscraping height. No stilts or boot extensions required. Drape a cavernous hood over his head and point him at Scrooge. Befitting in retrospect, for it was during the court proceedings Judd Russell would meet *his* future yet to come.

They were deep into the trial when the prosecutor wanted to bring in new evidence. Up to then the proceedings limped along with circumstantial proof the husband murdered his wife. They found a hiccup in the man's out-of-town alibi, and a motive—since he was about to lose a mountain of money in their divorce settlement, he turned homicidal.

Spinning a different story, the defense submitted testimony to the wife's erratic mental history. How she became severely depressed about the divorce, then suicidal. After draining a DUI's worth of bourbon, she stepped from their lakeshore mansion, wandered aimlessly across the ice in nothing but ballet slippers and pink kimono, broke through and froze to death faster than she could drown.

The Judge, an imposing bald eagle with beaked nose, white hair, and black robe, asked the prosecutor the nature of the last-minute evidence.

"I wish to show the court what the victim saw before she died. Exhibit 21." The prosecutor held up a flash drive. "I beg the court's indulgence. This evidence is a scientific breakthrough. It rivals such astounding discoveries as X-rays and DNA. You and the jury will see images from a brain scan showing the defendant murdering his wife. I have experts who will explain the source of the evidence more clearly than I."

After a rabid objection from the defense, the Judge punched the white noise button and waved the attorneys to the bench.

By this time Judd had abandoned his first impression of the defense attorney and began to savor the man as a character worthy of study. He nicknamed him Sterling Chrome. "Observe and value another's mannerisms," an acting teacher once instructed. "You may draw on it someday."

The defense attorney exuded wealth and aplomb with his impeccable, famous-to-somebody suit and hair dyed virility-black. He strutted around oozing a cologne of confidence that he would acquit his client.

Across the aisle, the prosecuting attorney looked ashen, her labored voice nasal from a cold.

As the attorneys returned to their stations, the Judge informed the jury, "I don't know where this is heading, but I'm willing to grant the prosecution's last request." He signaled to the back of the courtroom.

Doors swung open. Two young men paraded in rolling equipment cases. They wore bomber hats, khakis under lab coats, and snow boots. A girl, eleven years old if a day, trailed behind carrying what looked like a big hat box.

"It's a Hail Mary," an elderly juror elbowed Judd.

Judd moaned. Just when he thought the trial reached the final act, along came another round.

Not being privy to the evidence beforehand, the defense had liberty to question the backgrounds of the brain-scanners before their presentation. The brothers, nineteen-year-old fraternal twins, Oakley and Chester Jolley, were sworn in. Their little sister remained at the prosecutor's table.

"Her name's Flannery," Chester informed the Judge. "But we call her Flea."

The defense attorney made a swift and thorough shakedown of the Jolley twins. He called them impostors with no degrees in science, let alone training in human anatomy, neurology, "or any ology."

"Must we hear testimony from unqualified Hobby Lobby hacks playing MRI video games in a garage?"

"An outbuilding," Chester corrected.

"My mistake, a pole barn. With all due respect Your Honor, I cannot allow these proceedings to veer into fantasyland while my client stands erroneously on trial for murder."

Chester asked the Judge if he could pose a single question.

With a nod from the Judge, Chester turned to the defense attorney and asked, "Where's the light source that illuminates your dreams? You have dreams, right, mister lawyer, sir?" Chester didn't wait for an answer. "So where's the projection booth that makes your dreams so vivid and colorful while your eyes are shut in sleep? Is there sunshine in your head?"

Judd never considered the question. Neither had the defense attorney, who crossed his arms and munched his lips as if tasting speechlessness for the first time.

"There's no headlights in your head," Chester continued, "but there are happy little circuits. And among the circuitry are optic nerves that run behind your eyes. These receive visual imprints of our experiences in the world. Some are stored, even cataloged, and some dismissed. Right now, your circuits are like pinballs binging-and- banging this way and that, wondering if what I'm telling you is important enough to store or flush like a deuce down your hypothalamoose."

Laughter pattered the courtroom.

The gavel tapped.

"Bullshit," the defendant grumbled.

"Zip your client's mouth," the Judge reprimanded.

The attorney waved a "calm-down" hand to the defendant, mouthing, "I got this," followed by a snide, it's-in-my-pocket wink. "Can't say I disagree with my client's assessment. Clearly this is a desperate, last-ditch effort to distract from the facts of the case with a hare*brained* hypothesis. Pun intended."

A rustling noise took the court's attention. The girl, Flea, opened the hat box and lifted an enlarged acrylic model of the human brain. She hoisted it over her head like a trophy.

The Judge curled a smile at her.

"Won't take but a minute," Chester urged.

"Your Honor!"

"Sit down, counselor."

The courtroom brightened. The Jolleys' energy boosted the brooding trial like a double espresso.

Flea scooted the model brain around the table to assist with Oakley's explanation.

"The nerves that run behind our eyes converge at what we call the optic nexus," he began.

The multi-colored model had movable sections. To show the location of the optic nexus, Flea yanked the brain apart in two hemispheres— a bit too forcibly. One of the eyeballs popped out and clacked across the hardwood floor.

"Whoops." Flea handed the left hemisphere to Chester and scurried to fetch the eyeball; her cheeks blushing with embarrassment.

"This nexus holds images for only a short time," Oakley said.

The jury swung its attention between Oakley's fingertip touching a slot on the plastic brain and the girl scrambling on her knees, grabbing the eyeball as it rolled to a stop under the defense table.

"By tapping into this pocket, it's possible to transmit the last things the dying person saw. An instant replay, so to speak."

Getting to her feet, Flea glanced across the table, froze, and sucked in a loud vacuum of air. Everyone looked at the girl, who held the eyeball right in the defendant's glum face.

"Your Honor!" The defense attorney leaped from his chair and clumsily positioned himself between the girl and the jury. "This circus must stop!"

"It's okay, Flea." Oakley tenderly guided her away. "She's never seen a trial before."

"Bailiff," the Judge called.

A dismayed Flea handed the eyeball to Oakley and left the courtroom with an escort.

"An unfortunate mishap," the Judge informed the jury. "Nonetheless, let us proceed."

Chester beamed at his brother and thumped his snow boots on the witness stand. "On with the show."

"Down boy," said the Judge.

The prosecutor cued a screen to lower from the ceiling. The courtroom dimmed and a dark rectangular shape appeared, fringed with flickering light.

"Here's the instant replay," the prosecutor said. "The shadow you see is the underside of a pillow pressed down on the victim's face. The side-to-side action of the pillow shows her resistance. She's fighting for her life."

For a moment the dark shape lifted away to reveal the strained face of the defendant, all teeth and bulging eyes.

"Here she wrestles the pillow away. For two seconds you can see her husband's murderous intent." The shadow returned and the screen went blank. "That's the last thing she saw before he smothered her to death."

Gasps and "Oh my gods" washed the courtroom. The defense attorney railed.

The gavel pounded hard.

When everyone quieted, the Judge asked Chester to explain their method. Chester gave a wry smile.

"Basically, it requires converting the optical electrochemical transmissions into digital imaging."

Oakley opened an equipment case and handed a camera scope to the prosecuting attorney, who held it up. "Exhibit 22."

Oakley went on, "We'd really like to tell everybody how we made the film, but we've been advised to keep it proprietary until our Death Sight Scanner is patented."

The defense attorney tossed his arms up, signaling a touchdown. The prosecutor wilted. Without a viable demonstration, the scanner came across as a cheesy sci-fi movie gizmo.

And that was that. The Jolley brothers wheeled their cases out the door.

After closing arguments, Judd and jury filed into the Deliberation Room. They scoffed and swiftly dashed the film as fake computer graphics. Much as Judd and another juror argued for the new evidence, the Jolley brothers' playfulness eroded any perception of competence. They looked more like carefree imps than inventive geniuses. The jury pored over the reasonable doubts. In less than an hour they returned with "Not guilty."

The verdict outraged Judd Russell. He couldn't shake the defendant's raging face in the film.

He killed her! How do you doctor that?

After the court adjourned, Judd cornered the prosecuting attorney in the lobby. Her weary eyes didn't deter him from pumping her for information about the Jolleys—how to reach them, by car, phone, email? He felt an invisible force tugging him to them—the lure of astronomical dollars.

# 3
# Oakley and Chester Jolley

Something felt familiar to Judd about the over-sized mailbox and large leafless maple trees flanking the snow-plowed driveway. It was one of those late December Minnesota skies, blindingly bright, brutally cold.

The Jolley brothers' residence was not the old white-washed farm house he pictured at the trial. This was a straw yellow, prairie-style dwelling nestled against a hillside three miles north of the little town of Marigold.

Judd shut the door of his Toyota FJ Cruiser and, for some strange reason, expected a dog to trot up and greet him. No dog came.

As he approached the front door, he saw footprints in the snow and did a double take. They were as big as his size fourteen. He planted his snow boot alongside one. The tread was identical to his Sorel's.

No way they're mine.

Instead of stepping onto the porch, he followed the tracks around the garage to the backyard. They mirrored his gait, stride for stride.

Odd. Like I've been here before.

He scanned the field sloping below the house, snowdrifts squint-white in full sun. Beyond them, cattails edged a frozen river, its milky ribbon widening into a lake to the west. Overlooking the river stood a structure the size of a small barn.

The "outbuilding" mentioned in court?

Before Judd could knock, Chester opened the door, his head tilted, a quizzical look on his face.

"Hey, hi Chester, name's Judd. I sat on the jury a week or so ago when you … when you and your brother … "

Chester stepped back for Judd to enter and said, "Watch your head."

Ducking the door frame, Judd touched the bump on his forehead. Could've come from anywhere.

The interior was clean and heated, a high ceiling with paneled walls, hooks for coats. The scent of cedar tickled a hazy recollection.

"Feels like I've been …"

Oakley appeared at the door to another room. "Well, if it isn't Judd Russell."

"What's going on? Was I here before?"

"Yesterday," Chester said.

"W-what? You kidding me!" Judd shuddered as if he lost his footing. "Yesterday? How could I have blocked that out?"

Before answering the question, Oakley asked what he could recall.

Judd hung his coat, took off his boots, and joined them at a round oak table with a tall shelf of books and white binders in rows at his back.

"Felt like I'd driven Marigold's Main Street before," Judd said. "And I got déjà vu when I came up your driveway. Do you have a dog?"

They glanced at each other, snickered.

"Come on guys, be straight with me."

"Must have been Arnie." Chester giggled.

Hard to tell they were twins by their looks. Oakley had a rounder face, heavier frame, and slightly darker hair than Chester's blonder thicket. They both dressed the same, black tees, jeans, and lab coats. Oakley's voice was a register lower than his brother's, and his reserved manner contrasted with Chester's spring-loaded movements and gestures. Similarities showed in their dimpled cheeks and an elfin gleam in their eyes when sharing an inside joke. That and how they finished each other's sentences as if on cue.

"Whoa," Judd said, his mind in tilt-a-whirl. "Then if I've been here before, you already know how I vouched for you in court only to have it shot down."

They nodded.

"And how I wanted to invest in your Death Sight Scanner," he added.

Not that Judd had much money. He saved fifteen thousand dollars, thanks to living rent free. But he figured the Wilders, the wealthy couple he'd been house-sitting for over a year, would jump at staking money on an invention of incalculable value to the justice system.

"Pay dirt," Chester said. "Make a glut of money—your words."

"So why can't I… what happened?"

"Couldn't let you go away with the goods," Oakley said.

"You wanted to know, scratch that, you *demanded* to know about our big breakthrough," Chester said.

"Breakthrough?" Judd tried to recall what it was but nothing came.

"Which we showed you."

"Well, a teaser," Oakley corrected.

"So you erased my memory?"

"We don't trust anyone," Chester said. "Not since the first break-in."

"Got us vetting people," said Oakley. "See who we can rely on. Our 'brain trust' so to speak."

"Somebody tried to bust in here four nights ago."

"Think it was connected to the murder?" Judd asked.

"Dude didn't know we had a tornado siren." Chester said. "Musta pooped his pants."

They laughed.

Given what Judd saw in court, it didn't surprise him that someone would want to steal or destroy their invention. But he no longer cared. He wanted to know what they did to his memory.

"We cleared a corner of your attic."

"You lost me."

"Temporal lobe stuff."

That Judd's memory blanked on recent events started to make sense, and it pissed him off. Invading someone's brain is criminal.

"You gave me amnesia."

"In a word."

"So how can I get my memory back? I won't divulge anything about your... breakthrough," Judd said, though he wanted to know everything.

They stared at him.

"That's a promise," Judd added. "Gimme it back. I'll sign something."

"You did," Oakley said.

After a silent, eyes-only conference, the brothers agreed. They escorted Judd into a large, vinyl-floored room with microscopes, diagnostic monitors, and technical equipment.

This was more than the defense attorney's hobby shop. This was a genuine working lab with highly sophisticated electronics. Between the wall cabinets were push-pinned diagrams and color-coded charts. Everything in order, spit-clean as a dentist's office, complete with dental chair.

"Remember the magniscope from the trial?" Oakley lowered a multi-faceted lens attached to a retractable stainless-steel armature.

"No, I..."

"How about this?" Chester held a flexible, helmet-looking apparatus. "The calvarium."

Judd shook his head as he rubbed the object between his fingers. It felt squishy as a gel pack and made a crinkling sound like cellophane. There were small depressions around its rim with nozzle-like appendages stubbed at the back.

Judd removed his wool beanie. The brothers hooked up clear tubes to the nozzles and fitted the pliable helmet on Judd's head like a skull cap.

"No worries, man." Oakley could sense Judd's unease. "You're not our first guinea pig rodeo."

"But he's our first *actor*," Chester said as he pressed something into one of the pockets by Judd's temple.

"Any disasters I should know about?" Judd asked.

"A few oopsies," Oakley said.

"'To have a great idea, have a lot of them.' Tommy Edison said that." Chester adjusted a nozzle.

"But no human fatalities." Oakley grinned.

"That's not reassuring," Judd said.

Chester raised an index finger. "Accidents and misfortunes plague every explorer of the unknown."

"Edison again?"

"No, me, Rochester Jolley."

"So what kind of accidents have you had?"

Bunbun came to mind, a rabbit whose brains exploded. They looked at each other and broke into belly laughs.

"You guys scare me."

Oakley started to fit arc welder goggles over Judd's eyes. "It's protection from…" his voice deepened, "the Aurora Ray."

Chester echoed, "Aurora, Aurora."

Judd held back the goggles. "Wait… the wha?"

"Our customized medical laser," Oakley said. "We call it the aurora ray to make it sound wicked-special."

"What's it do?"

"You want your memory restored?"

"All of it," Judd said.

The twins looked at each other.

"All of it? Are you *sure*?" Chester asked.

Judd gave a rot-sniffing sneer. "Every frickin' minute."

The twins looked at each other. "He's sure," they said in unison.

Oakley tightened the goggle strap to Judd's head. "Then every frickin' minute it will be."

Unable to see what they were doing, Judd tensed up. The brothers mumbled code words he didn't understand. A soft fizzing sounded as air filled the feeder tubes, and the calvarium inflated like a blood pressure cuff around his scalp.

"Feels tight," Judd said.

"Try not to move too much. It's a finessy thing."

Judd could hear tapping, a keyboard, he assumed. The brothers batted numbers and techie terms back and forth like air traffic controllers dishing out vectors and coordinates. Judd felt a warm tingle followed by faint pulses. Within seconds, another tingle, different, spasmodic, starting at his temples and undulating across his forehead. The room swelled with silence. He drifted off.

Air whizzed. The cap deflated. Judd came to as Oakley removed the goggles.

"No cavities," he said, chuckling as he walked Judd out of the lab. "Your memory won't come back all at once. More like a time release."

"Where's your brother?"

"He went to meet Flea at the school bus."

Judd sat on the bench and stuffed his feet into his snow boots, still disoriented.

"You okay?" Oakley asked.

"Other than stressed out at being someone's specimen."

"Hey, you pressured us, ya know."

"So you say. Can't wait to remember how I agreed to that." Judd struggled with his boot laces. He wanted out of there. His mind leapt ahead to that evening: closing night of *A Christmas Carol* and a late date with Bianca BaLore, his favorite actor and unspoken love interest.

Hearing the honk of a Canada goose, Oakley dug a phone out of his pants. "Got to take this." He stepped back into the lab. "Until next time."

*There's not going to be a next time. I'm never coming back.*

But Judd didn't tell him that. He grabbed his wool cap and was about leave when the door flew open and in came Flea.

"Hey Judd! You promised me an acting lesson."

# 4

# Ezra Katz

Oakley pressed the phone to his ear. "Hey, Ezra."

A thousand miles away in a suburb of Ithaca, New York, Dr. Ezra Katz steered a '99 Porsche Boxster into his garage.

"Did you guys see my revisions?"

"We did, yeah." Oakley stepped to the counter and lifted the printout of a six-page article, Dynamic Apurtenances in Neuroscopic Studies of Cellular Clustering. "And, other than the title …"

"A bit dry, I know."

"Ya think? Reading it is like being bonked in the eyeballs by a herd of elbows. I still like Chester's, The Sleeping Nougat in Our Noodle."

"Yes, but the editors won't. To meet the publication's criteria, it's imperative we use technovative terms." Ezra cut the engine and pulled the keys. "Anyway, the journal assured me at least two board members will attend the conference in DC. Of course, I urged them to meet you. Can't wait to see their faces when they hear you activated each other's autobody thermostat."

Ezra didn't believe it when Oakley told him they opened a node in the brain that regulated body temperature. So they sent him a video of Chester, shirtless in nine below, goosebump-free.

"Burn your thermals. It's springtime all the time," Oakley said.

"Talk about living off the grid," Ezra said.

"We've got news for you too. We found a couple more."

"What? More nodes?"

"Once you know what to look for."

"Oh my god of gods, are you kidding me! What do they govern?"

"Haven't opened them. Thought we'd wait for you."

"Wooo!" Ezra jangled the car keys in celebration. "That makes five! Do you know what this means?"

"Your idea about a crown of jewels in our heads?"

"Oh, if that were true!" Ezra thumbed the remote button on the visor. The garage door lurched a metal-on-metal screech as it curtained the snow-clad evergreens outside. "It also means you two should prepare to meet Alfred Nobel in Sweden. He's been dead for over a century, but he'll revive once he hears this."

Ezra stepped out of the car, a short, wiry man, days from turning 48. "Your father would be ecstatic. Hell, I'm ecstatic! This is more astounding than stars! So... so.... have you told anyone?"

"You're the first."

Typically, after a day of teaching Neuro-musicology at Cornell, Ezra chose one of his wind instruments and, depending on mood, play an appropriate tune. These varied from a ballad on oboe to an earthy drone on an aboriginal didjeridoo. Now, with Oakley's incredible news, he'd bagpipe a Scottish Highland jig. He was on the verge of dancing on the garage floor when a low rumble came from inside the house.

"Hang on …" He opened the service door and listened. Nothing.

Couldn't be Cora. She called to say she was picking up dinner at Pizza Resistance. Must be the ice maker.

Ezra stepped into the two-story Cape Cod, on alert for any odd sound. The house quiet, but hairs stiffening on the back of his neck signaled something vaguely ominous. He waited a beat. Still nothing. He lifted the phone back to his mouth.

"Sorry about that." As he kicked off his shoes, he heard a breathy whisper from down the hall. He set his car keys on the kitchen counter and called out, "Hello?"

Two figures waited in his study. They wore transparent ponchos, black gas masks, and rubber gloves. One grabbed him as he entered. The other stuck a pen-shaped instrument up his nostril and pressed the ejector, emitting a spray of odorless white pollen.

Ezra's phone plunked on the throw rug. He tried to force a sneeze, but within seconds he folded into the killer's arms.

"Ezra?" Oakley said. "Hey, I lost you."

A gloved finger ended the call.

The intruders lowered Ezra's body to a chair, wheeled him to his desk, and set his head on the keyboard. As if rehearsed, they stuffed their ponchos and headgear in a duffel bag, put Ezra's files, laptop, and thumb drives in another, and strolled out the door.

# 5

# Things in the Puffs

After losing the connection, Oakley called Ezra back and left a message. "It's Oakley. Where'd you go?"

Outside the Jolleys' lab, Flea gave Judd the standard Minnesotan goodbye: "You drive safe."

Given winter's icy roads it's easy to lose the wheel, spin into another car, roll into a ditch, flip over, and end up airbagged in a snowbank. Hundreds of accidents can occur in a single commute. Body shop job security.

Not the case with Judd's return to the city. The danger wasn't the roads; they were clear and dry. It was the windshield. The glass lit up like a movie screen showing the Jolley brothers' faces in picture and sound. It was his first visit, the one he couldn't remember, when they told him about their after-death scanning discovery.

"Took in a frozen cat hit by a car," he heard Chester say. "And when we got the license plate from its optic nexus we knew we'd found something enormoso."

Judd pulled over. Before he could scream, *What's happening!* the movie faded away.

"Pah!" He let loose a ragged breath and drove on, shaken. "What the hell. Am I hallucinating?!"

A couple miles later the projection picked up where it left off. Oakley's face, life-size, stared at Judd above the steering wheel. "Our mother contacted morgues and medical examiners," he said. "Pressed them to call us immediately when they found a frozen body and to keep it iced."

When Oakley said "mother," she appeared on the windshield. Her face overlayed his, one memory on top of the other.

Windshield wipers couldn't erase the startling visions. Judd rubbed his eyes, tried to blink them away. They didn't budge.

"Go away! Go away!" He slapped at the glass. "I can't see!"

He turned into a gas station, killed the engine, and let the memory play out— their mother at the front door of the house, a high-cheeked Scandinavian, shoulder length hair, blonde-going-twilight gray. The kind of woman who was country plain in her teens but gained a rich, soulful beauty with age. She cracked open the storm door and pointed. "You'll find the boys in the building down around back."

Her face vanished, but yesterday's meeting with the brothers continued. Judd shut his eyes. Still, he could hear the twins talking as if passengers in the car.

"A few weeks later, we got Edgar, our first humanoid," Oakley said. "The geezer was taking his trash out to the curb one night, slipped on the ice, and lay unconscious in five below. Garbage men found his body the next morning hard as a salt lick."

"We had to bring our scopes and equipment to the morgue," Chester added.

"Yeah," Oakley said. "Extracted a moving image of the night sky with streaking stars and the moon. Last thing Edgar saw before he hit the ground.

"Goodnight moon."

"Then the drowned woman in Lake Minnetonka," Oakley said.

"What we found in her head pumped us up," Chester said. "We made inquiries. But the trial got delayed and delayed and we went on to other things. Didn't want to wait around for the next frozen corpse."

"That's the problem," Oakley said. "To access the optics, you have to freeze the head immediately."

Judd heard himself ask, "Ever think about taking your findings to MIT?"

"Did that. MIT, Cal Tech, Stanford," Oakley said. "They ignored us. We pushed. They scolded us, some harshly. Said to stop tampering or they'd seek an injunction."

"Which they did."

"Cease and desist. "

"We took that to mean we were close to something."

"And we were."

Judd opened his eyes. Oakley and Chester stared at him on the glass.

"So we went under the radar and discovered other things in the puffs," Chester said.

"Puffs?"

"Folds of the brain."

"Such as?"

They didn't answer.

"Show me," Judd heard his voice command. But their faces vanished. He stared out the windshield, his nerves sizzling like bacon grease. He never thought a Holiday gas station could look so heavenly.

# 6

# They Hacked My Brain!

That night, at the Guthrie Theater's final performance of *A Christmas Carol*, Judd fidgeted in the wings hoping nothing strange would happen onstage. Turns out it did, but not because of him. The actor playing Scrooge ingested too many muscle relaxants. As he rose from the four-poster bed, he tripped on his nightshirt. Judd braced him the entire scene so he wouldn't do a face plant on the planks.

Meeting up with Bianca BaLore afterward was not so much a date as a casual, "Let's grab a drink after the show." Casual for her, not Judd. He had a crush on Bianca since the first *A Christmas Carol* rehearsal. A natural actor, morphable as a chameleon, destined for stardom.

Even though Judd's height always stood out, Bianca paid no attention to him during rehearsals. Not that he was ugly or disgusting. He worked out, had a decent face with chiseled Gregory Peck features mellowed by hazel eyes and coffee brown hair.

It wasn't until the dramaturg asked Bianca and Judd to do a read-through of his tone play, *Duet for Three*, that she noticed his deep voice. After the reading, the dramaturg confessed his love for her to Judd.

"I want to canoe into the grotto of her eyes and reach the estuary where her spirit resides and whisper, 'Walter Newsome's the one, the one you truly need.'"

Judd met up with Bianca at the Ziggurat, an oolotic limestone-walled café bar frequented by theater people. By then he'd calmed down from the Scrooge debacle and his hallucinatory drive from Marigold to the Twin Cities. The movie on his windshield long gone.

So he thought.

When Judd looked across the table at Bianca's dark gypsy eyes, Oakley Jolley appeared on the window behind her. He was pulling a human brain out of a freezer and setting it on a counter. It looked like a giant gray walnut with little red, blue, and yellow pushpins stuck in it.

While Bianca spoke about rehearsing as Roxanne for the upcoming staging of *Cyrano*, Chester and Oakley filled Judd's ears with talk of nodes in the neocortex.

"A teensy-tiny huddle of cells with a smooch in the middle. Opening them revives long lost wonders."

Not here, not now! Judd watched two scenes at once, speed-blinking and twitching, trying to shake off the picture.

Give it a minute. Maybe it will pass.

It didn't. The situation went beyond awkward and raced headlong toward eternal humiliation.

Call off the date, man! Exit! Cleanly, apologetically. Don't make it look like it's about her, that you have misgivings, withdrawals, or incontinence.

Instead, he decided to go with it, acting 101, only in this case, blend the two realities. He pirouetted the conversation segue-free.

"You're an intelligent woman," he said. "Have you ever thought much about your brain?"

Bianca gave him a smug, "How dare you interrupt me" look. But Judd wasn't about to stop.

"Did you know the cerebral cortex has nodes tucked away that, when carefully aroused, can bring out much, much more of you?" He channeled Chester near verbatim like a TV news anchor fed information through an ear prompter.

Bianca looked bewildered. Fortunately, the artichoke dip arrived and he could ramble on while she ate.

"These nodes don't wake up because you want them. If you were a node, would you open your door if the last time you did you were enslaved? That's why neuroscientists haven't discovered them. They poke around, activate lobes with electrodes. But it's not about stimulation. It's about seeking permission with the proper prismatic light and frequency of sound."

Judd went on feeling like a ventriloquist's dummy mouthing a runaway ramble, until Bianca cut in.

"Really? Like what?"

"Huh?"

Her question stopped him cold.

"You said there are more marvels to my brainscape."

"Oh yeah, l, l-like ..." he stuttered. The projection shut off. He took a sip of wine. Nothing came. His mouth caught in a sinking gulp.

"Hey-hey, Bianca." Two cast members pulled chairs up to the table. Terry Roulet and Adam Van Zee, veteran actors he resented. But given the bizarre scene, they gave Judd momentary relief. He let them talk and pick at his food. He didn't know she asked them to show up in case he bored her.

At one point he excused himself, his coat half on as he exited the café. The icy wind that slapped his face did nothing to cool his rage.

They hacked my brain!

Shivering down Washington Street, he dug out his phone, careful not to do a header on the icy pavement. He called the twins. No answer. So he left a message: "You assholes screwed me up! I'm coming to your place tomorrow. You better be there!"

No memories lit up the windshield as he peeled away from the curb. But that didn't ease the panic.

"You fool!" he berated himself.

Later that night, in the Wilders' mansion he'd been house-sitting, Judd raided the wine cellar. As he slunk from room to room getting bombed, Bianca called.

"You took off."

"Yeah, sorry … needed to get some air," he lied.

"I know, my friends are tiresome. Anyway, I called to say what you said about my brain was really lovely."

"Oh? What …"

"You said, 'Think of your head as a sunflower with a hundred brain buds yet to bloom and seed the world.'"

Brain buds? Those were Oakley's words.

"I didn't know you were so …" she paused.

"Yes …?"

"Anyway, I want to hear more. Maybe we can pick up where you left off?"

Let the unexpected happen, he learned in improv class. Bianca's impression of their short get-together was the last thing he expected.

After they set a time, Judd swooned on the couch and tried to fill in Bianca's unfinished sentence: "I didn't know you were so ..."

So smart? Visionary? Deep?

He settled on deep. But the swoon didn't last. Within minutes, his anger at the Jolleys made him seethe and stomp the polished marble floor.

# 7

# Theodore Theroux

The geodesic sweat lodge stood on a plateau overlooking the high desert of northern New Mexico. Inside, Theodore Theroux's physical body sat naked with eyes closed, while his psychic body was long-distance-viewing, an ability the 38-year-old mastered, known as "bi-location."

News of Dr. Ezra Katz's sudden death prompted a flash mob of chatter throughout the neuroscience community. To Theroux, who walked the ridgeline between brain research and mysticism, the death was too coincidental. Ezra was poised to give the keynote speech at the upcoming neuroscience conference in Washington DC. He promised revelations about the "transformative" findings of his proteges, Chester and Oakley, the sons of Foster Jolley. Which made the timing of the man's death suspect.

Theroux had physically been to the Jolleys' Minnesota lab twice. The first time to meet Foster, the famous author of *The Isness*. Years later, after hearing about his sons' exploratory work, Theroux visited them and left unimpressed. Just brats in lab coats. But that was months ago. Could they have been playing him, or did they actually stumble onto something? Something worth killing Ezra Katz?

Theroux kept imprints of the brothers in his vibrary—a catalog of vibrational signatures collected from people he met and places he'd been. Having shaken hands with the boys at their lab, he could key into their biofield and project his psychic body to wherever they were.

After tuning in to the site's unique frequency, bi-locating there was immediate. A ruffle of air and he stood on their property. The white snowscape and stark shadows looked like an artist's charcoal sketch.

Theroux moved his psychic body to the north wall of the lab, careful his specter would not to be spotted. Through the window he saw Oakley pushing a handcart stacked with cardboard boxes. Hearing an engine, Theroux turned to see a car speed up the driveway. A tall, young man emerged in full winter wear and marched past the house toward the lab with some urgency.

So fixed on the scene, Theroux didn't hear a vehicle approach on the remote desert road, or footsteps come up the narrow dirt trail from his New Mexico villa.

A woman stood outside the sweat lodge, buzz-cut hair, clipboard in hand. She wore a black jacket with FBI in yellow block letters on the back. For a moment, she glanced at the distant peaks of the Sangre de Christo Mountains.

"Mr. Theroux? Hello? I'm with the FBI. Your caretaker said you'd be in here."

Theroux trembled as if stung by a chill. He blinked, drew in a pelvic breath, and returned to his physical body. Taking a wooden spoon from a bucket, he ladled water onto a cairn of stones heated by a small wood stove.

"Mr. Theroux?"

"You may enter," he said.

The woman pulled back the cowhide door flap and a swarm of steam escaped. She squinted, pinned the flap on a hook. In the triangle of light, she saw a bearded man cross-legged on a blanket. A sheen of sweat coated his skin. From where she stood, she couldn't tell if the discolored streaks on his body were birthmarks, scars, or tattoos.

"I'm Special Agent Daisy Franks from the Santa Fe office. Like to ask a few questions."

"Be my guest."

His silky, hypnotic voice made her skin creep. She gestured to his groin.

"If you don't mind …"

Theroux covered his genitals with two ends of the Navajo blanket.

Franks handed him a photo. "Recognize this man?" It was an enlarged image from a driver's license. "He'd been missing four months. A helicopter pilot spotted his remains in a desert canyon out in Hell's Ass, Arizona. Bones picked clean by buzzards. The wallet ID'd him."

Theroux studied the face, fingered his long beard as he read the man's name, and shook his head.

Franks unclipped a flyer with Theroux's picture on it.

"We found this in his rental car."

Theroux recognized the one-day seminar at Sedona he gave back in September.

"Do you remember him at your …" She hesitated before reading the header on the flyer, 'Mindgasm Training Intensive.'"

"There were more than a hundred attendees," he replied.

Yeah, she thought, and at $350 a pop. Where do these people come from? Franks had done a background check on

Theodore Theroux's peculiar appeal. His intermittent online newsletter reached thousands of international subscribers. And his "Radical Unlearning" retreats gave him notoriety among celebrities, some of whom referred to him simply as "The The."

She reclipped the flyer and held up the man's photo again.

"Anything about your workshop that could cause a man from Seattle to hike alone where even cacti don't grow?"

Theroux smirked. "In times long ago, aspiring prophets ventured into the barren desert to face their demons. The trek challenged them to overcome the sun's fire by matching it with the waters of their spirit. Many met their death."

"Something like a vision quest?"

"It's called Walking the Razor. Theroux calmly flicked water from the bucket by his knee. The stones hissed. A puff of hot mist rose to the agent's eyes. "And to the question you are about to ask—no, it's not part of the workshop."

"Walking the Razor."

Theroux lifted his palm to her.

"Interested in seeing your inner demons, Daisy Franks?"

"Nah, too busy dealing with the ones in the outside world."

She named another attendee who remained missing.

"Told his partner back east he needed some alone time to process things. Now, did he have a mindgasm or do we need to scour the desert for his bones?"

Franks stepped back as Theroux stood and wrapped the blanket around his waist. He was a head taller with an exposed ribcage and a dark mane of hair draping his shoulders. She followed him into the morning light. His long nose and pulpy lips reminded her of an Egyptian pharaoh.

"Sorry I can't be of more help." Theroux extended his hand.

She noticed a reddish streak on his forearm.

"All FBI agents should be named Daisy," he said, releasing her hand. "It brings a smile to a meeting with law enforcement."

As she headed to her car, Franks called the office.

"Some people are a piece of work," she told her supervisor. "That dude's the whole fuckin' job."

Theroux inhaled the desert's herbal scent as Franks's black government vehicle shrank in the distance. He could have told her about other undiscovered skeletons in the desert. Maybe someday one of his followers will survive Walking the Razor and return more enlightened. Not that he'd let anyone out shine him.

He strode down the path among prickly pear and ocotillo cactus to his winter home, a traditional adobe with wrap around terrace and floor to ceiling windows. He lifted a knife off the windowsill and sliced a leaf from an aloe vera plant in a clay pot. He squeezed the clear gel from the leaf onto the red swelling on his forearm and pondered what his psychic body saw.

Were the Jolley brothers packing? Remodeling? They didn't look like they'd made a "transformational" discovery. They looked distraught. Grieving their mentor's death? Hard to read. But something happened. Looks like they're moving out. I'll stop by their lab after my engagements back east.

And who was that tall visitor? He looked harried.

# 8

# Every Frickin' Minute

Judd pounded his fist on the door of the Jolleys' lab building.
"Not open," came a muffled voice inside.

"You better be, or I'll kick it in!"

Chester cracked the door.

"Can't see you today."

He looked sick. Slumped shoulders. Bloodshot eyes.

"Tough shit." Judd planted a snow boot on the threshold, forced his way in, and took a seat in the mudroom. "You didn't get my message?"

"Go away. This is not the time."

Judd pointed a finger at Chester's sullen face.

"You shitheads screwed up my brain! Now you're going to fix it!"

He went on to describe the forehead projections.

"Sounds like a memory trace."

"This was more than a trace. This was televised! Plain as the nose on my ... hell, it was smack dab in front of my nose!"

"Pineal recall." Oakley, also looking worn, came in from the lab rolling boxes on a dolly.

"Pine what?"

"Third eye. I'd a few flickers of that once." He stood the dolly up and pressed his finger to the middle of his forehead. "Any pressure here?"

"Yeah, burned like hell. I'm driving around seeing double, swerving, delirious."

"Mine wasn't that dramatic."

"What do you expect, he's an *actor*," Chester said.

"If I'd been pulled over, I'd have flunked the drunk test, gone to jail, and missed my date."

Judd expected them to chuckle. They didn't. He kept it up.

"Then, last night, you appeared on a window during the date. You two were talking at me. I finally synced my speech to your words to keep from looking psychotic."

Still, no giggles. They seemed like two different people.

"So what the hell did you do to my brain?"

"You asked for your memory back."

"Every frickin' minute, remember?" Chester said.

"No. Yes. Okay, I said that."

Chester pointed to the door.

"Now you need to go 'cuz we're in an epic time crunch."

"Like Noah."

"I'm not going anywhere! You don't set it right, I'll make your doom my mission in life!" Judd headed into the lab. It was nearly empty. The walls barren of graphs and illustrations. He glanced back through the doorway. "You got things to do, fine, so let's go, snap-snap."

The brothers huddled nose-to-nose, murmuring to each other, out of earshot.

Judd sat in the dental chair. "I'm waiting."

They came in, opened drawers, logged on a computer, and fitted the gel cap on his head. Peering through a scope, Oakley called out calculations Judd didn't understand.

Chester stepped away. "I'll boot up the Maestro."

Oakley connected the tubes. Flowing air puffed out the cap, squeezing his temples as it inflated.

"This time walk me through *every* step."

"Sure thing, Your Majesty."

"It's basically a sound-and-light show." Oakley held a large milky pearl between his thumb and forefinger. "We start with pearlie here."

"What's it do?"

"Puts you in a watery state of absolute slack." Oakley inserted the pearl into a pocket of the cap.

"Ready tone." Chester tapped on a keyboard, out of Judd's sight.

As Oakley strapped safety goggles to Judd's eyes. Judd heard a deep undulating sound like underwater thunder. His eyelids drooped. Their words drifted away as if they left the room. Judd's rage evaporated, replaced by a sense of floating on swells of loving air.

He woke up almost an hour later, stretched his arms and yawned.

"Back from Dreamland," Oakley announced, as he collected instruments off the counter.

"All right, so ...?"

"Good to go." Oakley left the lab. "And good luck," he muttered to himself.

Judd felt sunstroke woozy as he pulled on his boots. Chester nowhere to be seen.

"Tell me what you did," he said.

Oakley hesitated, choosing his words.

"We gave you full service."

"And ...?"

"And now you need to go." Oakley opened the door.

The cold air felt invigorating.

"Will I have more hallucinations?" Judd asked, his wits returning.

"Every brain is different. Look at me and Chester, born only minutes apart. Our brains are not alike. How can I speak for yours? There may be side effects, okay? But whatever comes, don't fight it." Oakley rolled the empty dolly back into the lab.

Judd put on his coat and stepped over to the bookshelf where a white binder caught his eye.

"What if I go off the rails?" he asked, and deftly as a pickpocket, slipped the binder under his coat.

"Then *be* off the rails!" Oakley shouted. "It will pass. Let it unfold."

Unfold, pfft, easy for him to say.

Judd couldn't start his car fast enough. He rammed it in reverse only to see a school bus blocking the driveway. Chester waited on the road, in shirtsleeves no less. The door opened and Flea hopped out. Thinking he should say goodbye, Judd lowered his window.

"Hi Judd!" she smiled.

"School out early?"

"Half day today. Hey, I memorized the lines you gave me with all the d's and t's. Want to hear it?"

No. Not really. "Yeah."

Judd recalled giving her an elocution lesson, a critical component in stage acting. "You can't mumble or mouth words in monotone," he told her. "You must project to the back wall of the theater. Your diction needs to be clear, crisp, no slop." He told her to stress the end of each word. "Don't say 'it.' Say, it-tuh. Exaggerate the 't' sound."

He had suggested a scene from Shakespeare. And, looking like a little rose-cheeked Eskimo bundled in a fur-lined goose down parka, she delivered lines from *As You Like It*:

"For your brother and my sister no sooner met-*tuh* but they looked-*duh*; no sooner looked-*duh* but they loved-*duh*; no sooner loved-*duh* but they sighed-*duh;* no sooner sighed-*duh* but they asked one another the reason; no sooner knew the reason but they sought-*tuh* the remed-*ee*."

"Hey, that's awesome!" Judd said, surprising himself with the cheery change of heart. Surely Bianca was on his mind when he suggested that scene.

"Y' think so?"

"Absolutely. You nailed the endings, and your breathing fell in rhythm with the words. Really awesome."

"C'mon Flan, let's get inside," Chester said, but the girl didn't budge.

"You don't have your own wow shout, do you?" she asked Judd.

"My what?"

"Everybody says 'awesome.' It's said so much its bland. Like eating rice cakes. You need your own wow shout."

Seeing his puzzled look, she explained.

"You know how people have personalized license plates? Come up with your own personalized wow shout."

"A made-up word?"

"Uh-huh."

"What's yours?"

"Balooge."

"Balooge," he repeated.

"Yeah like, 'That's so balooge!'"

"Well, your reading of Shakespeare was truly balooge!"

"No-no, you can't use mine. You need to make up your own!"

"I'll get right on that." Judd waved goodbye and backed out of the driveway.

*Let it unfold.*

Wary of his brain ambushing him, he drove strictly right lane, under the speed limit, ready to pull off the road and punch the hazard lights the moment a movie lit up the windshield.

None appeared. Still, something didn't feel right about his encounter with the brothers. They seemed distressed.

Caught up in his own predicament, he didn't ask. Or care.

No matter, I'm fixed and done with them!

# 9
# The Pivotor

Nothing happened until everything happened. For three days Judd experienced no flashbacks, hallucinations, or drama. A return to the glory of normal.

He began the morning in a sound booth narrating a Spam pâté commercial. Thanks to his vocal cords, Judd had steady income. Whether selling leaf-blowers or life insurance, he could count on his subterranean pipes making him good money without having to chain smoke. Acting gigs may be few, but when it came to voice work, Judd Russell was a golden goose—booked more than any other mouth in the Twin Cities. Ad agencies and production companies tolerated his overpuffed grandiosity and even scheduled sessions to his timing.

Headphones clapped to his ears, Judd lifted his eyes from the script and looked out the sound booth window. At the audio console, the producer and engineer mulled over the last take. As Judd waited, his father's face appeared on the glass.

"Aah!" Judd blurted, forgetting his mic was on.

"What's that?" the producer asked.

"Nothing-nothing." Judd groaned.

But it was far from nothing. He hadn't seen his father in eight years, not since leaving home after his fateful sermon.

"Okay, Judd, let's do that last bit again." The producer brought him back to the present as his father's face vanished. "This time punch the *mer* in A*mer*ica."

Judd let out a staggered breath and counted out loud, "Three … two … one … Hormel's Spamanade. The taste of A*mer*ica. A spread ahead of its time."

"Mark that," the producer told the engineer.

Judd left the production studio, still shaken by the sight of his father.

"Shitheads," he blurted as he brushed a mat of snow off his windshield. "I'll kill them!"

But no way was he going back to the Jolleys.

Could've been worse, he thought as he drove home. Didn't hear the old man haranguing me: "You can't stop botching things, can you boy!"

No, not his rancor, just his rhino-gray face, glaring at him, case-hardened with resentment.


The Wilder house was a glass and stucco extravaganza on a rise overlooking Lake of the Isles near downtown Minneapolis. Judd had it all to himself. As house sitter, his duties were meager—shovel snow off the walkways, bring in mail, take out garbage, water plants, vacuum, dust the Brazilian furniture, and manage the mousetraps in the wine cellar.

He normally handled his weekly chores in an afternoon, and today was that afternoon. Instead, he worked out in the exercise room lifting kettle bells to banish his father's grim face from his mind. He almost succeeded until his mother called. They hadn't spoken since Thanksgiving.

"There's something I need to tell you. Your father passed away this morning. A stroke," she said.

Judd shook. Not by his dad's death, which was not a surprise given his failing health. No, it was the face he saw in the audio booth.

That was not a flashback. That was my father's ghost giving me a fuck you farewell.

"He's with Jesus now." His mother waited for an affirming reply. It didn't come. "We don't expect you to attend the funeral."

She knew he wouldn't set foot in Trinity of Christ Church for the Second Coming, let alone his father's service.

"How are you holding up, Mom?"

"Okay enough."

She named well-wishers who called with condolences. He pictured their home in Baxter. Her friends stuffing the refrigerator with tater tot hot dish, lingonberry jam, and Alana's savory piroshkis with marinated meat and pumpkin seed pesto.

"Heard your voice on TV the other night," she said. "The pet-friendly ice melt commercial. So proud."

Judd felt an emotional dam about to burst.

"Mom, I love you, but all this dad stuff it's … I got to go. I'll get back to you."

"Soon?"

"Yes, soon."

He ended the call and headed for the wine cellar. He didn't need projections to remember his father's wrath or the sneers of disgust from the faithful after his "Save our Savior" speech.

"You brought shame to our family!" His father ordered Judd to apologize door-to-door and admit the sermon was his own idea, a sacrilege at that.

Gently, as was her way, Judd's mother took him aside and said everything would be all right. "A youthful mistake," she told their nosey neighbor. But desecrating Jesus labeled him a menace to the sanctity of the Church overnight. Those who believed in Judd, and there were many, felt betrayed, heartbroken. Others saw it as a test of faith. A heathen deceiver vanquished.

As for Judd, it's hard to enjoy those last days of high school when you're called "The Anti-Cross" by fellow students, and hear Chelsea's parents declare, "She's not your girlfriend anymore."

So be it!

No way would Judd ever show his face in that church again. No atonement blather could make him apologize. Instead, he fought back. He called it hypocrisy for Christians to espouse "May peace prevail," while displaying an act of unthinkable cruelty.

When Judd left home the day after graduation, his father's last words were, "You'll burn in hell!"

Did he miss the church? Absolutely. Not the religious part. Not the choice of sin or salvation. No, he missed the spot-light of attention, the rock star celebrity. But the high of stardom was gone. Judd's future, a desert. Until the night at the Comstock warehouse, a canned corn distributor where he drove a forklift. The Lakota custodian, nicknamed "One of Few Words" for his quiet presence, came to work earlier than usual and caught Judd stuffing green bills in his jacket pocket from the office safe. The same small, undetectable amount he stole every month. "A temporary loan," he claimed. But the custodian didn't buy it. He gave Judd the option—get fired, go to jail, or take a trip with him that weekend.

Habitat for Humanity was doing a multi-home build on a reservation. Volunteers came from all over to construct a dozen houses among the tall grass plains. Judd actually enjoyed the rough carpentry work and team effort.

On the drive back, One of Few Words spoke.

"The more you take what does not belong to you, the less you are complete. Every theft punches a hole in your spirit that you try to fill with more stealing. You end up a hollow gourd. Why don't you use what you've been given? Your voice is a deep river. Ever think of acting?"

With this Lakota man, Judd Russell met his "pivotor," a person who may appear only briefly in your life, a chance encounter when you've lost your way, and points out an unexpected path to follow.

Judd took drama classes at Moorhead State, a university in Minnesota, two miles east of the North Dakota border. He performed in a number of plays including *Our Town* and *Doubt*. He may have lost his identity, but acting freed him to portray others.

By the time he turned twenty-one, Judd saved enough money to go for the big time. Crossing the Mississippi River on the way to New York, his Ford van conked out, closing off a lane. Rain poured on the bridge. Horns ranted. As Judd waited for a tow truck, he watched the rain dive into the roaring river, high and massive from spring snowmelt. The sight touched something he'd never felt before. A verse from Ecclesiastes came to mind: *All streams flow into the sea, yet the sea is never full. To the place the streams come from, there they return again.*

While a mechanic repaired the engine, Judd read about all the theaters in the Twin Cities, and decided to stick around. Although acting jobs did not come easy, the money his voice earned became an ever-flowing stream.

# 10

# The Star of Reality

"I've been thinking about the beauty of my brain ever since that night," Bianca told Judd as they stood on the shore of Lake Harriet, clipping boots on cross-country skis. She wore an ensemble of burgundy and rose-colored ski pants, a tight knit sweater and quilted vest, topped with a fur-lined wool cap. Stunning as ever.

Bianca chose the lake. He wanted Lake of the Isles, to be within walking distance of where he lived. Invite her over after skiing, share the news of his father's death, move on to drinks and sympathy sex. But he acquiesced. Don't push it, he coached himself. Let the intimate stuff arise organically. Work to extend the run, another date, back by popular demand.

He woke that morning with a vein-bulging hangover, his head a hive of vampire bees. He reached for his trusty coffee, ibuprofen, and hair-of-the-dog remedies. By the time they met at eleven o'clock, he was coherent, the temperature a balmy twenty degrees. They set off across the frozen lake in a sensual glide, the snow smooth as flour. His initial nervousness at being in her presence eased with each stroke of the poles.

Before meeting Bianca, Judd rejected long-term relationships. Not only with a woman, but pets, goldfish, ferns. Acting is a transient profession; you can't let yourself get tied down. How many times had he babysat an actor's labradoodle or calico cat? Chances are he'll be going away, join a touring company, get cast in a TV series. Better yet, a movie on location, gone for a time. No wonder he'd only had a few one-night stands since house-sitting the Wilders. Although he questioned why they're called one night "stands" when they're "lays." No, he made it clear with bed dates that getting serious and clingy was not going to happen.

Not until Bianca BaLore. Although he only knew her from her web bio, what better chance to connect than skiing shoulder-to-shoulder under a silent sky with snowflakes drifting down like feathery stars.

As soon as they started off, Bianca took a call.

"No, no, it's not Baylor, it's Ba-Lore. Capital B, small a, capital L, small o, small r, small e."

"I changed agents," she told Judd, closing the call. "Major upgrade. Okay now, let's see ..." She scanned the lake. "It's a skiing scene. I'm with the tall guy."

The *tall guy?* Judd wasn't sure Bianca said what he heard. She attached her phone to the grip of her ski pole to record the moment.

"I'm going to miss this place, the four act seasons, the lakes, the ultra-fresh air ... oh, and the smell of lilac in spring ... and the big fluffy hippo clouds in summer. This is where it all began, the launch of my journey ..." She kept on, full voice, turning the heads of passing skiers.

Judd tried to edge in a comment only to feel walled out by her monologue.

"You wanted to pick up on the brain stuff?" He finally interjected.

"Yes, yes, the brain. Oh, what was it? A thousand buds ready to blossom. You know I love sunflowers. I wrote a poem about sunflowers. I call it, "Under the Spell of Yellow.' Paint my portrait with pastel yellow petals …"

He watched how she postured and delivered her words for all to hear. Some children have imaginary friends. Bianca played to an imaginary audience. A stage manager referred to her as "the star of reality," but Judd thought it meant her acting talent. This was plainly no act. She truly believed all the world was her stage.

Judd realized that if anything romantic materialized, he'd be confined to a minor, supporting role. It wasn't the first time he'd been out-narcissized, but it was the first time he felt so devastated by it.

Me, a spectator? Not on your life!

"… with swallowtail wings flashing in the lemony eyelashes of the sun …'"

Judd's vibrating phone interrupted Bianca's recital. Her face momentarily distorted as he stabbed his poles in the snow and took the call. The voice on the other end sounded frantic, asking Judd if he skated.

"Who's this?"

The man hurdled the question.

"Our actor came down with pneumonia. We need a replacement."

"What's the gig?"

"Oh, sorry, it's *Waiting for Godot on Ice*. You'd play Pozzo. Can you do it? We'd need to rehearse you like ASAP."

The caller made it sound as if Judd knew who Pozzo was. Of course, he'd heard of the play. Who hadn't? But he'd never seen or read it.

"Okay. Where?"

"Hubert H. Humphrey Hockey Arena."

"Wabumba!" He howled, stuffed the phone in his pocket. "I got an acting job!"

"Wah-what?" Bianca sounded irritated. Her scene upstaged.

"Wabumba, my personal wow shout." Judd agreed with Flea, or Flannery as she insisted on being called. "You know, instead of saying 'awesome' or 'fantastic,' which are stale and redundant, you coin your own wow shout."

Bianca's head tittered, she had no place to put that and felt offended at having her rhythm dislodged.

The call gave Judd an out.

"Say, I'm sorry to cut this short, but I gotta go. They need me to rehearse like now."

Bianca struggled to accept the scene shift. As for Judd, he couldn't ski back fast enough. When they said their goodbyes, a passerby recognized her with a wave and she brightened.

Judd tossed his skis, poles, and boots in his SUV. Won't be hearing from her again. Back at the Wilder house he downed more ibuprofen and dropped on the sofa, his Bianca-fantasy in rigormortis.

"How was your date with BaLore?" Mel, the transgender Guthrie dresser called. "Had to ask."

"A one-sided disaster."

"A few of us once stopwatched how long she could go without bending the conversation to herself," said Mel. "Eight seconds. If there was a Guinness Book of the Self-Absorbed, she'd be on the cover." Mel held back telling Judd he'd be the centerfold.

Could have been worse, Judd thought on his way to the wine cellar. If it's any consolation, my brain didn't go bug wild out there. Maybe my head is weird-shit-free. Now that's something to celebrate.

# 11
# You're Having a Heart Attack!

Normally, Judd would join the New Year's Eve revelers at the Mississippi Model and Talent Agency, then move on to Minnehaha Media, a production company that often hired him for voice-overs. But this year the Guthrie Theater invited him to ring in 2016 with the acting company. Not to be missed, even if Bianca Balore would ignore him.

He planned to spend the rest of the afternoon reading *Waiting for Godot* online. He didn't get far into the Beckett play when he felt a clenching sensation in the middle of his forehead. The room blinked. He jolted at the thought of another presence.

Shit! My father's ghost again?

This was no Dickens apparition. A pulsing light funneled from his head onto the wall with images shuttling by so fast he only caught glimpses: Bianca on skis, the checker bagging his groceries at the co-op, the Spamanade producer's fake-tanned face.

It didn't take Judd long to realize that the projection, like a choppy vintage newsreel, was a non-stop rewind of his past—walking the Jolley's driveway, uncorking a bottle, sitting in the jury box, uncorking another bottle. Everyday occurrences, many forgotten, flickered by in a torrent.

He tried to shake the flashbacks. He walked about the living room, ran in place. But wherever he turned the playback appeared—on the basalt fireplace, the teak window shades. He couldn't shut it off or mute the skittish traffic of sounds. Further and further back in time they raced. Long days driving a forklift countered by oblivion nights, blinking casino lights, the hurt in Chelsea's eyes.

Memories with an emotional charge held up a few seconds longer, causing him to buckle from hurt, or burn with anger. He re-lived the impact his words and actions had on others. Like the fateful sermon that sent him packing.

What was I thinking? Why did I tell people to chop down the crucifix? It's their logo for God's sake. That's like ripping the American flag off every pole.

"Stop it!" he cried out, as more of his past sped by like a bullet train making him re-experience the fear, the heat of lust, the adrenaline surge of petty theft.

You're having a heart attack! Call 911!

He slapped his scorching forehead. But it didn't stop the stampede. He made his way down to the wine cellar spraying the racks with snapshots of his youth— learning to drive a stick shift, walking with crutches, sitting with his Bible tutor, his mother cramping, hunched over the kitchen sink.

Judd stuffed balls of tissue in his ears, turbaned his head in a towel. Then he uncorked a bottle and repeated an actor's vocal exercise out loud—"Red leather, yellow leather, red leather, yellow leather …" until he blacked out.

The clap of a mousetrap twitched Judd awake on the concrete floor of the wine cellar. It took a minute to recall how he ended up there. His shirt was spotted with hacked-up bile, his pants sopping wet from sleeping in a puddle of Pinot. His head pounded as he stood on wonky legs, a dime-sized blister in the center of his forehead.

"Assholes fixed *nothing!*"

He roamed the house in a bathrobe holding an ice cube to his third eye, wondering why he ever wanted to meet those devil twins.

What was my motivation?

Money!

Damn right, armored trucks of it from investing in their Death Sight Scanner. There's no money in theater. Voice work might be good for a time, but bummers happen. Hell, polyps could grow in my throat. Someday the Wilders will return. Then I'll have to pay rent. And at the rate my acting career's going, I'll have to look for some Joe job.

Money was the mover, all right. Judd wanted the Wilders' luxury lifestyle—a ski lodge in Park City, a beach house on the Big Island, a bay window overlooking the thirteenth green at Pebble. Every day a vacation.

To fulfill his dream, Judd planned to get the Wilders to invest in Oakley and Chester's Death Sight Scanner, and more. The twins said they'd uncovered marvels. Like what? Levitation? Invisibility? Chances like this came around never.

So much for swimming in a river of cash. Judd had to admit his fantasy had been sabotaged. He couldn't predict what would burst out of his brain next. And no amount of makeup could mask the scarlet splotch on his forehead. He stood at the mirror in the master bath slathering ointment on it. His reflection shatter-cut like a Picasso while his headache ranted with his father's voice: "You fool! Temptation blinded you, and you're paying dearly for it!"

"Yeah!" Judd shouted back. "Well now *they're* going to pay!"

# 12
# Fine Bits and Splinters

Something felt different as Judd sped to the Jolleys that afternoon. Normally void of cars, the winding country road out of Marigold was bumper to bumper.

Must be a fallen tree, Judd figured. Or a power line down, overladen with snow.

Nearing the property, he saw red flares and an authority figure waving drivers along. Yellow CAUTION tape cordoned off the driveway. Where the house once stood was an upheaval of rubble. The line of cars stuffed with gawkers inched along. Big news in the boonies.

Judd lowered the window.

"Nothing to see here," said the man. He had an insignia of some kind patched to the breast of his hooded parka. "Move on. No stopping."

"What happened? Is everybody okay?" Judd craned his neck but couldn't see the lab beyond the rise.

"Go on. Move it!"

"Jesus!"

He drove on, but wasn't about to leave without answers. He parked on Main Street and entered the Marigold Café, a century old, two-story, red brick building, straight out of a Hopper painting with green sash windows.

Sidelong glances and the smell of fresh coffee met him at the door. The warm café was packed and humming, a chinkle of dishes from the kitchen.

Judd scanned the long, rectangular room, round tables with blue-and-white checkered oil cloth, a few booths toward the rear, all taken. Large men in flannel and denim lifted steaming mugs to their mouths.

Seeing Judd, a ponytailed waitress said, "Look who's back," as she lowered the blinds on the front window to mask sunlight blazing in from the west.

Judd kept his cap on in case pictures shot from his forehead. He took a swivel stool at the counter by the register, a caddy of condiments and silver napkin dispenser within reach. Next to him sat a wide load. The man's belly bulged so far the brass buttons on his overalls looked about to pop off.

"Say, maybe you can fill me in," Judd said. "I missed all the ruckus out on River Road. Know what happened?"

"Depends who you ask. You a reporter?"

"No …"

"My guess, the water heater blowed up and exploded."

The man on the next stool with a white, walrus mustache under a frayed John Deere cap, tipped his glasses.

"Those boys were making bombs. Why else would ordinance disposal specialists be siftin' through it all."

Bomb squad? Judd flinched. Did something backfire?

"No-no," said Overalls. "If that's the case, where's the dogs?"

"Dogs?"

"The bomb sniffers."

The waitress stood over Judd, *Roslyn* on her name tag.

"The kitchen closed twenty minutes ago."

Judd looked up at the red, rooster-shaped clock above the register—2:22.

"Oh, just coffee, black."

The place reminded him of a diner in Baxter, same floral tin ceiling, same homey smell of bacon and toast. No espresso machine here. Like going back in time, pre-cappuccino.

"So what happened to them?" Judd asked Overalls.

"The boys? Nobody knows. Musta hightailed it. Found no body parts what I hear."

"How about their mother and the girl?"

"Marsha was teaching at the university," Overalls said. "Her daughter was at school when it happened. So they're okay."

"If you call losing your house and all your belongings okay." Roslyn set a fat-lipped mug in front of Judd. "And Marsha's sons have gone missing. You see any okay in that?"

Judd stared at the steam uncoiling from the brew.

Shit, those two better not be *gone* gone, and no one to fix my brain.

"Time's up everybody!" Roslyn flipped the sign on the door to CLOSED.

She looked like someone Judd had met before but couldn't place.

The patrons paid their bills, zipped up their winter coats, and headed out. As Judd sipped his coffee, he stared out the big front window and pondered taking a back way to the boys' lab.

After finishing, he bused the cup into the kitchen where Roslyn and the cook were cleaning up.

"Say, can you tell me how I get to the river?"

Roslyn read his mind as she took his cup.

"You looking for trouble?"

"Me? No, looking to get out of it."

"There's a river park with access. It's that way." She pointed west.

He took in her striking bronze eyes.

"Thanks ... Roslyn."

Judd drove the two blocks to the river park. He changed into ski boots, clipped on skis, and cautiously slid along. Wind had swept the snow thin on the frozen river. In some spots his skis scraped bare ice.

He figured the Jolleys' lab was about three miles out of town. But the windy river made it longer. By the time he got there, long blue shadows stretched east. Cattails lined the bank, their seed heads like hot dogs on a stick. At first, he thought he'd overshot the property.

He hadn't.

"Oh, God!"

Like the house, the lab was demolished. But he couldn't leave without taking a close look. He unclipped his skis and climbed the slope. No guards in sight as he stepped over the crime scene tape, passing cedar boards half-sunk in the snow, some blasted to fine bits and splinters. Tufts of insulation flitted about. No charred wood or smell of smoke.

It made no sense. Chester and Oakley may have taken an experiment too far. But why would it blow up their lab and the house?

Judd caught the sheen of something standing upright in the wreckage. It looked like a flag-pole, straight and tall, minus a flag.

A memorial? Did somebody die? God, not the twins?!

When he saw that the shiny shaft was actually the aluminum handle of a roof rake, upturned by the blast, he let out an audible sigh.

A scruffy dog sniffed among the piles of debris. Judd pulled out his phone and clicked off quick shots of the scene as if busy-making would lessen the shock.

"Hey you!" someone shouted. "You're violating a crime scene!"

Spotted! Judd hurried to the river.

"ATF! Freeze!"

A man's voice, this time louder. Judd acted like he didn't hear him.

"Stop or I shoot!" The man hustled down the slope.

The dog barked: "Arr-urff!"

Judd scooped up his skis and ran.

A gunshot rocked the air.

"That's a warning! Next one's in your ass!"

"Okay, okay!" Judd froze, held up his skis.

The ATF agent stopped on the wooden dock. "Get back here!"

Turning, Judd saw the dog come running headlong and ram the back of the man's knees. He flopped on the deck with a loud grunt. The weapon sprung from his hand and skimmed across the ice.

Before Judd could question why the dog would do that, it sprinted down the bank toward him.

"Arr-urff! Arr-urff!"

He thought it was going to attack, so he waved a ski pole at it. The mangy, long-haired mix of strays looked up at him with strange, pin-wheel eyes, then loped off toward the lake. After a few yards the dog held up and barked at Judd as if beckoning him.

"What the hell?"

Judd clipped on his skis and followed. Reaching the lake, the mutt veered toward the shore and stopped at a small boat dock.

"Arr-urff!" It barked again before disappearing between huge cottonwood trees.

Judd unclipped his skiis and followed a utility vehicle track as twilight withered away.

"Okay!" He called out to the dog, "Now where?"

Nothing. The dog didn't show. Judd felt the temperature dip, his cheeks going numb. As he passed a barn, a man's voice rang out.

"You lost or stupid?"

Judd's skis rattled on his shoulder. Busted, he thought and kept walking.

"What were you doing over at the Jolley place, do ya know?"

"Looking for Chester and Oakley."

Out of the shadows a stocky shape appeared.

"You a reporter?"

Again that question.

"No."

"Then why take pictures?"

How could this guy have seen me from way over here?

"Best you go back where you came from."

"Best I do." Judd didn't look at the man. He switched the skis to his other shoulder, dreading the long, frigid trek back to Marigold.

"Here, I'll give you a lift."

The man entered the barn and climbed behind the wheel of a late model Ram pickup. Judd set his skis in the bed.

As they drove down the road, the man asked about Judd's connection to the twins.

What do I lose by telling the truth?

Judd shared how Chester and Oakley messed up his brain, and how he came back to get it reset.

"Do you know where I can find them?"

"They saw it coming," the man said. "Didn't expect to get bombed though. If it's who I think, you better make yourself scarce."

"Me? I'm nobody."

"Everybody who's been around them is a somebody. And if that air strike is any indication …"

"Air strike? Hey, where you going? I said my car's at the river park."

"Little detour. Only take a minute."

The man slowed the truck and turned into a commercial facility: ARNIE'S ECONO SELF-STORAGE. A motion detector lit up a snow-plowed gravel driveway flanked by rows of storage bays.

"Follow me." The man opened the rollup door of a unit high enough for them to duck inside. "Wait here. Don't pee on anything."

"What?!" The door slammed shut, enclosing Judd in blackness. "No, hey-hey!"

The truck wheeled away. Judd groped for a light switch only to collide into boxes and furniture. The space smelled of moldy uphostry. At least it was heated.

Ten minutes later the door lifted. Marsha and Flannery stood next to the truck driver. Ballooned out in down coats, they looked like aliens under the yellow cast of security lights.

"Told ya, mom," Flannery said, "It's Judd. He's an actor."

"Judd, huh." Arnie said, as overhead fluorescents strobed on.

"Could have told me about the light switch," Judd said.

"Wanted to keep you in the dark."

"Our house blew up," Flannery said.

"I know. I was just there."

"I remember you." Marsha Jolley spoke as if each word weighed a hundred pounds. "You came to see them."

"So where'd they go?" Judd recalled seeing her on his windshield.

"Where they won't be found."

"That's unacceptable! They screwed with my brain!"

"Right. And what, they did it while you were sleeping?" Arnie said. "Without your permission?"

"Just tell me where they are!"

"No one knows," Marsha said. "And it's best you know nothing."

"Come on, I'm losing my mind! I got pictures pouring out of my head! I'm an artist! It'll kill my career if it doesn't kill me first."

"You got a problem with your hearing or your listening?" Marsha stepped into the light of the unit. A big-boned woman with aster-blue eyes. "My boys have become targets. By association, *we* are targets. If you value your life, you'll get as far away from us as you can."

"Value my life? Look at me! I don't have one! I'll never get another part!"

Arnie confronted Judd. "Hey! Marsha's home was destroyed, her sons are running for their lives, and she just endured a five-hour grilling. So ease up."

"Yeah, well my brains are mush." He darted a finger at Marsha. "Your sons did this to me."

"Me-my-me." Marsha scoffed. "So get help, listen to Bach, surf your brain waves." Marsha clasped Flannery's mittened hand. "Arnie, take Me-My-Me to his car." And walked off.

Arnie hit the light switch and closed the storage unit. As they wheeled away, Judd noted Arnie's name on the facility's sign.

"You own this?"

"Yep."

Turning onto Main Street, Judd reflected, "She said, 'Best you know nothing.' Know what?"

Arnie didn't answer.

"Come on, man."

"Ever hear of the gold rush? Well, we're in the thick of a brain rush. Everybody wants to get their mitts on it. The boys' were closing in. Word got out."

"You lost me. Closing in …?"

"The treasure of treasures. People will kill for it, or stop anybody from having it."

"It? What's the *it*?"

Arnie glanced at Judd. "The Godhead Spot."

"In the brain?"

Arnie nodded.

"Oh, spare me."

# 13

# Get Help

Actors have numerous ways of coping with stage fright, self-doubt, and rejection. But no special amulet, mantra, or controlled substance was going to alleviate Judd's personal apocalypse.

Back at the Wilder house, he dove into online sources to learn about mental disorders. Things he never wanted to know. He would try anything, even convulsive shock therapy, to have his brain reset.

He downloaded Dr. Alton Pabbo's e-book: *SOMA SPEAK: How to Talk to Your Body in a Therapeutic Way.* Each chapter focused on a part of the human anatomy to be read aloud—*Good morning, heart. Thanks for keeping the beat. I'm so glad to have you.* The author's warm, ingratiating words were meant to encourage the organs of the body to work in harmony. However, the two-page chapter on the brain left Judd wanting. Statements like—*You are a wonderful wonderer whose thoughts can travel great distances inside a skull. And—You are a wizard at calculating equations but try not to be uppity when it comes to matters of the heart. You need the heart to fully understand.* Not a word on how to prevent overload, or ways to restore sanity.

Judd pored over web sites until he couldn't absorb any more information, his brain overwrought, all one hundred billion neurons of it.

"Get help," Marsha told him. Which, at the time, sounded like "Get lost."

Feeling more and more desperate, he called Mel, the dresser at the Guthrie. She was into pseudoscience and alternative healing modes. He kept his symptoms vague and left out the flashbacks. Mel told him, "You could be on the verge of a break*through* or a break*down*" and suggested two people who might help. The first was Sara, the "Second-Opinion Psychic" who charged ten dollars a minute. She looked him over and said, "You're having a spiritual emergency. Good luck. That'll be fifty bucks."

Mel's other recommendation was craniosacral work, basically skull massage. Kate, the practitioner, in whose hands Judd placed his head, made an immediate assessment— "Brains move. Yours is tight as a coconut."

Some places she prodded made him wince, her fingertips hard as bolts. She asked about trauma. Did he ever have a concussion or black out?

Yes.

After she finished, he felt more pliant, as if a vent had opened and his brain could breathe. Kate suggested blueberries and turmeric, booster foods, and recommended he remove wheat and grains from his meals. "Anything sprayed with pesticides and herbicides." She also encouraged him to look into university classes on mind-body gymnastics.

"Taught by Foster Jolley's wife," she said.

"Foster *Jolley*?"

"Were you a Foster fan?"

"N-no."

How could I have overlooked the connection? It's not like there are a lot of Jolleys in the world. Marsha's husband is that inventor who became a charismatic spiritual somebody before disappearing. Foster, yeah. Of course he's Chester and Oakley's *father*. No-brainer there!

# 14

# Red Snow

As the wheels of his private jet lifted off the tarmac, Theodore Theroux decided to take another look at the Jolley twins. The last time he checked, it appeared they were moving out of their lab. He shut his eyes and keyed in on the vibrational autograph of their Minnesota home. At first, he thought his bi-locating misfired, but surveying the snowy landscape he realized it was the right place, only the house was leveled.

He moved about the site, tree to tree, shifting his point of view by mere thought. On the road plumes of vapor poured from tailpipes. A man in a jacket with ATF emblazoned on his back stood next to a stretch of yellow crime scene tape. He wore a black, balaclava face mask and stamped his boots as he directed the steady creep of cars to keep moving.

Taking in the scene, Theroux sensed a mechanical sound wave—a generator? Beyond the rise, he spotted the peak of an immense pole tent pitched at the site of the lab.

"What's this?" came a voice from inside the tent.

"Looks like some sort of diagnostic device. Set it with the keeper pile."

*That's not the twins talking.* Theroux peeked in and saw two federal agents on their knees. As he started to identify the instruments, a ranting noise pulsed from the river. Two snowmobiles crushed the stalks of cattails as they bounded up the bank.

Hearing the high-pitched whine, one of the agents went outside.

"Shooters!" he hollered as a dozen bullets tore tent fabric. One struck the man. He let out a wail, clutched his shattered elbow, and slumped to the ground. The other agent crawled out of the tent on hands and knees, staying low. Bullets whizzed overhead. He fired back as the invaders circled the tent, whooping and shooting at anything that moved.

A bullet rippled Theroux's psychic body like a breeze buffeting a sheet. If he were physical, he'd have a hole in his gut.

Hearing the gunfire, the masked ATF agent, came running from the road. He shielded himself behind a tree as a chip of bark burst from the trunk.

Theroux slipped into the tent. In one area he saw piles of busted boards and debris. At the other end, an upturned dental chair, a waveform monitor, and an electrode meter.

Clearly the bombing was a tactical strike, he concluded. Precise and efficient—destroy everything. As he scanned the rubble, the ski of a snowmobile lanced a corner of the tent and threw the driver, who stumbled away from a barrage of bullets and spouts of snow.

Theroux sprang from the tent as the other snowmobile retreated down the incline toward the river. It didn't go far. The kneeling agent stood, steadied his weapon in both hands, and fired three successive rounds. The last punctured the gas tank. The sled burst into flames. The driver crawled out of the black smoke, his clothes on fire. He struggled to pull his melting helmet off and collapsed.

The masked ATF agent tackled the other snowmobiler, who'd been shot in the neck; blood seeped between his knuckles. He pulled off the snowmobiler's helmet, revealing the sweaty face of a young man.

"Who the hell you work for?"

The snowmobiler's lips moved, but Theroux couldn't hear the answer. Neither could the ATF agent who leaned down and yelled, "Who'd you say!?"

The young man spat blood in the agent's face.

Gripping his shattered elbow, the wounded ATF agent stumped over the prone man, his eyes pinched with pain and rage.

"Well, take this to your boss in hell."

Before the other agents could stop him, he emptied his firearm into the man's head. Globs of brain and blood sprayed the snow tomato red.

"What the shit!" The masked agent threw up his hands. "Now we'll never know!"

Theroux rushed back to his physical body. Buckled in a seat on his private plane, he worked to calm his breathing. He couldn't shake the image of the pure-white snow soaking up the blood like a sponge. As he tried to blot it out, he felt a bruise-like sensation in his stomach. He suspected a skin lesion. But it was where the bullet passed through his psychic body.

The actual lesion, a side effect of bi-locating, would soon appear. He was prepared for it, and within minutes felt a searing itch on his left shin. He unzipped a small travel pouch, unscrewed the top of a vial, and applied a clear gel to the rash-like stripe. As he wiped his fingertip with a cloth napkin, he stared out the aircraft window at a layer of cottony clouds and ruminated on recent events. There was Ezra Katz's sudden death. Then the Jolleys' laboratory blasted to smithereens with ATF agents combing the scraps. And now two kamikaze-types invade the site.

So the onslaught has begun, which means only one thing— the rumors are true. The boys found something momentous in the brain and ruthless forces want to seize it at all costs.

Theroux knew a number of laboratories looking into the brain's ability to access the so-called Godhead Spot. The Holland Institute and the Munich Neurobiology Center, among them. But those were geeky scientists. They wouldn't hire assassins. As for the bombing, a larger entity must be behind it. The Russians? Possibly. US government? Wouldn't put it past them.

Theroux thought of Kira King, an avid admirer who worked at Neurokey, a Virginia brain lab. She had set up a meeting for him with some higher ups in the Defense Department. "A little demonstration, if you're game," she said. "They're curious about your amazing psychic skills."

Theroux savored the synchonicity of it all.

Fortuitous? Could be a chance to find out if they attacked the Jolleys' place. That in itself will make the meet-up worth my while.

# 15
# Black Ice

Setting *Waiting for Godot on Ice* was the brainchild of director, Zach Kitchener, a native Minnesotan who moved to Los Angeles seeking fame and fortune with less than lackluster results. Zach stood center ice, blocking the scene where Judd skates in from the hockey players' bench. Judd tugged a thick, coarse rope attached to the neck of an actor playing the enslaved and ragged Lucky.

"There's no such thing as a small part" is an oft-repeated saying in theater circles, and Judd was determined to make the most of his part.

This is it. My launchpad to stardom. I'll show them a bravura performance! A portrayal so masterful, so quintessential, forthcoming actors will try to emulate it and they will fail.

For Pozzo, an autocratic character, Judd channeled his father, emphasizing the man's rigid, lion-tamer domination. With one hand gripping the leash, the other snapping a whip, Judd shouted his lines above the dirge of a Zamboni shaving the ice at the far end of the rink.

"I am Pozzo!"

Zach's sweeping arm gestures choreographed Judd in wider and wider arcs. He steered him close to the front seats, then sent him in a swift figure eight, tugging Lucky, who lugged a bulging suitcase.

"Pozzo! Does that name mean nothing to you?" Judd shouted.

"Good, good, and keep the rope taut!" Zach yelled and turned to his sound man. "What pipes he's got! The acoustics are crap but that's your job."

Round and round Pozzo and Lucky whirled. Judd was loving the madcap frenzy of it, especially after the principal actors playing Estragon and Vladimir arrived and filled out the scene.

The four rehearsed together for half an hour before Zach stopped to take a call. When he howled, "No!" the skaters froze. He waved them over, his face sour.

"Bad news. We lost our primary funder. I'm afraid we gotta go on hiatus."

Profanities echoed throughout the arena. Judd felt like he'd been sucked down a drain, his dream in free fall. Every actor faces rejection, but this felt like fatality. A ball of stardust landed in his hands only to darken and die.

Zach took in the glum faces.

"Yeah-yeah, it's crappy-crap. Nothing I can do about it. But listen, I know people. If this doesn't pan out, I'll find a way to make it all up to you. I promise."

Judd strangled the rope in his hands.


An icy rain pelted the parking lot. Three o'clock in the afternoon and already the sky cast a world's end gloom. Gray plumes of vented smoke trailed from the Minneapolis skyline like pennants on a ghost ship. As Judd scraped his windshield, he glanced around, sensing someone looking at him.

No one there.

The feeling of being watched haunted him as he drove back streets, avoiding the gridlocked highway. He pulled up to the Wilder's garage relieved to reach the house before the freezing drizzle made driving treacherous.

As Judd stepped out of the car, a door slammed. Two men in wool overcoats jumped him. They wrestled him toward a silver van idling at the curb. A fleshy, slab of a hand muffled Judd's shouts for help. He twisted to free himself, jabbed at them with his elbows. They struggled to hold him, slipping on the ice. One stripped off Judd's arctic parka, lost his footing, and hit the pavement with a guttural yowl. Judd slid to his car and clung to the bumper as the other abductor grabbed the back pocket of his jeans.

"Help!" Judd bellowed.

The assailant yanked so hard the pocket ripped open. He tumbled on his butt and spun a triple axel down the driveway all the way to the curb.

Judd gripped the rail of his roof rack and hand-over-hand skim-stepped to the driver's door. Once behind the wheel, he sprang the engine and crammed it in reverse, nearly backing over the fallen man.

"What the hell!" He swerved onto the one-way street that orbited Lake of the Isles. He wanted to floor it, but the freezing rain coating the asphalt made speed out of the question. The ice shone like glass.

"Who were those assholes!"

Judd had no time to speculate. Those assholes swelled in his rearview mirror.

"Shit!" He tried to accelerate. But anything faster than eight miles an hour spun the Toyota.

All-wheel drive and studded snow tires have zero traction on black ice. Which was also true for the thugs maneuvering the van. Attempting to catch up, their rear end careened sideways. It slammed the fender of a parked car busting a tail light, then scraped the side panel of another with a nerve-ripping screech.

Judd made a wide, swively right turn over a flattened street sign. If he gripped the wheel any tighter his white knuckles would break skin. He passed a car upturned in a ditch. People stood by, motionless with absent eyes.

At the next corner a Range Rover drifted onto the shoulder, jumped the curb and clipped a tree. The driver opened her door.

"No!" Judd banged the horn, tapped the brakes. The driver ducked back in her car as his SUV bashed the Range Rover's door off its hinges. The door vaulted in the air, landed on the road, and lodged under the front tires of the abductors' silver van.

Judd took the next right in a slow-motion glide and merged into a motorcade lumbering west. He thought he was free of the thugs. As he exhaled relief, his forehead throbbed and pictures lit up the windshield.

"Fak!" He yelled, as glimpses of his youth flitted in front of his eyes—North Dakota, his hand swiping a twenty from the church's offering plate, his father sandblasting a gravestone, white sheets flapping on a line.

"Stop that!" Judd clapped his left hand to his forehead to see ahead. Brake lights flared. The sluggish procession stuttered to a skidding halt.

Judd considered wrapping his neck scarf around his skull when he heard a honk behind him. He didn't notice the light turn green. Accelerating on ice from a dead stop causes tires to slither sideways. He carefully eased down the gas pedal. His FJ Cruiser, along with other cars and trucks, fishtailed right and left before straightening out.

As he crept across the intersection a siren blared. Red lights flashed behind him. Cars veered into the right lane to let the emergency vehicle pass. Up ahead a semi was jack-knifed. Its cab canted on its side, crushing the guard rail. Smoke spooled from the engine.

"Gahh!" Judd shouted. Instead of a cop or ambulance, the silver van he thought he'd outrun appeared in his side mirror. It swung into the open lane and nosed up alongside. Frozen raindrops dotting the side window magnified the driver's eyes in twenty lenses. Judd cranked the wheel hard right. He bounded up a curb and twirled a 360 to a squealing stop, blocking the drive-thru of a burger joint.

The van driver whipped the wheel in pursuit, but the tractionless tires betrayed him. The van spiraled across the center line where it was T-boned by a sand truck. The collision sounded like a detonated bomb. The van somersaulted, flung metal and chunks of glass, and scudded to a halt, a battered hulk, wheels up and whirling.

The cashier in the drive-thru window gaped at Judd as if he could see the pictures beaming from his forehead. Judd drove around back and parked. His heart thudded so hard he thought it would bust out his ribcage and never come back.

As he wrapped his head with his neck scarf, he spotted the van driver in the side mirror limp toward him on a bum leg with something in his hand.

Judd lowered his window and yelled, "You got the wrong man!" But the guy kept coming, snorting like a bull.

"Who are these people?!"

Judd jammed the Cruiser in reverse and crept out the side exit.

Okay, now what? Go to the police? No, get the hell out of here. But where? Not back to the Wilders, that's for sure.

He thought of calling friends, but opted for the only person who might sympathize with his predicament.

When he reached Marigold an hour later, Judd drove straight to the Econo Self-Storage facility and called the number on the sign.

Hearing him describe the incident, Arnie asked, "What'd they look like?"

"The driver had a rodent face, upturned nose. The other wore a ski mask. Might not be from around here. Dude didn't know how to steer into a spin."

"They say anything?"

"Only groans from the guy who hit the asphalt."

"Foreigners?"

"Dunno. Groans are the same all over."

"You in debt to anybody?"

"No?"

Arnie was silent.

"What are they after?" Judd asked.

"What's everybody after."

"The Godhead Spot?"

"You betcha."

"Why me?"

"They must figure you got something. Think your brain's a mess now? They get their mitts on you it's creamed corn. Meet me behind the café in an hour."

# 16

# Arnie and Marsha

Arnold "Arnie" Arneson was a frisky, fifty-four-year-old jack-of-all-trades who looked like a Swiss army knife with all the implements sticking out. He had a gray bristly beard, short, porcupine-spiked hair, and a gleam in the eyes as if grateful to be alive. His gregarious nature made him the first choice as interim mayor of Marigold after the former passed away.

A consummate handyman, and a wizard at wheeling and dealing, Arnie loved trading for properties. Besides the eighty-acre farm where he lived, he owned two houses, a duplex, the self-storage facility, and the 1904 brick building in town that housed the café. You'd never know how wealthy he was by his faded work clothes.

Arnie was not surprised to find the road to the Jolleys gridlocked with onlookers. Rumors of a raid on the property sent jitters through town. He hadn't heard such a hen house of gossip since casino robbers buried their loot in the area in '09.

A guard stood before a line of orange cones stopping traffic. He only let those pass who lived beyond the property. Arnie saw Marsha at the home site hunched in her goose down coat, poking a broom handle into the ruins. She had permission to dig for valuables the ATF agents deemed inconsequential.

Arnie figured the best place to shelter Judd was on the apartment couch above the café where Marsha and Flannery temporarily lodged. The way he saw it, someone who knows about brains needed to watch Judd. And being a professor on the subject, Marsha filled the bill.

The guard checked him out and let him through. He hiked past roofing panels slammed against tree trunks and shards of window glass glinting in the snow. Seeing Arnie, Marsha frowned.

"Now I know how tornado victims feel."

To Arnie, the way she held up under the circumstances was heroic. He wanted to hold her, comfort her, but that would bust a boundary. He stuffed his love for Marsha so deep not even Henna Pino, the nosiest busybody in Marigold, could see it.

He told Marsha about Judd's abduction and asked if she'd let him sleep on her couch.

"He'll only be there the one night. I'd have him stay at my place but it's a mess with the remodel," he said.

"That's all I need, an oversized ego to babysit."

"He sounded shook up."

"Who isn't!" Marsha let out a ragged sigh and punched the broom handle into the pile. "You said whoever did this had thermal imaging. Do you see one scintilla of regard for human life here? It's a kill zone."

Arnie stared at the mangled jumble of busted sheathing, the billowy pink fiberglass poking through crumbles of drywall.

"But why would they want the boys dead? They're far more valuable alive, doncha think?"

"Hmph. Well they didn't murder me and until they do my every waking moment will—" Marsha was interrupted by the hiss from the brakes of an eighteen-wheeler.

With some crafty maneuvering, the semi backed up between the maple trees and parked at the top of the rise.

"Evidently someone attacked the lab site," Arnie said.

"So I hear," Marsha said. "Listen, I'm grateful for letting Flan and me stay in your building. So it's your call."

"Tell you what. I'll run it by Roslyn. See if she's okay with him sleeping on her couch."

Marsha didn't say anything as she watched the ATF agents load busted remnants of the lab into the back of the truck. She may have been silent, but Arnie could see in her eyes a smoldering defiance.

"I'll let you know," he said.

Marsha watched Arnie walk away, skirting the upside down refrigerator half-buried by debris. Part of her wanted to pack up Flannery and leave town. But she couldn't. Not yet. She needed to shop for clothes and work on a eulogy for Ezra Katz at the upcoming Neuroscience Conference. Besides, the land where she stood belonged to her parents. Not something she was willing to surrender outright, or at all.

Looking back at the heap, something caught her eye. She took off her glove, reached down and plucked a framed photograph of her sons sitting with their father on the riverbank. They must have been fourteen.

It's said a loving mother is blind to her children's defects. Not Marsha. She was keenly aware of her boys' changes as if they happened to her. Their resilience was a blessing. It took no time for them to adjust to Minnesota after living in California. They did well at school, made fast friends, played soccer in the summer, hockey in the winter. Teenage normal until Foster, their father, vanished. Then the boys were excluded from parties and overnights. She watched their moods darken. Known for playful hijinks, their pranks turned mean. Several times the high school called her in.

Foster's lab became their sanctuary. Arnie would stop by and check on them. They trusted him. He shared what he knew about Foster's research. He also found them jobs snowplowing driveways and mowing lawns.

But their father's disappearance stigmatized them. And maybe it was just as well. While other students gravitated to drugs, drinking, sexual escapades, and parental rebellion, the boys turned to science. They dug into Foster's experiments in neuro-archeology. They picked up his optical instruments and began to explore. Later, Marsha connected them with Ezra Katz, who became an exuberant mentor.

The more the twins experimented the less they shared with their mother. Arnie found people to craft equipment for their research. And from time to time, he shared their latest findings with Marsha.

She wiped snow and crud off the photograph.

If only I could go back to when I took this picture—back when my family was whole. Before *The Isness* shattered it.

# 17
# The Drone

As Bob Zeebart muscled a fifty-pound sack of turkey grit into his truck, he heard the whirring of a dentist drill in the sky.

"What the hell we got here," the bearded, forty-eight-year-old grumbled.

He walked to the middle of Marigold's Main Street to get a broader view. The thing appeared a block away.

"There you are," he said.

The white drone lifted and lowered. It circled the thrift store, then whirred off in zigzag passes between the river and the town.

"This here's a no-fly zone, dickhead!"

Seeing nobody near, Zeebart figured the pilot was parked some distance away. He figured right. Chewing a thumbnail, the drone operator sat in a box truck two miles from Marigold with a metallic hedge of antennae and a satellite dish on its roof.

Zeebart got behind the wheel of his fresh-off-the-lot GMC Sierra and tracked the drone. It was hard to see in the fading light of day, but he was determined to chase it back to the source.

"I got you in my sights now!"

When the operator saw the truck on his screen tailing his drone, he jumped in his chair and steered the 'copter skyward.

"What, you afraid of me!?" Zeebart shouted, heading south along the icy River Road. "Y'oughta be!"

So fixated on the drone, he didn't notice the curve until it was too late. His pickup skated off the blacktop, plunged down a gully and up the other side where it struck a power pole. Zeebart's nose smacked the steering wheel. The pole tottered and tugged down the next one. Lines snapped. Sparks spat across the road.

Zeebart stumbled out of the cab dazed. He straightened the red baseball cap on his head.

The drone banked a U-turn and buzzed directly above him.

Zeebart unkinked his neck. He waved a beckoning hand.

"Come on! Take a good look!"

The drone hovered for a minute, then, as if to gloat, descended.

"That'a girl," Zeebart said. He unclipped his twelve-gauge pump action from the gun rack behind the seat.

The drone whirred louder and soared.

Blam!

The damn thing hopped in the air, pitched, and plummeted to Earth.

Zeebart clumped through deep snow and picked it up. The drone was three-feet wide, twice the size of the one he'd seen a neighbor kid maneuver. He stared into its camera.

The drone operator's chair rolled back, bumping against the wall of the truck as Zeebart's bloodied nose pressed against the lens.

"Hey there. You be lookin' at Bob Zeebart. Don't like robots. Don't like spying on. But this is your lucky day 'cuz the soft center in me is willing to let you take your bird back. You still got two propellors look to be working. So, put some thumb muscle into it."

The two props spun.

"That's it. Faster!"

The disabled drone rose from his hand.

"There ya go!" Zeebart shouldered the shot gun, drew aim, and smiled. "Nothing more fun than a movin' target."

The drone operator's screen disintegrated into a black and white square of boiling bee-bees.

# 18
# The Side Yard

Judd turned down an alley and parked his SUV behind the Marigold café. A day that began on a high note in a hockey rink plummeted into an aborted play, a near abduction, a frenzied chase, a car crash, and a sweaty drive into the unknown.

He unfastened his fingers from the steering wheel. But his hands would not stop shaking.

How can this be happening to me?

He wanted to cry. He wanted to punch somebody. He could almost hear the thin ice of his mental state hairline-cracking. Nowhere stable to stand. No guide rail to grab.

Breathe. Be in a bubble of calm.

He felt for the frightened driver whose car door he busted off. "I'm sorry," he half-whispered. "I was being chased, couldn't stop or go back."

He unclipped his seat belt.

Come on! Bubble of *calm*!

When the tremors subsided, he removed his scarf. The projections were gone. But one image stuck in his mind—the side yard, a thistle and knapweed lot next to his family's two-story home on the outskirts of Baxter, North Dakota.

The yard was an orchard of blank headstones. In the center stood a weathered board and batten shack. It had a back booth where his father sandblasted names and dates onto slabs of granite. Most of the epitaphs were long forgotten. A few stayed with him. The saddest were for children: *Far too soon to be forever in our hearts.*

Judd began helping his father at twelve. He printed and cut rubber stencils for people who died of old age, cancer, farm accidents, overdoses. He adhered the stencils to the stones. His father grooved them out with silicon carbide sand.

Judd hated working there. He hated the scorch of blasting sand that took him away from friends and sports.

On occasion, he assisted at the cemetery, lowering the memorial stone by winch. One day, while his father loaded the truck in the side yard, the cable snapped. The monument dropped on Judd's left foot. The bones never healed completely. After the cast came off, he had a slight limp and cringed when stepping on uneven ground. The injury took eight long months out of his life. No baseball, no dances. The time stolen from him hurt more than the bone fractures. To rebel, he began to steal chocolate bars and breath mints from the 7-Eleven. His motto: rightfully take from the world what was taken from you. The adrenaline rush he felt from each theft fueled a craving for pricier goods.

Staring blankly at the back of the café, he didn't see Arnie pull up alongside. At the slam of the truck's door, Judd's head hit the roof. Shooting stars raked his vision.

Arnie understood. He'd be just as jumpy if assaulted.

"Follow me." He waved a finger on his way to the back door.

"Hold on." Judd stumbled out weak-kneed, as if he'd stepped off a trampoline. He grabbed a satchel from the back seat. Then checked the front bumper, barely a dent.

But something was missing. He reached for his wallet and found the pocket torn away. The wallet gone. He searched the car. Under the driver's seat he found a white binder labeled DEATH SIGHT SCANNER. "What the hell," he muttered as he flipped through its optic nerve illustrations and blocks of type. "Oh, shit, that's right," he admitted, as if he'd been concealing the memory of stealing it from himself.

Judd was beginning to realize how thievery had lost its thrill. It had become a routine habit without the "got away with it" kick. The laptop he lifted from a dressing room backstage, the Ray-Bans he pocketed at the optical store. Not so much as a tickle. He stuffed the binder back under the seat.

"Assholes got my wallet." He slammed the car door.

"If that's the worst, count yourself lucky." Arnie unlocked a deadbolt. "Never thought glare ice could save a person's life."

They entered a long storage room with shelves of kitchen supplies. Arnie climbed a flight of stairs. Judd struggled to keep up. The stairs led to a landing and a long, dark hallway.

Feeling the need to say something, Judd asked, "Any news about the boys?"

"Not a peep."

"You know them pretty well?"

"Yep." Arnie flicked a switch. Ceiling fluorescents lit up a carpeted hall. There was a faint, musty smell of mildew. "They were hiding in my tornado bunker when it happened. Scared the crap out of 'em. Now they're domestic terrorists."

"Who do you think's behind it?"

"The bombing?" Arnie sorted through his keys. "Could be the government, a secret society, or some power-hungry billionaire."

"Secret society? You mean like a cult?"

"You got those who want to destroy the discovery and those who want to possess it." Arnie opened an apartment. "This is Roslyn's. You can hang out here, or down in the café until she's back from class."

"She okay with this?"

"For one night."

Arnie had called Roslyn. She was not okay with it. She felt her space invaded. However, this was Arnie asking, her friend, her boss, and the father she never had. She accepted, begrudgingly.

Her apartment was clean and uncluttered. It had a hardwood floor, colorful throw rugs, and shelves of books. There was an easel in the corner with a painting of yellow-and-orange triangles, a glass jar of paint brushes beside it. In the kitchen, Roslyn's café uniform draped over an ironing board. A poster of a tree branch with a cluster of monarch butterflies hung above the sink.

"I'll wait in the café for now." Judd followed Arnie down the stairs. "So how'd those thugs find out where I live?"

"Coulda spied you at the boy's lab and tracked you."

Once in the café Judd went straight to the big picture window and peered through the blinds. No one on the street. He set his satchel on the counter.

"Thanks, Arnie. 'Cause right now I'm afraid to go back home."

"Just so you know, Roslyn's doing me a favor. You go weirdo, it's good riddance."

# 19

# Head's Don't Do That!

It was dark when Marsha and Flannery arrived.

"We been shopping," Flannery said.

Judd helped them carry bags of store-bought clothes into the café. He sat at the counter and watched them snip price tags and collapse cardboard boxes.

"Our second Christmas," Flannery said, holding up a pair of Red Wing boots. "I love these, Mom!" she shouted to Marsha in the kitchen.

What an incredible girl, Judd thought. She just lost everything.

"Here." Marsha handed Judd a cup of fresh coffee. "There's creamer and sugar packets, you need them."

Marsha asked Flannery to take her new clothes upstairs while she got dinner ready.

With Flannery gone, Marsha took a stool next to Judd.

"So what happened?" Marsha said.

"They were waiting for me."

"They who?"

"I don't know. Strangers. Never seen'em before. They knew where I lived!"

"Someone stalked me at the university last week. I'd show you a picture but the Feds confiscated my phone."

"What do they want from me?" Judd took a gulp of coffee.

"I warned you to keep away from us."

"Is this about the God thing?"

Flannery danced into the dining room wearing her new shoes and humming to music in her ear buds.

Marsha stood. "I need to get dinner started."

Judd went upstairs. He was hungry but didn't want to impose. Sitting on Roslyn's couch he pulled the laptop from his satchel and looked up Marsha's husband, Foster Jolley, online. One short biography said Foster graduated from Stanford with a Master's in neuroscience and how he invented an optical scanning device. While there, he met Marsha. They later married. She gave birth to twin boys, Oakland and Rochester, named after Foster and Marsha's birthplaces. Eight years later Flannery was born.

Another article showed a book jacket with a René Magritte painting of a man in suit and tie whose head was a ball of light. The title, all caps: *THE ISNESS*. Subtitle: *A field guide to lighting the fuse of self-salvation.*

Judd bristled at the word "salvation." At least Foster made it clear no one can save you but yourself.

He looked around the apartment. Propped on an artist's easel, Roslyn's unfinished abstract painting caught his eye. It had the same golden orange colors as the monarch poster above the sink.

"So that's it," he muttered. She's picturing the butterfly through a prism like a kaleidoscope.

Flannery entered without knocking. She wore bright-blue flannel pajamas with beluga whales printed on them.

"Do you have another acting lesson for me?"

"Maybe tomorrow."

"I've decided I want to do *musical* theater."

"Ohh …" Judd moaned. "That's…" He almost said "too bad." Musicals made him gag. He hoped it didn't show. "Do you miss your brothers?"

She thought about it and said, "Yes and no. They teased me a lot, and sometimes cruelly."

"Flan?" Marsha called.

"G'night."

Judd found a three-year-old magazine article online: "Come Back Foster Jolley—The Isness is Wasness Without You." Under the title was a color photo of Foster signing books. His facial features resembled his sons, most notably Chester, the straight nose, the sharp V contour of the jawline, the tousled dirty blond hair.

"Where are you Foster?" the article began. "You abandoned your followers in limbo-ness. Stories of your disappearance range from falling for a hottie to achieving the ultra-heavenly state of 'Is-vana.'"

Indistinct voices percolated up from the street. Looking out the window, Judd saw a police cruiser at the curb, Arnie talking to the driver. When Judd dropped back on the couch, he felt a pressure between his eyes like someone depressing a button to start his brain.

No-no, *not now!*

Split-second flashbacks lit up the wall—Susie Tash slapping his hands away from her breasts, his father dragging him by the ear, the grill of a police car, wind whipping flames from a rolling hay bale.

Judd had no choice but to let it play out—chased through corn rows, echoes in an empty silo, blood dripping off barbed wire …

The pictures shuttled further and further back in time. With his attention riveted, Judd didn't notice the door swing open and shut.

Hurry up, he pleaded, hoping the memories would rewind to his birth and fade to black.

"Hello?"

It was Roslyn.

Judd looked up to thank her for letting him sleep on her couch. But when she saw the beam of light flash from his forehead onto her winter coat, she gasped and ran out.

He heard knocking and Roslyn shouting, "Marsha! It's Roslyn, next door."

The two entered Roslyn's apartment.

"Good God," Marsha said.

"You can see it?" Judd was shocked as well. The pictures kept racing back in time, younger and younger. The point of view lowered—a man kneeled, extended huge hands.

"Can you hear it?" he asked.

"No."

Roslyn shuddered, "What's happening?"

"My sons ..." Marsha said.

"Your son's what?" Roslyn stepped back, both captivated and shaken by the freak show.

"I told you, they messed up my brain!" Judd convulsed as his projections continued: a woman's bright eyes followed by an interval of darkness.

"Are these past events in your life?" Marsha asked.

"Yes," Judd said. But his experiences didn't stop at birth as he hoped. The visuals reached beyond the womb—a storm at sea, bearded men in armor, fingers fletching an arrow, a camel pulled by braided rope.

"I have no control. It just happens," he said.

The memories finally stopped. Judd withered on the couch. He pointed to the ruddy patch of skin on his forehead.

"And it burns."

The two gaped as Judd shut his eyes.

There was a two-knuckle rap on the door.

"It's me." Arnie peeked in. "Hey there, checking in. Hi Roz."

Marsha herded Arnie and Roslyn into the apartment across the hall. "Keep your voices down," she said, and went off to the bedroom to check on Flannery.

Seeing Roslyn's pale, pale face, Arnie said, "You look spooked. You okay?"

"No," she said. "Nowhere near."

"Here." Arnie gestured to a chair for her to sit.

Marsha left the bedroom and closed the door behind her.

"What happened?" Arnie said.

"What happened is my sons turned Judd's third eye into a movie projector."

"Say that again. Movies?"

Marsha pointed an index finger to her forehead. "Out of here."

"And he spasmed the whole time." Roslyn said.

"Talk about your life passing before your eyes." Marsha paused. "No … can't be."

"Can't be what?" Roslyn said.

"His Life Review," Marsha said.

"What's that?"

"It's called the Life Review or the Great Remembering. After death we re-experience the life we lived. We face our actions, our choices, the harm we caused, the joy. That would explain the gyrations. Oh my God, he wasn't only replaying his past, he was re-*feeling* it while alive!"

Roslyn pointed across the hall. "Heads don't do that!"

"They do now," Marsha said.

Roslyn blew out a long exhale. "Shouldn't he go to a clinic or some place that looks into these … these abnormal …?"

"Probably. I'll say this, he definitely needs watching," Marsha said.

No one spoke.

"Well, I got something." Arnie said. "Been talking to Sheriff Buck. The rumor is true, Marsha. There was a raid on your property. A bloody one. I'm worried for you and Flannie's safety. Maybe it's best we pull her out of school until things settle."

"Can we discuss it when I'm back from the conference?"

Arnie nodded, turned to Roslyn.

"Roz, how would you feel about homeschooling Flan after the breakfast rush, rent free?"

She didn't answer.

"Think about it."

He went next door to check on Judd.

Roslyn looked at Marsha. "Guess I should be glad I never got to know your sons.

"What would make them do that to him?" Marsha asked. "And what's to come of it?"

"Sorry. Nurses' training doesn't prepare for this."

Arnie came back.

"He's conked out, Roz. But, don't worry. I'll set up a makeshift bed in the utility closet."

Roslyn removed her knit cap, stopped at the door. "Guess I'll be seeing a rerun of this in my Life Review."

# 20
# The Conductor

Inside the Smithsonian Museum in Washington DC, a young intelligence analyst spotted Inman Hayes, Chief Consultant for the Department of Defense. He was fanning through a pamphlet at the information table.

"Chief …"

"Walk with me," said Hayes, an imposing sixty-one-year-old with an over-sized head, visor eyelids, and a world-suspicious stare. His credentials gave him access to every government building in America, yet only a handful of people knew he oversaw clandestine missions beyond the purview of the DOD. Hayes answered solely to the Secretary of Defense, who in top secret briefings simply referred to him as "The Conductor."

The two strolled down the Hall of Human Origins.

"Ever been here?" Hayes spoke through a burlap throat.

The analyst looked at the glassed-in dioramas of early man. "I have not."

"It's good to get away, get perspective on things." Hayes didn't care for the analyst the Secretary picked for the assignment. Just another Ivy League academic who never spent a night alone in the wilderness or unclogged a toilet with his bare hands.

"So catch me up," Hayes said.

The analyst opened a folder. "The committee came up with possible scenarios based on there being a genuine conduit to the Creator."

"Gimme the worst."

"In terms of national security and America's economic stability, it could incite cataclysmic changes."

"I'm listening."

"Consider the entire population infected by boundless altruism."

"Whoa …" Hayes stopped to eye a young woman sauntering past—his kind, Rubenesque, pillowy. He was struck by the contrast between her smooth-skinned looks and the backdrop of hairy cave people. "You were saying."

"A plague of benevolence, sir, and with it, possibly a complete decline in global hostilities. There was a long debate about a credible peace scare. Even the D-word came up."

"Disarmament?"

"Weapons of war obsolete. There'd be a drastic tanking in arms sales if every person became enlightened. Missiles and munitions-makers out of business. General Dynamics, Northrop Grumman, kaput."

"That's absurd. War's not going away, too many benefits. Think of the advances in science, not to mention breeding control. We're an invasive species. We spread. War is a natural prophylactic. Besides, violence is hard-wired to our existence, like hunger. And, when it comes to God, there've been religious wars since the Crusades, hell, since hell began. Did anybody mention that?"

"Yes, the committee addressed it and …"

Hayes stopped at a Neanderthal man spear-hunting a mastodon.

"Have you done that Paleo diet thing? Ladyfriend put me on it."

"No … I …"

"Got the trots."

The analyst had been coached not to become frustrated with Hayes's attention deficit. Must come with the job, the young man figured, a side effect of being privy to crucial issues of national security.

Actually, Hayes used verbal diversions to keep people on their toes. No one knew what he was thinking. And no one existed with whom he would completely confide.

"Now, who was on the Spitball Committee again?" Hayes asked.

The analyst shuffled through pages to the Think Tank list.

"General Meeks …"

Hayes checked a text on a phone while the analyst recited a series of names with acronyms including the NSA and CIA, plus a Georgetown professor of religious studies, a theoretical physicist, and a science-fiction writer.

"Quite a diverse group," the analyst said, as Hayes stopped at a display showcasing replicas of million-year-old heads.

"Say, you think way back then those Homo erectus men ogled the babes? Makes you wonder if the more extreme slope of the forehead made the female more … seductive."

"I …"

"You were saying …" Hayes pocketed his phone.

"Right. So the committee agreed that staggered intervals of peace are good, but not long term. And other occupations and pastimes will surely take a hit."

"Such as?"

"Who needs drugs or therapeutics when your life is unburdened?"

"That's a stretch."

"In the theology professor's words—'Consider being enrapt in the inexhaustible light of divine grace.'"

"Light of divine grace ... that doesn't sound half bad."

"No, it doesn't, and he wondered if religions would end when everyone had a pipeline to the Almighty. Who needs churches, synagogues, mosques? All religious leaders, whatever denomination, ministers, rabbis ... poof!"

"No chance in hell," said Hayes. "Shit happens, even in Utopia. People fall down. Die before their time. Where do you go to for solace and consolation? What, everyone's a fuckin' saint? Gimme a break. People are crazy. Even shrinks need shrinks."

"Other institutions will flatline too."

"Such as?"

"Law enforcement. The courts. Governing bodies like the Department of Defense ..."

"That's lunacy!" Hayes shouted at the analyst, turning heads of museum visitors.

After a momentary pause, the analyst continued.

"The conversation then devolved into quantum physics, God as an equation."

Hayes gestured to a display.

"Ever think about Charles Darwin? Now there's a guy who faced a firing squad of flung dung after his boat trip. Talk about a buzz kill. Hey everybody, your ancestors are orangutans!"

The analyst cleared his throat. "Bottomline, we're talking a cultural tsunami that would capsize the status quo, undermine everything American—the way things are, the way things are meant to be!"

"Gimme that." Hayes set his attaché case down. He snatched the folder, thumbed through the pages. "Did anybody determine with any degree of certainty what kind of God the God of this Godhead Spot is?"

"No, but they...."

"No is a no."

"Yes. But, what if it's not a Christian god? Or what if it comes with a thousand commandments? You know, like: 'Thou shalt not barbeque.'"

A beeping sounded.

"Hang on." Hayes handed the folder back to the analyst and pulled out his phone. "Got to take this."

The analyst murmured on. "What if it manifests as a god-*dess*?"

Hayes turned to the analyst. "Got a Cardinal Barberi on the line. Been trying to reach me for days. How do I address him?"

"A Cardinal? Your Eminence, or Your Most Reverend Eminence."

"Good morning ... your Em-nence. What can I do for you? What? ... Ha! You can't imagine the rubbish we hear every day. Who? His Holiness?" Hayes gave a perplexed look. The analyst mouthed, "The Pope." Hayes nodded. "I see. Say again? ... Ho-ho, that's a good one. No-no-no, standard rule of thumb—keep rumors and conspiracy theories under the tongue until you know enough to know enough. Right ... Will do. You as well."

Hayes pocketed the phone, picked up his case and smoldered. "How the hell did he ..." There's only one way this Cardinal Barberi could know. A leak. Ears were everywhere, like roaches in the walls. His first suspicion—someone on the Spitball Committee.

Hayes and the analyst came to the end of the hall, turned, and walked back toward the lobby.

"All right, so that's worst case, what's the best?" Hayes asked.

"Depends on your point of view. Personally, I think the worst case *is* the best case."

"Did I ask your opinion?"

"No, but ..."

Hayes sped up his stride.

"Listen," he said, "I appreciate the work of the committee. But there are no known knowns that raise this to an actionable threat level. Even if true, surely it would require some sort of procedure, an injection, or brain surgery."

"Maybe not," the analyst replied. "Could be catchy, a kiss, or airborne. An angelic pandemic."

"We're all varied individuals, young man, different DNA, idiosyncrasies, what-have-you. If anything, it will affect you differently than me, like ... like cilantro."

"Or make us all the same. Mass mind control. 'Communionists' as General Meeks speculated."

"Bah!" Hayes grabbed the folder from him. "I trust you will destroy every speck relating ..."

"Absolutely."

"That'll be all." Hayes gave a slack wave of his hand as he exited the museum. He wasn't about to let the analyst know what was really going on. Keep him in the weeds. Besides, the kid knows way too much already.

As Hayes stopped to put the folder in his case, a sleeve of photos fell out onto the rain-soaked walkway.

"Aw, shit!" he hunkered down, flapped water off them. There was one of Oakley Jolley, another of Chester, and one of

Judd Russell outside the twins' lab, holding something white partially concealed in his coat.

Over the years Hayes handled a number of classified operations. Many ended deadly, their existence obliterated. He could demand electronic surveillance, intel analysts, scouts, soldiers, drones. He was a strategic magician who'd seen more shit than a sewer, and when he bit down he never let go.

But this one, *Operation Mind Control*, was an odd duck. The department assured him it was not a joke, and he came to understand why they assigned it to him. God is one touchy subject. Best kept detached from the mothership. Wherever it led, the department could deny involvement.

The job—capture and remove "the significants." Seize their materials and determine the efficacy of their discovery. All good, but the wear and tear of commandeering so many covert missions had crept up on Hayes. Although unspoken, he vowed to make this his last assignment.

He pulled a different phone from his overcoat and punched a name.

"Activate the the task force. Have them sweep the town and, goddammit, track down those runaway jackals! They're twins, you find one, you find both. What? I don't know how they could have known … Of course somebody tipped them off … Who? God knows! And as for the analyst, see that he's grounded … with a spade."

# 21

# Victor King

Back at the Pentagon, Hayes called Victor King, who ran Neurokey, a brain laboratory across the Potomac River from the Capitol.

When the call came through the landline, Victor was in his mezzanine office. Before him, on a large screen, a photograph showed objects from the ruins of the Jolleys' lab.

"Chief Hayes, what a coincidence. I was going to call you about our contract." Victor gave an assured grin to the camera, belying his urgency. The slick-haired forty-six-year-old was dressed in ivory white T-shirt, black blazer, designer slacks, and gold-tinted glasses—going for a casual, euro-manly look with a shadow of manicured stubble.

"What can you tell me about a Cardinal Barberi?" Hayes asked.

"Hang on, let me put you on the jumbo ..."

Victor punched a button. Hayes's pink face filled the screen, huge as Zeus. The sight gave Victor a start.

"Woo! There you are. Okay ... Cardinal Barberi ..."

"Claims he's an envoy for the Pope," Hayes said.

"The Vatican's had feelers out since word of a divine portal in the brain first surfaced. Consider the threat it poses."

"Not following."

"Imagine a wrecking ball smashing the bell tower of Christian dogma. The anxiety over the Dead Sea Scrolls pales by …"

"So how did Barberi …?"

"Not from me, but I'm not surprised. The Cardinal shows up at conferences to eavesdrop on new developments. He toured our lab a while back and pressed us about achieving ecstatic states by stimulating temporal lobes with electromagnetic pulses."

An over-salivator when tense, Victor wiped spittle from the corners of his mouth. "I wouldn't worry about Barberi. I'd be more concerned with the Chinese. What if they tap the spot first? We know they're looking. They're all looking. What if a Russian becomes all-seeing, all-knowing?"

*All-seeing, all-knowing.* Hayes took the thought to a scary place, rare for him. *The ultimate spy.*

"Hold on a sec. Got to take another call," he said.

Victor heard Hayes railing, "How'd they lose him? Ice? Did you say 'ice'? That's their excuse!?"

Victor stamped his foot. He couldn't let Hayes go off track. They had verbally agreed on a contract that assured his laboratory of desperately needed funding. It also gave him exclusive access to everything the ATF pulled from the remnants of the Jolleys' lab.

Don't let him delay any longer, Victor berated himself. If you have to pitch Neurokey ten more times, pitch and close the deal!

Hayes returned.

"You find anything useful in the hangar photos?"

"Standard lab equipment. Nothing out of the ordinary. Those boys must've ditched the real important ..."

"Evidently your daughter Kira knows somebody who can track them down. She claims the guy's got superhuman extra-sensory powers."

Victor slumped. Why Kira summoned Theodore Theroux to locate the Jolleys was beyond him. No way should a Defense contract hinge on the success or failure of a psychic warlock.

"Kira's network is wide," Victor conceded. "Still, I have a more effective plan. The twin's mother is speaking at the upcoming neuroscience conference. I set up a meeting with her where I'll offer a win-win proposal that'll bring her sons back. But to make that happen I need the DOD contract in my hands for leverage. Can you messenger it over?"

No response. Hayes left Victor dangling again.

Shit! Don't let him slink away!

"Where were we?" Hayes returned.

"The contract, Chief. May I remind you that we offer the brightest stars in *the* most exceptional brain lab on Earth." Victor knuckle-swiped the corner of his lips. "And ..." he cleared his throat. "... you have *me*, guiding the ship ..." Victor stopped. Did Hayes just chuckle?

"Looks like atheists may be in for one helluva whiplash."

"Chief?"

"Mean to say, it'll be quite the deal if true."

"What's that?"

"How all the while there's been a direct phone line to the man upstairs tucked away in our noggin."

"Yes, well, they don't call it the God*head* for nothing."

# 22

# Small Towns Have Big Eyes

Locals packed the café gabbing about "the ka-boom" Gladys Smith witnessed on the river. Judd sat across from Arnie at a booth in the back, eating farm fresh eggs, crisp strips of bacon, and golden hash browns. A borrowed purple Vikings cap covered the blister on his forehead. Out the front window a man shoveled snow off the sidewalk.

"So what was it?" Judd asked "Another bombing?"

"Somebody raided the site, guns blazing. Things don't go unseen here. Small towns have big eyes." Arnie held up his coffee mug for Roslyn. As she refilled it, she avoided eye contact with Judd and walked away.

"You sure frightened her, and she doesn't scare easy," Arnie said, lifting the mug to his lips.

Judd wanted to say that the projections freaked him out too, but his mouth was full.

"She hasn't had an easy time," Arnie went on. "Parents divorced and left her at fourteen. Fended for herself ever since. She works days at the café and takes night classes at Mankato State for a nursing degree."

Judd watched Roslyn take an order at the counter. She had a fluid grace. Chestnut brown hair gathered back in a ponytail. Soft features contrasted by piercing bronze eyes. Eyes that have known hunger. And when they look at you, they drill so deep you feel your honesty x-rayed.

Arnie thought the world of Roslyn. He knew that, although wary of others, at 23, she was willing to let her heart go full out. Hoarding her love created as much pain as losing it. In her time at the café, she'd inspired several upgrades including a Vulcan stove and new refigeration unit. Her idea to replace the fisherman photos on the walls with artwork from school children brightened the atmosphere.

"She's like one of those roadside daisies." Arnie went on. "The ones that get tossed about by the wind of passing motorists and still hold a bloom."

After speaking with a few regulars, Sheriff Billy "Buck" Thorne stopped at their booth. Arnie introduced Judd who thought the two looked hewn from the same block of stone—stocky builds, similar age, crow's feet. Judd wasn't surprised to learn they were football teammates in high school. Arnie the affable one, Buck no-nonsense.

"Anything more about the raid?" Arnie asked.

Buck held up two fingers. He lowered his voice. "Foreign types on snowmobiles."

Arnie looked at Judd. "Buck doesn't buy it's all charade." He turned back to Buck. "Did you see how fast those ATF guys arrived at the site? Like they knew it was going to blow before it did. I'm tellin' ya, they aren't looking for bombs. They're after the boys' experiments."

"You're almost making me a believer, Arn," Buck said. "And this shit's gotta stop. Folks started locking their doors."

"So where'd they truck the lab rubble?" Arnie asked.

"Hangar at Flying Cloud." Buck glanced at the clock. "Oh, got to grab some joe to go. Catch up with you later."

Arnie followed Buck to the door to speak privately.

Judd took a sip of coffee and looked around. Not everyone was talking about the raid. A burly man in the next booth was reading a newspaper article out loud. Three booths away a couple were telling Roslyn about visiting their daughter for Christmas in San Diego.

"Whoa," Judd blurted, surprised he could hear what people were saying ten feet away amid all the hubbub and kitchen clatter.

Okay, what's the white-haired man at the counter saying?

"It's a sure sign you're aging when you start watching the behavior of crows."

Unreal, Judd thought. So, how far can I go and listen in?

He aimed his attention at a table by the front window where an elderly man sounded off to a guy half his age.

"Hell, we had none of this technology and farm analytics back in the day. Didn't need it. To know the soil's fertility, we'd grab a handful and chew it down to a foamy gruel. We'd gargle it like mouth wash, spit it out on a platter 'n read the grit like a book."

Every word sharp. Judd couldn't recall ever being able to cone his hearing with such clarity before.

"Wabumba," he said under his breath.

He ate the last of the hash browns, nudged the plate away, and wiped his mouth with a blue paper napkin.

Arnie returned. "You done?"

"Yeah, thanks. I'll pay you back, after I sort out my accounts with the bank."

"Oh no, you'll pay me back now." Arnie stood. "Let's go."

# 23
# Cardinal Barberi

Cardinal Barberi was a short, energetic Italian with a Buddha-round face and an inner-tube belly. Although living well in Washington DC, he was homesick for Vatican City, the center of his universe, where he felt infused with the Christ. But Barberi's spirited intensity aroused concern in Vatican chambers. The elite feared he was becoming more popular than the Pontiff, his outspoken opinions more persuasive. A rising star they didn't need. So they sent him abroad.

His relocation coincided with Foster Jolley's *The Isness* book climbing the non-fiction bestseller list. Vatican powers sent Barberi to America to investigate and denounce Foster's revelations as well as any other neurological developments related to the divine.

Barberi's disarming, compassionate personality enabled him to make friends with everyone from street vendors to branch heads of government. If he wanted an invitation or information, he could simply ask. No one suspected his motives as anything but pious.

After five years in the states, Barberi sought reassignment. He found Americans to be shallow, over-stimulated, and consumed by their looks. Still, he did as told. He played the curious enthusiast and took tours of laboratories across the country. In time he spoke fluent neurology, asked smart questions, and filed his findings with the Holy See.

Barberi had nothing ground-breaking to report until he met Dr. Ezra Katz at Cornell University a month before the man's death. Katz was ecstatic about his protégés' discovery. He told the Cardinal he'd be introducing the boy's work at an upcoming conference at the Capitol's convention center. Of course Barberi would attend, meet the brothers, commend their achievement—and debunk it.

However, days after visiting Katz, the Cardinal became obsessed with the possibility of a Godhead Spot existing in the human brain. What if the brothers actually opened a channel to the Supreme Being? Why defraud such a miracle? Wouldn't that be sacrilege? Why not have it? Do I fulfill *their* mission, or the world's salvation?

Barberi felt a mix of relief and sadness when he heard Katz died. Days later, when word came of the Jolley brothers' disappearance, he made inquiries. A dismissive call with Chief Inman Hayes of the DOD told him everything he feared. The Pentagon was all over it.

Would they destroy the portal or use it to brainwash the masses?

# 24

# Name's Lester

Helping out a handyman was the last thing Judd Russell wanted, but what could he do? Obligation buckled him in the shotgun seat of Arnie's pickup, off to who knows where. If it was any consolation, his craziness subsided. And maybe, he thought, some physical labor might take his brain off his mind.

Lester Moore's farmhouse stood in a panoramically flat snowfield. Arnie's truck bumped along the rutted driveway and stopped in a turnaround by the porch. Along the facade of the house, a row of long icicles hung off the roof like shiny stalactites.

The front door opened. A woman filled the frame with the fleshiest pumpkin face Judd had ever seen. At her feet yipped a dog the size of an insect.

"Mornin' Joy."

"Arnie's here!" Her strained voice hollered back into the house. "At least there's still a man around who can do something."

"Said you had some old pantyhose," Arnie said.

"Got 'em right here." Joy reached around the storm door and handed out a paper sack. "Question for you—what in God's name did those boys do now? Got everybody on edge."

Arnie turned to Judd. "Go ahead and pull the ladder out of the truck and set it up under the ice dam here while I get the de-icer."

Judd stood the aluminum ladder near the concrete stoop. Back at the pickup he watched Arnie scissor-cut a bag of a salt-looking substance on the tailgate.

"Need you to hold this open." He handed Judd one of Joy's nylons.

"What's it for?"

"To melt the ice dam." Arnie tipped the bag, poured calcium chloride into the pantyhose three-quarters full and knotted the end like a big sausage.

While filling the nylons, Judd asked, "This guy Foster? You knew him pretty well?"

"Met him shortly after they moved here. Marsha inherited the place from her folks. He knew nothing about maintaining a property. Hired me to help him construct a laboratory for his work with optical lenses. Showed me a scope that could see through bone and under the human skull."

They finished stuffing six nylons.

"Okay, now lay these along the ice dam so they straddle the rain gutter."

Judd only needed to step onto the second rung of the ladder to reach the roof.

Arnie handed the sausages to Judd and directed him to place them a couple feet apart.

"So what happened to him?"

"Foster? He found something in his head and wrote a book. Gave a bunch of talks. Plenty of people sought him out.

Some say the fame got to him. Up and vanished on a speaking tour. That was four years ago. The boys pretty much took up where he left off."

Arnie struck the icicles with a hammer. They shattered on the ground.

"I'd help them out best I could. Find people to make things for the lab—harnesses, retractable arms, some strange looking skull caps."

Skull caps. Judd recalled the one they tightened on his head.

Arnie eyeballed the roofline. "You think you got had by the boys? Well, Lester Moore in there, he's another example of watch-out-what-you-wish-for."

"How so?"

Arnie didn't say. He sent Judd to find out if Joy had more pantyhose.

Hearing no response after knocking on the door, Judd went in.

"Hel-lo?"

Joy sat in the kitchen in a floral house coat watching television at top volume. Seeing Judd enter, her hairball of a dog had a yipping fit.

"Squire!"

"You don't happen to have any more of those …?"

"It'll take some digging. Haven't wore 'em since last century." She picked up the dog and waddled down a hall, her heels slap-slaping in fuzzy slippers. Judd followed and stopped at a doorway to a living room where a man, turning from a window, strode toward him with a broad smile.

He looked like an overstuffed chair at a garage sale. Fiftyish with an oatmeal complexion and a splash of frightened hair.

He was dressed in slept-in slacks, a Scottish plaid flannel shirt and an olive green cardigan stretched long in the pockets.

"And a good morning to you," he said.

The room smelled of pipe tobacco. Judd removed the glove from his right hand. "Name's Judd."

"Ah-ha, the ritual of shaking hands," the man announced as he offered his right hand with a sparkle in his eyes. "A cordial how-do-you-do that elicits a psychophysical assessment of each other's character. Albeit brief, it sets a tone, beginning with the arm extension, is it short, stabby? Or at length, generous? Do the eyes meet with fresh appeal? Disapproval? Do they meet at all? There's the telltale tactility in the touch of the flesh. Is it the asperous skin of a gardener treaded with callus? Is it smooth and talcumy as a baby's bottom, cloistered from shovel and mop? Is it the clutch of mutual accord? Or the vice grip of control, punctuated by a tug of dominance? A medical sensitive might diagnose a malingering malady in the clench, a cirrhosis prognosis perhaps. While a Chinese chiromancer could predict a lifetime of prosperity. Certainly, a plethora of unspoken attributes and clandestine intentions can be perceived in the meeting of the meat."

Lester released Judd's hand and raised his wiggling fingers.

"Historically, one could surmise such a greeting gesture revealed the appearance of peace, the hand devoid of sword or dagger. Clearly it is a naked junction where the intimate fates mapped in our palms cross paths. Name's Lester."

Arnie found Judd in the living room. "There you are. Come on, we're done."

"Arn." Lester gave a side-tilted bow.

"Can't talk now Lester."

"What goes up, try, try again." Lester winked.

As Arnie and Judd passed through the kitchen, Joy explained to Judd, "My brother used to envy smart people. Took up with those rascal twins. Next thing you know he's talking non-stop. Quit growing corn. Doesn't do much of nothin', just blathers about. Ella left him. His son doesn't come by. The only visitor is some pipe-smoking professor-type. They foam at the mouth for hours."

"Let's go, Judd," Arnie said.

"So are those boys dead?" Joy picked up her dog. "Hope so. Doing the devil's work 'n all."

Arnie didn't answer. He folded the ladder and set it in the truck bed.

"Some days you can almost understand what Lester's talking about."

"Must be one of those days." Judd climbed into the passenger seat. "Who else's brains have they tinkered with?"

"Not many." Arnie snatched the keys off the dashboard.

"Marsha?"

"No-no. And Flannery's off limits, Marsha's law. All young brains forbidden. But there've been a few volunteers, myself included." Arnie started the engine and pulled away. "The boy's helped me regain a childhood talent ..."

"What's that?"

"Shape-shifting."

"Get outta here."

"It's not how folks tell it. You don't grow fur and howl under a big moon. No, you join the creature's spirit."

"Of course."

"Heh! Says the man who spits pictures out his head." Arnie steered the truck away. "It's not easy to be in the body and mind of an animal and see through their eyes, hear with their ears, feel their hunger, the tug of their instincts. It's quite intimate. And it can only happen with their okey-dokey."

"You mean like, 'Hey there raccoon, mind if I jump in your body?'"

"Can't force it. They'll reject you. And it's not like you're in the cockpit. It's not remote control. They still have their ways."

Judd flashed on the evening he first met Arnie.

"The dog! That barking mutt on the river. That was you?"

"Name's Fetch. Town dog. Feed him sometimes."

"You're joking. You jumped that ATF guy on the dock?"

"Used to shape-shift when I was a kid. People thought I made it up. As I got older the ability rusted shut. Happens a lot, doncha know? We're born with skills and stuff that gets shoved aside. But the boys gave my brain a little WD-40. Re-opened that door."

They came upon a Jeep Cherokee stuck along the shoulder of the road, rear tire spinning, spurting chunks of frozen snow.

Arnie lowered his window. "What we got here?"

"Hey Arn. Big buck come outta nowhere," the driver said.

"Let's help Mortie out." Arnie cut the engine. He pulled a wide board from the bed, handed it to Judd.

"So what kinds of animals do you …"

"Not many critters out in winter." Arnie grabbed a snow shovel. They crossed the road. "Dogs are pretty agreeable. Cats, it depends. Crows, no way." Arnie shoveled the snow in front of a rear tire. "A kingfisher was incredible. Couldn't top that until I joined a great-horned owl and saw the night world come alive."

He told Judd to wedge the board under the tire for traction.

"Okay now, you're the muscle. I'll stand on the bumper while you push."

Judd dug in his boots, bent his knees, and propped his hands on the Jeep's bumper.

Arnie called out. "Okay, Mortie, let'er rip."

The driver gunned the accelerator. Arnie bounced up and down as Judd pushed. The tire spun, burned into the grain of the wood, and wheeled away with a grateful wave of Mortie's hand.

Arnie retrieved the board and kicked off crusted snow.

"It's easy to imagine what it's like to be the bird or the fish, but it's a whole nuther thing to be inside them. You realize we're all passengers here, animals, trees. They got souls, only they've taken on a different body for learning this life."

Judd picked up the snow shovel. He'd underestimated Arnie. The man had a worldview like no one he ever met.

Back in the cab he asked, "So what's the weirdest creature you shape-shifted?"

"Bat, hands down. And I stay away from bugs. Once managed to be a horse fly for half a while. Never do that again. Took a long time to unscramble."

"A fly?"

"Looking out its eyes made me delirious. Must say though, didn't know shit could smell so good."

Judd doubled over, snort-laughing nonstop. He hadn't cracked up that long and loud since he smoked a joint in high school. After wiping the tears from his eyes, he asked what Arnie was looking to shape-shift next.

"Oh boy, I'd love to join the wind."

"The wind?" Judd looked out at the skeins of snow snaking across the asphalt road. He knew all kinds of wind. It was a constant in North Dakota. But he never considered it a living being like a dog or an owl.

Arnie's truck phone chimed. Marsha on speaker. She asked if Judd was with him.

"Yeah, I'm here." Judd said.

"Are you staying the night? I've got a wild idea."

# 25

# The Pleroma

The Department of Defense field office was an inconspicuous gulag-gray shed next to an unnamed air strip in northeast Virginia. Jurgens, Theroux's pilot and loyal follower, didn't receive the exact coordinates from the control tower until the plane was seventy miles away.

A slouch of a man met Theroux on the tarmac. He had silver hair like shriveled wire. A flesh-toned Breathe Right strip saddled the bridge of his nose.

"Ennis, Operations, et cetera, et cetera," he said, with the hard-lined lips of pallbearer. He wore a baggy, polyester sport coat with a necklace of key cards.

Theroux followed him into the squat, corrugated metal building and down a flight of concrete stairs. At each step Ennis grimaced with little zipper teeth.

"Wrenched a lumbar," he said. He gestured to his back. "Got a battery- operated nerve-stimulation unit. Don't do shit."

The guy's a relic, Theroux thought. A cadaver who should've retired years ago.

They reached a landing with an elevator. Ennis slapped a key card against a security screen. "Kira King's not coming," he said.

The elevator door opened.

"I know." Theroux said. She had texted him:

```
Sorry I can't be there, love.
Putting out fires in advance
of the conference. You'll have
to wow them without me. Can't
wait to see you.
```

Against her father's wishes, Kira had set up the meeting to gain favor with Inman Hayes and the Department of Defense. However unorthodox, she felt Theroux's uncanny psychic ability to find the Jolley twins would help cement the contract with Neurokey, the lab she represented.

"Kira hyped what you call bi ... something ..."

"Bi-location," Theroux said.

"Right, another word for mumbo-jumbo." Ennis punched the lowest of five buttons on the control panel. "So you know where I stand."

The door shut. The elevator made a hiss and descended.

Ennis had done his homework. He'd read about the son of Heston Theroux, the American shipping magnate and Ursula, his mother of Grecian descent. Among his notes was the article in *Alchemy Now* magazine entitled, "Mystic or Monster?"

*Feasting on his father's wealth, young Theroux led a freestyle flying carpet ride of ultra-debauchery, lounging hash-headed on luxury yachts anchored in topaz waters, reveling in an orgasmic express of island-hopping all the while toga'd in the finest thread count linen.*

The article speculated that his mother's death caused the twenty-two-year-old to abandon his hedonistic, drug-addled lifestyle. Actually, Theroux changed when he encountered people he couldn't buy. So he took the guru route and sought to amass followers by delving into old and new age spiritual practices. He studied with teachers of the Kabbalah and Hermeticism before trekking the twilight lands of the occult and shamanic.

The elevator doors opened on a wide corridor flanked by walls of black plate glass.

"Kira said you can send what you call your "psychic body" to a specific place and record what happens."

"To paraphrase Paracelsus from the sixteenth century: Man possesses a power by which he can see his friends and the circumstances by which they are surrounded, although such persons may be a thousand miles from him at the time."

A woman in a marine-blue uniform came out a side door carrying a sheaf of papers. Through the open door Theroux caught a glimpse of an enormous arena where banks of blue screens displayed satellite images of cities and landscapes. Rows of silhouetted operators punched keys and spoke into headsets.

Has to be the biggest underground surveillance center in the world, Theroux thought. As they walked on, he felt a whir of data zip through miles of fiber underfoot.

Ennis turned a corner. "So how does what you do differ from remote viewing?"

Theroux knew the Defense Department's past remote programs had mixed results.

"It's not about coordinates. I simply need to touch the place beforehand or meet the person I want to locate. Obtaining the signature is essential."

"The signature …?"

"Everything carries a unique vibration. Think of it like the Dewey decimal system. But instead of a number in a catalog, you have the vibratory autograph. By attuning your mind to the vibe, you can be where they are."

"Yeah-yeah." Ennis opened a door. "Take a seat."

Theroux entered a carpeted room. On a long table were a carafe, cups, and a plate of pastries.

Ennis made a call.

"We're here." His tone sounded annoyed. Like this was another waste of time to add to an Everest of wastage.

Still standing, Theroux added, "Bi-location also differs from remote viewing in terms of exposure. I am not invisible. Not a hidden camera. My psychic body is like a hologram or a ghost. If you intend to spy on someone, an installation or foreign agency, you aren't shielded from sight."

"They can recognize you?"

"If seen, yes, perhaps not by name, but certainly by description."

Ennis grunted and turned around to the door.

"You hear that? The dude can be seen!"

"How about a demonstration?" Came the gruff voice of Inman Hayes in the doorway.

Theroux was waiting for this. Kira promised them he would give a show-and-tell.

Ennis introduced the Chief Consultant for the Department of Defense.

No hands extended.

"Someone or some place in particular?" Theroux asked.

"As a matter of fact." Ennis slid three photos across the table—Oakley, Chester, and that of a tall guy, the one Theroux saw when he last bi-located the Jolleys' lab.

"Kira says you knew Foster Jolley," Hayes said. "And you met his sons. Did she mention they are dirty-bomb makers presently at large?"

Theroux looked over the photos and thought—If they're dirty-bomb makers I'm an armadillo.

"We need to catch them for the safety of America," Hayes said.

Ennis tapped the photo of Oakley. "Do you have his signature? If not, I have something that might help." He set a busted hockey stick on the table.

Theroux declined the stick, convinced it came from the bomb site.

"Psychometrics does not play a part in what I do."

"Whatever." Just more horseshit, Ennis thought.

"The electromagnetic field in here is pretty strong," Theroux said. "Too buzzy. But I'll try."

"You do that." Ennis bit hard into a glazed donut.

Theroux moved his chair to a corner and sat. He rubbed his hands, took a deep breath, and let out a long, guttural sigh.

Entering the site was always tricky when bi-locating a person, especially if they're in a confined space. Theroux could frighten anyone within eyesight. Like the time he looked in on a wedding and so frightened the groom he pissed his tuxedo pants. Outside was always better. But the target would be where it would be. All he could do was take a peek and go or, if concealed, stay.

Theroux pinpointed Oakley in his vibrary. He felt a flurry of wind as if sucked through a vacuum, and saw a jittery frenzy of color. A bustle of people came into focus at a shopping center of some kind. A figure stood with his back to him— Oakley Jolley. He wore aviators and full desert camouflage, like a soldier stationed in the Middle East, complete with high boots and boonie hat.

Feeling exposed, Theroux slipped behind a pillar. Oakley stood alone at a railing watching shoppers move in and out of stores, up-and-down escalators. Sensing someone staring at him, Oakley slowly swiveled his head.

Theroux shuddered as he returned to his physical body. "Give me a moment." He inhaled a gulp of air, then reported, "Oakley Jolley is in Minneapolis. Place called Mall of America."

Hayes tapped Oakley's photo. "Get that into the hands of every security guard and salesclerk in that mall. Have local law enforcement lock the exits the moment he's identified."

Ennis grabbed his phone and punched a number.

Theroux added, "He's dressed in desert camouflage."

"Camo? Like a soldier?" Hayes asked.

"Yes. He was on one of the upper floors but that may have changed by now."

"We've got a lead." Ennis yelled into the receiver. "Minnesota. Mall of America."

Hayes turned to Theroux. "Can defense personnel learn your technique?"

Theroux recalled his arduous training on a tributary of the Orinoco River in South America. The boiled fungus soups he vomited. The delirious nights he spent alone in a rainy jungle, twitching with every tickle of sound, his skin riddled with bites. One morning he woke up in a grass hut, a spindly man stood over him and in broken English said, "You saw another side. Now you learn double sight."

The curandero taught Theroux to travel psychically to the Cape Cod mansion where he grew up and observe the comings and goings. Theroux returned to the states with the ability to bi-locate along with an affliction that caused a patch of his skin to erupt after each psychic body excursion.

"Bi-location can be taught," he told Hayes. "But learning how is difficult."

The only time Theroux attempted to teach an admirer, she couldn't find the way back to her physical body. She became lost in limbo, or what his teacher called "the hall of a hundred locked doors."

"Kira said you've been to their lab. So, were you able to see what these boys found in the brain before they bombed their place?" Hayes asked.

Hayes knows more than he's telling. Theroux was certain.

"Some believe the human brain is more than a switchboard of neurons relaying data inputs like a computer," Theroux said. "Hidden in its rumpled mass is a portal to unrealized states of being, and possibly a link to the pleroma, or universal mind."

"Pleroma. Is that like a God Spot?" Hayes asked.

"Are you familiar with Dr. Ezra Katz?" Theroux was fishing to see if the DOD authorized Katz's murder. Other than a rise of his eyebrows, Hayes didn't speak.

"Ezra was the Jolleys' mentor," Theroux explained. "He believed that as there are sacred sites where people pilgrimage to commune with God, we carry one in our brains. A Mount Sinai if you will, and each of us its Moses."

"And what's your take on this pleroma, a fairytale?" Hayes asked.

Theroux felt an itching sensation in his armpit. The skin was ulcerating. He resisted scratching it and said, "There are nectars hidden deep in the jungle yet to be tasted."

Hayes wagged his index finger. "If this pans out, we may seek your skills again. What would you require in return?"

Theroux was quick to answer. "Exclusive access to the boys' instruments and methods."

"Agents are on their way to the Mall," Ennis reported.

# 26
# Mall of America

Oakley stuffed his mouth with sweet potato french fries at a food court. Yolanda, a high school friend who worked in cosmetics at Macy's, just told him he could no longer stay at her Bloomington apartment.

"I don't know what to believe," she said. "All I know is I can't be dragged into it. I need to keep my job. Sorry, Oaks, but I can't let you stay another night."

Yolanda suffered from severe migraines during her senior year until Chester and Oakley minimized their frequency. She felt indebted until she saw the twins' faces on a local television newscast.

Oakley scanned the whirlwind of shoppers bundled in down jackets, clutching bags, pushing strollers. Sounds of carefree buying-is-living muzak mingled with the idle banter of teenagers on their phones. He pondered what would change if he and Chester opened the node in their brains that regulates body temperature. Would clothing stores go out of business? Everyone in shirtsleeves and shorts? Bikinis on ice skates? Probably not. It's all about having the latest looks and styles. Stand out or blend in.

Up to then, Oakley's army disguise was a safe way to hide in plain sight. Most people don't give much notice to servicemen. But as he gobbled the last fry, he felt walls closing in. His antenna node was warning him of immediate danger.

Somebody's coming! Get out of here! But where?

The Mall had everything imaginable, a complete world, lacking only a place to shower and sleep.

He took the elevator to the third floor and surveyed the canyon of shops below.

They're coming for me, whoever they are.

Sure enough, in the atrium near the Boot Barn store he spotted a man in a tactical vest showing a security guard a sheet of paper.

How'd they know I was here? Yolanda swore she didn't tell anyone. Yeah, but she would if confronted. Can't go back to her place, they'll be waiting, and that means losing my duffel and most of my money!

Somebody tagged me. Time to move, ditch the army clothes fast. Can't go to the Halloween store for another disguise. They'll see me.

"Thank you for your service." A man brushed past, startling him.

Oakley quickstepped around a corner into Nordstroms. He ducked behind a rolling clothes rack with a winter clearance mishmash of fleece jackets and wool sweaters. He shed his camo shirt. But as he reached for one to replace it, a stock employee pushed the rack across the floor. Oakley tiptoed behind it. The wheels stopped in a storage room. After the footsteps faded, he snatched a red, plaid, wool shirt off a hanger and cautiously slipped back into the store where he frog-walked over to a carousel of sport coats. He lifted the closest one, a houndstooth mesh blazer, tucked the hat under his arm, and nonchalantly left the store.

Oakley's costume change didn't lessen the force field bearing down on him. His pursuers were so near it felt like a fire hose in his face.

Change pants! Chuck the hat!

One level below, a security woman stopped shoppers as they stepped off an escalator and pointed to the screen on her phone.

Oakley dropped the hat and aviators and rushed into North Face. He gave the greeter a phony smile. No time to waste. All kinds of pants on sale hung on a corner wall. The only two his size were a pair of dark fleece joggers and papaya-orange parachute pants. $29 each. A deal.

In line at the register, Oakley spotted a hard-eyed suit pass the front window pulling people aside. The man held his boonie hat.

Oakley backed from the counter and ducked into a dome tent on display. Adrenaline boiling, he pulled the parachute pants over his camos, retied his boots, and fled the store.

Someone shouted as Oakley hopped down the stairs two at a time. Hard to be inconspicuous when you're dressed in a harlequin clash of stolen clothes.

He dashed out the front doors and across the street toward an IKEA store. Walking past, two young women swung their heads. "Oh," one said, "I want *that* look!"

# 27

# Grand Canyon

Chester stepped off the Greyhound bus stiff from the long drive from Minneapolis. He shoved his arms through the straps of his backpack and set off toward the South Rim Visitor Center. He chose the Grand Canyon after reading about Foster sightings posted on the internet. Two different people said they saw his father at the park within the last three weeks.

The bus ride was exhausting. The rank stew of sweat and old people smells made his throat clutch. Typical of Chester's analytical mind, he noticed one thing about long bus trips. Listening to the chit-chat pattern of passengers, he deduced an auditory waveform. Prior to each stopover, their talking increased. For the first mile after departing, there was also a heightened decibel level of chatter. Then the passengers would quiet to a murmur, until the driver announced they were nearing the next stop and the vocal volume would rise again.

Once inside the visitor center, Chester plucked a photograph from his windbreaker. He held it up to a park ranger slotting postcards.

"Excuse me. By any chance have you seen this man?"

The photo was the most recent of his father, midforties, with ruffled hair and pointy goatee. He sat at a table, a stack of *The Isness* books at his elbow. One hand rested on an open volume. His blue eyes looked up at an admirer seeking his autograph.

The ranger scrutinized the photo.

"I've seen someone who looks like him."

"Really? When?"

"Oh, a week or so ago."

"Was he alone?"

"Not that I recall."

Chester stared at the photo as if sheer willpower could make it come alive.

"Wait now." The ranger tilted her head to see the picture again. "He was wearing one of those Australian bush hats with one side of the brim pinned up."

Dad was not much into hats, Chester recollected. But who knows, maybe he's gone incognito.

"You saw him where?"

"I don't remember. Sorry."

"My father," Chester said.

"Thought so. There's a resemblance." She started to go back to the postcards but did an about-face. "And if I see him?"

"I'll check back. Thanks."

Chester bought a park map and hiked to the rim of the canyon. He took in the panoramic view of limestone and sandstone cliffs terraced with ropes of snow. "The Crown Jewel of America's Natural Treasures," he read on the cover of the map. He'd seen pictures of the canyon before, but they didn't come close to its monumental dimensions. He sat and watched the interplay of orange-and-gold colors on the far cliff shift in the changing light. The air was ultra-quiet. He thought of a quote from his father's book—"Listen to the Is-ness. It sounds like a choir of silent fizz."

He couldn't wait to tell his brother what the park ranger said.

Dad's alive! Has to be him!

The last night Chester spent with his brother was at a hotel near the university. They were in a panic, debating what to do. The two agreed to communicate after a week through a particular website.

Chester took out his wallet and counted his money—$438. Arnie pitched in $1,100 cash, which he and his brother split. Rooms at the lodge were expensive, and full anyway, so he hiked to the campground, feeling lonely and disconnected without a phone or laptop.

Afraid of snakes slithering up a pant leg in the night, Chester made his bed on top of a picnic table chained to a spindly pine. Unable to sleep, he recalled the old lady in a curly brown wig who sat next to him on the bus sharing her aches and pains.

"Nobody talks about aging like it's an epidemic," she told him. "I've got the bug, you've got it, everybody on the bus does. Or rather, it's got us. Now you think about Abraham. He lived 400 years. Did he have all these vitamins and meds back then? No. He went around eating figs and drinking wine. So what changed?"

Chester wondered if a node in the brain governed anti-aging. He stared at the spectacle of stars, feeling homesick for the Marigold lab.

# 28
## It's It!

"Visualize a spiral staircase." Marsha directed Judd into a hypnotic trance. "Now with each descending step, count back from ten, and with each count, allow your body to feel more and more at ease."

Hypnosis was Marsha's "wild idea" to see if it could slow the replay of Judd's projections.

"Maybe it will reveal my sons' state of mind, and what they did to you," she reasoned.

Judd was willing to try.

"Have to admit, I'm a bit afraid," he told her.

"Most fear is about loss of ego," she said.

Judd and Marsha sat at the café kitchen's stainless-steel prep table. Roslyn and Flannery were upstairs, Roslyn to study anatomy, Flannery to watch an animated Disney movie on her iPad. Arnie shut off the overheads. He knew Marsha was a hypnotherapist, but had never seen her in action.

"Show us the last time the boys worked on your brain," she said.

Judd felt the familiar sensation prod his forehead. Within seconds a light flashed on the wall between shelves of pots and pans. Images zipped by too fast to identify.

Seeing the pictures for the first time, Arnie blew out a, "Good God!"

Marsha asked Judd to find the projector in his head. "Imagine a dial that adjusts the speed of the movie. Right now it's stuck on fast forward. But you can slow the speed of pictures by turning the dial until it plays in real time."

Gradually, the images slowed.

"Hold up there, that's it!"

The projection revealed the twins moving things about their lab.

Seeing her sons, Marsha sighed, "There they are."

"You did it," Judd said.

"*We* did it."

"I must be sitting in the dentist chair."

They watched Oakley set a cubby-holed box of rough gemstones on a table.

"Foster's rock collection," Arnie said.

Marsha shook her head. "All those times I wanted to sell them, but the boys refused."

Oakley moved in to fit the gel cap on Judd's head.

"They're attaching air tubes to the cap," Judd said. "I can hear the rushing sound as it inflates."

Oakley strapped welder goggles to Judd's eyes and the projection on the wall went dark.

"What happened?" Arnie asked.

"It's the goggles, to protect my eyes. Guess I can't show you what I can't see. But I'll tell you what they're saying."

*We're starting with this pearly one.* "It's Chester, he says," *Play the tone generator, maestro.*

"Now I'm hearing a drone, kinda wavy-like." Chester asks if I can hear him. I don't answer. I must be out, which is odd, because I can still hear everything."

"Like what?"

"Movement. Shuffling feet. Now Oakley says," *All right, Mr. Judd, we're planting the ruby.* "I feel something pushed against my head. Must be a pocket in the skull cap."

"And now?" Marsha asked.

"Now … I don't hear anything … wait … *Ahh-nuu!* One of them yells. Not sure what that's about."

"Mean's 'really good' in twin talk," Marsha said.

*The emerald is next.* "Chester says. And I'm hearing chimes."

Marsha listened, transfixed by the protocol her sons developed—applying uncut gemstones to the cranium, then infusing them with laser light, while playing precise tones.

How did they come up with such a complex process? she wondered. It's like each tiny node has its own waking anthem of sound and light.

*Now for the Temple of Topaz. Brace your bones, man. We're entering unknown territory.*

"Another push in the cap, tapping sounds. And … nothing," Judd said. *No workie.* "One of them says. They're jostling around, muttering." *Okay, so we go with newbie number two. What do you think, try the diamond first or …?*

"The little shits are toying with my brain!" Judd shouted.

"Stay with it," Marsha urged.

Flannery came down the stairs singing, "And can you feel the love tonight … how it's laid to rest. It's enough to make kings and vagabonds believe the very best …"

"Flannie, shh," Arnie said.

"But it's from *Lion King!*"

"Not now please, Flan," Marsha implored.

Flannery stopped on the bottom stair. She saw everybody looking at a black space on the cinderblock wall.

"What's going on?" she whispered.

"Judd?" Marsha asked.

"I don't know," Judd said. "They must be trying another stone."

Marsha wondered if the nodes in the brain had ever been open before. And if so, what shut them down?

*Let's try the green garnet.* "Chester says. I guess the last one didn't work either. Ohh … wow!"

"What happened?" Marsha said.

"I can actually feel something! Little bursts," Judd replied. "Like electric surges around my scalp."

*Ahh-nuu! That's the one!*

"My whole body is tingling. Chester's whooping. "*Look! Oakley, look! It woke up others! Ahh-nuu! Never ever saw that coming!*

"Others?" Marsha said.

"That's what he said. Now Oakley is shouting." *It's IT! It's IT!"*

"And …?" Marsha said.

"More movement …" Judd said, "… rustling sounds, like they're taking things away."

*Hey, you in there.* "It's Chester." *Nobody tells us what to do. Not you, not nobody. You come here and threaten us, you're asking for trouble, you soat!"*

"Soat?"

"More twin talk," Marsha said.

*So here you go.* "Oakley is saying." *We opened nodes we only recently found. The fifth one popped seven others, like a chain reaction. That makes twelve! You hearing this? You're gonna light up like a Christmas tree!*

"Oh, God," Marsha gasped.

Roslyn came down the stairs as the wall lit up with a projection of Chester's face as he pulled the goggles off Judd's eyes.

"What's that?" Flannery asked.

"Something Judd can do. Hush," Arnie said.

Judd dipped his head.

"I need to stop."

Marsha apologized and brought him out of the trance. He clutched the edge of the table, his upper body see-sawing.

No one spoke at first. Then Flannery asked. "Can you show me how to do that?"

Marsha turned to Arnie, "In all my years of study on brainwaves ..."

"What happened?" Roslyn asked.

"They sprung a bunch of nodes in his head," Marsha said.

"Twelve," Arnie said.

"And that means ...?"

"Means I'm deranged for life," Judd said.

"I really can't say. Arnie, help me," Marsha said. "What were the two earlier ones they opened in each other?"

"One was a thermostat that adjusts the body's temperature. Too hot, it cools you down, too cold, it warms you up."

"That explains that," Judd muttered, having seen Chester standing outside in freezing air wearing only a flimsy shirt.

"The other one," Arnie went on, "is like an antenna that senses threats. That's how the boys felt in danger. They didn't know who was behind it or what form it would take. They just knew trouble was coming. So they scuttled the lab and hid in my bunker. When it all got bombed, well you know the rest."

"You said twelve. What do the other's do?" Roslyn said.

"No idea," Marsha said.

"They had it in for me!" Judd pounded on the table.

"They'd strike back at anyone who pressured them," Marsha said. "That doesn't absolve them, Judd. But understand, they just lost Ezra. He was their champion. They didn't know what they found in the brain would bring havoc and death. You come along, insisting—"

"So what now?" Judd said.

"Have to wait and see. Best you stick around."

Judd combed his fingers through his hair.

"What's with the funny words like 'soat'?"

"It's common for twins to make up their own language," Marsha explained. "They've got words that only they know the meaning."

"Yeah, well I've got a word for them."

# 29

# What If They Catch Me?

Oakley took the light rail to the University of Minnesota campus. The VW he and Chester had parked on Oak Street was gone. Towed away. He trudged around looking for Elliott Hall, where his mother taught. She might know what to do, get a lawyer, something.

After four days on the run, he was worn out from lack of sleep. Spending the night on a mattress rack may have been the best place to hide in IKEA, but he woke up every ten minutes afraid the security chub making the rounds would find him.

Oakley had been to Elliott Hall once before but still needed directions. Walking a long echoey corridor he looked for his mother's name tagged to a professor's office door. The promise of a safe haven exceeded the humiliation of "going to mom." After all, she might have news about his brother.

Although some twins claim to have a telepathic connection, this was not the case with the Jolleys.

"I'm finding Dad" was the last thing Chester said before the two split up.

"Good luck with that." Oakley felt no desire to see their father. He was furious at the man for deserting the family and wished him dead, if he wasn't already.

He asked passing students where he might find Ms. Jolley. None knew. He kept walking until a young woman with schoolbus-colored hair overheard him.

"You're looking for Professor Jolley?"

"Yeah. Know where I find her?"

"Not here anymore. Fired. Her kids are terrorists."

Oakley gulped. It hurt to think that he and Chester cost their mom her job. Then his alarm bells rang.

"Thanks for telling me," he said and hurried off.

"Yeah," she said. "Like your outfit."

Through the entrance doors to the building, Oakley saw police bursting from patrol cars. Someone had identified him and called it in. He climbed the stairs and ducked into a classroom on the second floor as students shut their laptops and filed out. He snatched a large hardbound book off a desk chair to shield his face as he joined a group chatting away down the stairs.

Once outside he broke free. Crossing a parking lot, he passed a small mountain of snow a city plow piled against a chain-link fence. He scampered around it and held up, knees knocking.

"Anything?" he heard a pursuer shout.

"Check over there!"

After the voices trailed off, Oakley scraped a shelf in the snow mound to sit and plan his next move.

So what if they catch me? What can they do? He thought of the three worst case scenarios he and Chester came up with the night they sped out of Marigold:

1) They electroshock our testicles. We falsely confess we're terrorists and get thrown in a rat-infested nowhere prison to waste away eating entrails and broccoli.

2) They electroshock our testicles. We give in, describe our methods and the barn where we stashed our instruments, only to be suffocated in Ziploc bags and stuffed in steel drums filled with flesh-eating hydrochloric acid.

3) They forgo electroshocking our testicles. They bury us alive in a coffin with ten thousand spiders.

The last scenario prompted Oakley to dig deeper in the snow. When his fingertips bled, he broke off the hard cover of the thick book he'd jacked—*Plato. The Collected Dialogues.* Using the cover as a trowel, he scooped out a cave in the snowpack—a winter survival tactic Arnie once showed him.

"Nobody can see me in here," he assured himself.

Oakley huddled until nightfall when hunger spurred him out. He found a pizza joint three blocks away. He ordered a 16-inch barbeque with pineapple, crawled back into the homemade shelter and devoured it. Fully sated, he nodded out.

Sometime later he woke up to the tap-tap of water dripping on his head. His thermostat warmed the snow so much the ceiling was melting. Suddenly the tunnel collapsed. The snow buried his legs and clenched him in darkness.

"No, no, no!"

At first, he squirmed and clawed blindly, unsure which direction was the way out. He didn't have time to calculate air space versus seconds of expiration. He only had one choice. He piston-pumped his knees to free his legs, blinking droplets from his eyes. Finding the book cover, he scraped the walls until he could swivel his body. Then stretching his legs, he kicked at the snowpack as he dug straight ahead. When the cover sunk into softer, crumbly snow, he punched with all his might until it gave way to a rush of open air.

Oakley clambered out, sopping wet from snowmelt and sweat. He vomited up a lime-green blob and slumped against the fence, panting.

"You doopid!"

Okay, okay, there's a downside to the autobody thermostat, he now realized. Stay out of snow caves unless you want to suffocate.

Regaining energy, he followed a bike trail along the Mississippi River and took the Stone Arch Bridge toward the bright Minneapolis skyline. It was late. Everything was closed. Seemed like the only cars at that hour were police, some aflare with lights and sirens. Fearful of being seen, he crossed back over the river and hiked down under the bridge to hide out. He came upon a ramshackle, corrugated metal and tarpaulin structure. In the faint light a scrawny figure rushed at him wielding an iron pipe shouting what sounded like "Backhoe!"

Oakley stumbled up the rocky embankment to the bridge and tromped away through slushy snow, looking back every six or seven steps.

# 30

# The Audition

The inflatable on the floor of the utility room wasn't exactly the Saatva mattress Judd was accustomed to. But that didn't cause his fitful sleep. He couldn't shake his outrage at the twins. Having thugs pursue him added a spike of paranoia, and being stuck in Marigold, of all places, boomeranged him back to a version of the North Dakota farm town he fled.

Hypnosis was the only consolation. He felt some refuge with Marsha, though guarded. In his theater world, she'd be called a BEW, a Big Energy Woman, or "BEWare."

Judd woke up to voices below in the kitchen. Marsha was telling Arnie about an upcoming conference.

"Only trouble is, I can't be in two places at once," she said. "Right after I give the eulogy for Ezra, I meet with Victor King. So I won't be able to attend the international labs exhibition."

International labs?

Judd wondered if one of them could reset his brain. The question stayed with him as he helped Arnie remodel his home. Arnie had wanted to do it for years. He drew up plans, stored lumber and materials in his barn, even poured a concrete foundation for the addition. Never got around to completing it until now. Given the devastation of the Jolleys' home, Arnie thought having an enlarged kitchen, two additional bedrooms, and another bath to his farmhouse might be acceptable for Marsha and Flannery to stay.

Tomás, the cook, was cleaning the stove when Judd returned to the café that afternoon. Flannery, her legs up in a booth, watched *Mama Mia* on her tablet and sang, "'Take a chance on me, take a chance on me ...'"

Roslyn and Marsha sat at the counter creating a Power-Point for Marsha's upcoming speech.

"Let's use that one of Ezra," Marsha said.

They were sorting through photos she'd saved on a thumb drive before the Feds took everything.

Judd poured himself a cup of coffee and coned his hearing to listen in.

"When Ezra found out about Chester and Oakley's scanning transmitter," Marsha said, "he became their mentor."

Judd came over.

"Say, I couldn't help but overhear you and Arnie talking about an exhibition in DC. You said it'd be good to know what those labs were up to. And I was thinking ..."

"Why not take you?"

"I can be your eyes."

"Good try, but it's exclusive to high rollers, invitation only."

"How rich do you need me to be? I'm an actor."

"Then you're used to rejection."

"Used to it, sure, but the trick is not to give in to it."

Marsha shook her head. Roslyn clicked a photo of Ezra with Oakley and Chester on the screen.

Judd stepped behind the counter.

"Listen," he said to Marsha. "I go. I take it all in. Then you hypnotize me and play back what I found."

That got Marsha's attention.

"Might work. I'd have to get you in as a board member of the Foster Jolley Foundation."

"I can be that."

"Anybody hungry?" Tomás's face appeared in the kitchen pass-through. "I can put together some tasty burritos with the leftovers."

Marsha looked up at Judd. "I'll think about it."

"At least let me audition."

Feeling uneasy by Judd's presence, Roslyn turned from the laptop. "Hey Flan, let's you and me help Tomás."

Marsha stared at Judd. "Okay. Understand, this is not a public expo. These are big brain labs strutting their goods for funding. You'd have to portray a mega-wealthy investor."

"I can do that."

"But, behind the guise, you're fact-finding to see what the labs are doing, especially Neurokey."

"Neurokey."

"I'll be miles away meeting with their CEO."

"Okay, what am I looking for?"

"Whatever you can about their neurotheological research."

"I can do that," Judd said, without asking what that was.

Marsha held up three fingers in Judd's face. "Three things you have to know. One, you need to exude riches. How do you do that?" She didn't wait for an answer. "With cool and confident ease."

Judd's shoulders dropped, he straightened his back, hands at his side.

"How old are you?" Marsha asked.

"Twenty-seven in two months."

"Play older. Five years older."

Judd thought about how to do that—unfettered eye contact; a worldly bearing, relaxed lips, not too smiley.

"Number two—detached curiosity," Marsha said.

Judd gave a cordial, attentive nod to invisible people as he strolled about the café floor.

"*And* you're playing hard to get. Remember, they want your money, in tonnage. Can you make them want it enough to reveal their secrets?"

"What if they ask about you, or bring up Foster?"

"Then shift from his disappearance to his achievements."

"You mean the optics, like the handheld Hubble and the peak experience while exploring his own brain?"

"Labs are mum about the metaphysical. But given your association with Foster they might go there."

"Eat up!" Tomás said as he, Roslyn, and Flannery set plates with tortillas wrapped around bacon, tomatoes, and shredded cheese in the pass-through.

Marsha and Judd sat across from each other. After a couple bites, Judd asked, "What was it like living with him?"

"Foster? In a word, tumultuous. True, he tapped into an elevated awareness and gave it a catchy slogan."

"The Isness."

"A term vague enough to tickle up a fan base and make him a high priest of the New Age. But he couldn't sustain the Isness. Nobody mentions that. Sure, there'd be days he'd be in a heightened state of perception, but then he'd collapse, shut himself in a darkened room, unreachable."

Judd smacked his lips. "So what happened?"

"Imagine if people believed you were an ascended being. There you are, rocketed to fast fame with the expectation you can sow miracles."

"Do you think he'll come back?"

"Who knows. I stopped looking. Actually, I never started. He abandoned us. Didn't leave a note. The boys would tell me about the latest Foster sighting they'd read online. One day he's at Ayers Rock, another, Mount Shasta. Anyway, let's rehearse. What are you?"

Judd stood. "I'm rich ... confident ... enterprising..."

"And curious about recent neurotheological breakthroughs."

"Neurotheo ... you mean the God Spot?"

"The God*head* Spot. It goes by other names: the Pleroma, the Ocean of Ultimate Consciousness."

"Do you believe our brains have such a thing?"

"I don't NOT believe."

Judd took a few steps, pivoted, and approached her as if she sat at an exhibition booth. He assumed a chin-high, suave manner.

"Hello and welcome to Synapse Solutions, I'm Vonda," Marsha reached to shake his hand, eyeing his make-believe badge. "The Foster Jolley Foundation, that's interesting. I was just talking to a colleague about him."

"The man was a game-changer." Judd lifted his burrito off the plate and partially unwrapped it as if it was the lab's brochure. "And what game-changing work is your lab up to these days?"

"Watch the snide, arrogant tone."

Judd repeated the question with curiosity and added, "Anything related to heightened states of consciousness?"

"You're going to need some clothes," Marsha said.

Judd's eyes lit up. "So ... I go?"

"If I can get you in as a board member."

Judd raised his burrito. "Wabumba!"

"Huh?"

"Kind of excited. Never put my acting to the test in real life. This isn't like theater."

Marsha picked up her plate. "It's all theater, clamoring for enlightened direction."

# 31

# Arson

Sheriff Buck's wife, Grace, was one of the early risers to catch the metro news report on channel 11:

"Fire alarms sounded at Flying Cloud Airport around 3:00 a.m. Our camera crew was there as emergency vehicles arrived on the scene. At first the fire inside the hangar appeared containable. But it suddenly erupted into an inferno. All firefighters could do was control the blaze until there was nothing left to burn."

On the screen, the hangar roof buckled and collapsed.

"The west metro airport leases its hangars to corporate jets and turbo props. However, this one housed the components of alleged terrorists Chester and Oakley Jolleys' bomb-making lab."

"Buck!" Grace called for her husband in the other room. "You need to see this!"

The newscast continued.

"Fortunately, no one was inside. The fire remains under investigation. All indicators point to arson ignited by the brothers to destroy evidence. They currently remain at large."

"Hey, Buck!"

"Now stay with us for today's weather after this short break."

Grace left the kitchen to find her husband as the station went to a commercial:

"Impress the guests at your next soiree with Spamanade, the all-American appetizer," Judd's voice boomed over the airwaves. "Coat a luscious layer on a toast point, or plaster the paté on a pita chip, or swab an ample blanket on a bagel. Mmm-hmm … moist … mouth-watering … Spamanade. Serve it hot. Serve it cold. Be it a banquet or a brunch, put a party in your mouth. Hormel's Spamanade. The taste of America. A spread ahead of its time."

# 32

# Let's Confront the Lies

Marsha used to accompany Foster to the annual Neuro-science Conference. They traveled to Zurich one year, London the next. Even after Foster's disappearance, Marsha attended the event to stay connected.

This year's conference was at the Convention Center in Washington DC. It featured Ezra Katz's much ballyhooed launch of her sons' achievements. But due to his death and disturbing rumors about the brothers, the conference director restructured the agenda so Marsha could deliver a eulogy for Ezra.

During the opening remarks, she searched the audience but couldn't locate Judd among the 300 attendees. The last time she saw him was at the hotel that morning pacing bare-foot around his room "getting into character."

The genial speaker, a well-regarded Japanese neurobi-ologist, welcomed everyone and announced the day's slate of breakout sessions and panel discussions.

"Now I want to introduce Marsha Jolley, who will pay tribute to our late friend and colleague, Dr. Ezra Katz."

Respectful applause greeted her as she stepped to the lec-tern, wearing a dark blue outfit consisting of wool pants, azure scarf, and pearls. A large screen projected a young Ezra Katz blowing a conch shell.

"We lost a dear soul," she said, "a short, wiry man with an open-source heart that knew no bounds. He and I met at Stanford and instantly connected around music's effect on brain waves. Our collaboration still serves as a template for college classes today."

Judd strode into the convention center, a bit out of breath. A text from the Wilders had held him up:

```
Returning soon.
Sorry for short notice.
```

Judd tried calling the Wilders to pin down their arrival but couldn't get through. That and trying to fit in the shoes Roslyn and Arnie bought for him led to his delay. They did a good job picking out the Prussian blue suit and vanilla silk shirt with mandarin collar, definitely high buck and tailored to his extra-extra length. But the handstitched tassel loafers were a half-size too small, even with his feet stylishly sockless.

Judd entered the conference hall as a slide showed Ezra and Marsha sitting at a brain wave monitor.

"But I'm not here to chronicle a life stolen from us," she said. "Ezra wouldn't go for that. He'd want you to hear about the remarkable findings my sons Rochester and Oakland discovered under his guidance.

"Some of you may recall when the Dalai Lama was keynote speaker at a meeting of the Society for Neuroscience. Asked during the Q&A what he would think if a surgical procedure could inspire a spiritual awakening in people, he answered— 'I'd want to be the first in line.'

"Well, you'll be pleased to know what my sons found won't require brain surgery. To quote Ezra: 'Transcendent states of being that have been slumbering in the folds of the cerebral cortex for who knows how long can now be awakened.'"

Marsha clicked to the next slide, a smiling Ezra, outside the Minnesota lab when he visited the past fall, his arms around Chester and Oakley.

"Now let's confront the lies." Marsha's mouth kept moving but no one could hear her. She tapped the microphone to no avail. Undaunted, she stepped off the stage and walked among the audience.

"As I was saying, let's confront the lies." She worked her way to the center of the space. "The murder of Ezra Katz was a deliberate attempt to keep the world from a scientific break-through beyond measure. His sudden death was not due to cardiac arrest, nor was the destruction of my sons' lab and our house in Minnesota an experiment gone awry."

Marsha clicked to a slide of the laboratory rubble. Judd heard gasps among the audience.

"No, it was a ruthless attack orchestrated to deny access to elevated states or AUM."

Marsha had the audience's attention now. She spoke pure fire. Some moved in closer. Others stood to hear better.

"I admire the work of this creative community. But the ul-timate creative act is honesty. So let it be known," she pointed to the slide, "gutless cowards committed this sabotage. But like heat, the truth rises. And soon Ezra and my son's achieve-ments will come to light."

Marsha walked away and, as if on cue, the sound system came back with a piercing shriek that deafened the swell of murmurs.

After the keynote speaker finished his humorous talk on Axonal Tradecraft, Judd stood in the double doors of the conference hall and waved for Marsha. She spotted him but a throng of attendees had corralled her.

"Well, I survived that," she said after finally breaking free.

"I lost my home." Judd told her about the text and how he needed to move out of the Wilder's.

"Know the feeling. Okay, let's see if we can get you back on a red-eye. Are you still up for the exhibition?"

"I guess. But these shoes are too tight."

"Remember, you're a high buck venture capitalist on a fact-finding mission. What are the labs touting? Is it anything that resembles Oakley and Chester's explorations? Could they be behind the attack? What's with the wiggling?"

"These shoes …"

"Stop with the shoes!"

"My feet are burning."

"So use it. Isn't that what actors do? Use their pain to heighten the drama?"

"If they can walk."

"Remember, do a serious check-out of Neurokey. That's where you'll meet Kira King. And be careful, behind her allure is a coiled python."

Marsha didn't let on about the stunts Judd's brain might pull. Didn't want to jinx him. But Judd read her mind.

"If things go bizarro and I spew a movie, I'll find the nearest men's room til the credits roll."

"You better get going."

"Wait, what's AUM?"

"It stands for Absolute Unitary Being. A feeling common among those who've experienced an ecstatic state."

# 33

# A Black Caravan

Sheriff Buck took a call from Gladys Smith asking about a caravan of sinister-looking black vehicles heading into town. Buck didn't have a ready answer. Minutes after hanging up, a Director Somebody from the Department of Homeland Security called to inform him about a military operation in his jurisdiction.

Two armored personnel carriers rumbled down Main Street followed by a military cargo truck loaded with gear, food, and an arsenal of weapons. Eight soldiers made up the counterterrorism task force. Their mission: scour Marigold for the brothers and anything resembling bomb-making materials.

They set up an encampment inside the Burger, Brew & Bowl, at the south end of town, that had been closed for remodeling. The soldiers had pulled tours in the hottest hot beds of the world, but never experienced the teeth-clicking chill of a Minnesota winter.

Buck got Arnie on the horn.

"They're hunting for the boys and their bomb stuff. Guy on the phone called the twins 'radicalized.' The task force

Commander is coming to the station midmorning tomorrow to brief me on their plan of action."

"They didn't make bombs, Buck. Time you believed that. And we need to tell folks it's a bald-faced lie before it spreads. Ya know, facts walk, but rumors run fast as pheasants clucking nonstop."

# 34

# I'm Sterling

Outside the doors of the exhibition hall, a tuxedoed young woman checked names on a guest list.

"I represent the Foster Jolley Foundation," Judd said.

"Oh-kay ... I see the name, Marsha Jolley."

"I'm taking her place."

"Oh? Hold on ... oh, yes ... per-*fect*." The woman plucked a Post-it Note off the list. "Mr ..."

"Sterling." Judd assumed the character of the attorney he nicknamed while on jury duty. He rehearsed the rooster strut and ego-sheen the man exuded in court.

"Okay, Mr. Sterling, here's a little program to help you navigate the hall."

After a security guard took his phone and patted him down, Judd entered the ballroom.

"Showtime," he said, and played a narrative in his mind: Act One, the setting, a spacious room, super high ceiling, peach-colored walls, a U-shaped surround of large open booths. In the center, a couple dozen high-top tables draped in white cloths. Old, upbeat Beatles music piped in, "Eight Days a Week."

"Time to find Kira … Kira King."

Judd didn't know people called her "Killa" behind her back. She earned the nickname from an encounter with an alleged rapist. Rumors ranged from a serial stalker to a date gone bad. None true. She was nineteen. The man was her father's business associate. They had an affair. He lied about leaving his wife to marry her. When she called it off, he kept pursuing, kept lying. One night he burst into her loft slobby drunk promising divorce. She resisted his advances. "What," he said, "that time of the month?" Kira leisurely reached for a large Chinese vase painted with orange blossoms and smashed it on his head. He regained consciousness to find her straddling his torso, her knees digging into his arms. "Got something for you." She opened his mouth, stuffed a tampon down his throat followed by a glass of Perrier. The tampon inflated. He couldn't hack it out. Kira snickered and whispered in his ear, "Lie to me now."

"Kira King," Judd repeated as he strolled the parquet floor.

High above the center tables, a hologram of a human brain the size of a Mack truck rotated in a slow circle. Given the diverse faces and attire, Judd felt he'd stepped into the U.N. Saudis and Africans moved about in flowing robes; others were tailored in posh and polish, some casual, tieless, headwear from turbans to his wide-brimmed Panama, which he wore to cover the unsightly blister on his forehead.

Judd adjusted his name tag.

The loafers scraped his heels as he made a slow orbit of the booths. He waved off a caterer with a tray of truffles flecked with edible gold. Although tempted, sugar would jangle the self-assured manner of his performance. Besides, he found he acted best on empty.

At one booth a woman spoke in eye-glazing terms about "transcranial neurulation." Another booth played a video of a smiling white-haired lady pointing a wired pen-like object to her head. "I once had migraines. Now with the simple touch of my *Stim Stick,* I'm free of 'em."

Spotting the Neurokey banner at the back of the ballroom, Judd walked with a regal stride to the display table and asked for Kira.

"She's not here right now. May we help you?" said the man with SENIOR TECHNICIAN pinned to his lab coat.

Judd noticed a woman seated behind the technician at a monitor with electrodes attached to her head.

The man followed Judd's eyes.

"Interested in a free EEG?"

"What does it tell you?"

"It's a way to learn about your electrical circuitry. It identifies brain wave patterns and abnormalities."

Up to then Judd was so taken in by the sights of the exhibit, he forgot to seek help for his own brain. Here was a chance. But he hesitated. *He* wanted to do it, but would his character?

# 35
# Yes or Absolutely

After calling the airlines to change Judd's return flight to Minneapolis, Marsha went about the convention center looking for Ezra's widow, Cora. They weren't friends. For a time, years back, she was jealous about Marsha working so closely with her husband on a project. Setting their sour history aside, Marsha phoned Cora the morning after Ezra died. Cora didn't return the call but sent a text:

```
Someone stole Ezra's files.
```

Proof he was murdered. But Marsha wanted to hear it from Cora and give her condolences in person.

She passed a room filling up with attendees. A placard outside the door caught her eyes: "IT'S ONLY PARANORMAL UNTIL IT BECOMES THE NORM." She poked her head inside and flinched at the sight of Theodore Theroux stepping to the rostrum.

Who invited *him*?

Unable to find Cora, Marsha retrieved her coat and went outside to grab a cab. A black limousine idled at the curb. A hunchbacked man with a Breathe Right nasal strip on his nose swung open the limo's door.

"Ms. Jolley, can we give you a ride to the Neurokey lab?"

"Do I have a choice?"

"You do. You can either agree by saying 'yes,' or 'absolutely.'"

"Fine," Marsha said. "Just what I need, a good flossing."

"Now-now," came a raspy voice from the back seat. "We want to share some developments. Name's Inman Hayes."

Marsha sat across from a man with an overly large head and sunken eyes. Hayes had his back to the privacy partition. He tapped twice on the glass with his ring. The limo rolled into the strobe of city lights.

"Quite the speech," Hayes said. He hit a button. Interior lights came on.

The Breathe Right man plopped two sheets of paper on her lap.

"What's this, another warrant?" Marsha said.

"Permission to do a body search and your hotel room."

"Permission? How considerate. Have you been taking mindfulness training?"

"Just sign it, lady." Breathe Right handed her a pen.

"Of course, as long as you leave the mint on the pillow." Marsha jotted a ragged signature on the line.

"And your phone, or phones."

"You never returned my last one." She handed the man her purse.

He plugged her phone into a brick-sized computer while Hayes made a call. "Tell me what you find."

"Look," Marsha said, "I have nothing new to report since the last interrogation. You won't find any phone calls to or from my sons. Another sorrowful tale of teenagers shunning their loving mother."

While Breathe Right scanned Marsha's call history, Hayes asked if she had any clue about her sons' whereabouts.

"Where would you go if someone blew up your place and made false claims about you being a terrorist?"

Hayes didn't answer.

"Your turn," Marsha said. "Tell me about these *developments.*"

"They found your sons' VW parked in what's called Dinkytown and towed it. The first parking ticket was dated the day after the incident at your home."

Dinkytown. Right by the U. This *was* news.

"You were teaching at the University then?"

"I was," Marsha whispered, suddenly distant, shuttled back to the day. She wondered if Chester and Oakley came to say goodbye and tell her where they were going. Or was it a decoy to throw off their pursuers? Either way, realizing her sons were that close made her heart sink.

Hayes held up a photo. "Recognize him?"

It took a few seconds for Marsha to identify a young man in a desert camouflage outfit and sunglasses. She didn't answer, but seeing her hand go to her mouth said it all.

"From a security camera at the Mall of America," Hayes said.

The masquerade would normally give Marsha a chuckle, but under the circumstances it made her feel sad, her Oakley hiding behind a disguise and stalked like a rabid dog.

"He managed to evade capture, but he's probably close by."

"And what do you expect me to do here in DC?" she asked.

The black limousine nosed into a parking lot like a sleek eel.

"We're there," said the driver.

"Here's your phone." Breathe Right opened the door for her. "I'll need to search you before you go in."

"Think about your sons' safety, Ms. Jolley." Hayes reached into his shirt pocket. "My card."

Breathe Right patted her down in the parking lot and asked, "Did your sons stash anything other than what they destroyed in the hangar fire?"

"What hangar fire?"

"Ahh," said Breathe Right, relishing the moment. "Breaking news. Your sons are accused of arson."

"You bastards don't quit!"

"Well?"

"I wouldn't tell you *if* I knew, and I don't."

"Best you start knowing," sneered Breathe Right. "We been talkin' reeeal nice, but don't be fooled."

"Gee, how'd you know about my fetish for death threats?"

Marsha watched the limo drive away and stuffed Hayes's card in her coat without looking at it.

As she headed toward the door of the Neurokey building, the encounter with Hayes brought everything into sharp detail.

There's only one way the government could know where I was going.

Victor King.

I should have thanked them for the ride.

# 36
## Kira King

The technician removed the electrodes from Judd's head. "Come back to the booth in a few minutes. We'll print out your brain's electrical chart."

"And you expect Kira here at some point?" Judd asked.

"Definitely, sir."

*Sir.* Judd liked that. He winced as he worked his feet back in the loafers. Then he gingerly stepped to the center court where semiclad women in white shorts and crimson halter-tops offered drinks and appetizers. He sipped a flute of Voulez '68, and took a bite of a tenderloin cromache, patting his lips with a cloth napkin, his character fully formed.

*If only I was being filmed.*

After eating, he stopped at a booth with the banner: INTELLIGENCE FRANCHISING. He fingered a colorful brochure with the subhead: "Those not owning the future will be renting their days."

A sprightly, rotund man appeared at the table. "Welcome to Geneva Laboratories. Name's Gordon Tully." Wide-rimmed glasses covered the saddlebags under his eyes.

"Sterling." Judd gave a firm shake of the man's clammy hand and angled his body to converse and scan the floor for Kira King at the same time. "Arrived a bit late, I'm afraid. Perhaps you can catch me up. For starters, what Intelligence Franchising is exactly."

"Surely you're familiar with the latest cartography of the human brain."

Judd glanced up at the flesh-colored image of a brain on the back wall of the booth and realized the cloudlike cerebral forms were actually a troupe of nude bodies bent and bundled on top of each other.

"Geneva Labs has turned charting the brain's neuron garden into a breakout enterprise front-loaded for profits unimaginable."

"You have my attention."

"Every millimeter carries as yet untapped potentialities. Maybe a meta-skill like psychometry, trauma memory erasure, or sleep induction. We've got a demo that shows how your soldier will stand at attention with minimal cerebral stimulation."

Judd fingered their brochure.

"I'm not following. You're selling real estate of the brain?"

"Access, specifically. Like owning the rights to part of a mineral mine, only it's brain-mining and it turns gray matter into gold bullion."

Something invaded Judd's vision. Strange fibers darted before his eyes. He tried to blink them away.

"So … I buy the rights. Who mines the gold?" Judd said, unable to shake off the ripply strands of light.

"Our lab. Unlike the others you see, we possess the special, patented tools to activate the area you purchase. Say it's a tiny speck of the neocortex. Anyone wanting to experience the super ability found in that patch of their brain pays you a fee."

That's whack, Judd thought, but instead said, "Wild science."

Tully raised his arms. "There are more things in heaven and earth than are dreamt of in … your lifetime."

"Well put."

"Hemingway."

A hose-like appendage moved from Tully's throat toward Judd's head. He rubbed his eyes.

Did they spike my drink?

"Mr. Sterling, you can be among the first to purchase a cranial site. However, the price per millimeter does not come cheap."

"Well suppose …"

A woman crossed the floor as if floating on ball bearings, bright as a tiger, and so vivid everyone else looked like a smudge.

"Wabumba. Could be Kira King," Judd murmured under his breath. "Here we go."

"Suppose? You were saying, Mr. Sterling?"

"Sup-pose …"

As the woman passed booth after booth, men swiveled toward her like heat-seeking missiles.

"… suppose I wanted to buy the right hemisphere?" Judd said, "Or for that matter, all of it?"

"The entire brain? Are you out of your mind?!"

Judd dropped the brochure and went for a closer look. The woman was sweat-hot gorgeous. About five-seven. Brown hair with reddish waves, like bacon. Flawless skin. Not overly made up. No need. She was dressed for comfort and luxury in an ivory satin pantsuit open down the front, cleavage accented by a cantaloupe scarf. Walkable short heels. No necklace, rings, or bracelets. Her body the jewelry.

She *must* be *her*.

But there was a problem—laser-like streaks confused Judd's vision. They shot from men's heads and pelvic regions toward the woman. It was so unnerving he wanted to leave.

Stay in control, he coached himself. Own the space. And look distinguished—whatever that means.

Judd revived a grin of unwavering confidence and followed the woman.

Kira King gave the first man who approached her an icy, "look at me don't" glare and veered away. Her skin glowed like liquid amber. Perhaps a mix of bloods, White with a dash of Peruvian, or Venusian for that matter. And he thought Bianca BaLore was Beauty's envy.

Another man wearing a Stetson stepped up to her. "Name's Art Darling. Richer than Jesus and just as lovin'."

She jettisoned him with a blink of her lashes.

Judd edged around the center tables to be in her path.

"You must find it greatly entertaining," he said as she swayed past, "to know all men want what they cannot have."

She lifted her chin, locked on Judd's eyes for a second. As she moved on, he saw a wave of energy extend from his body toward her.

Enough! This is insane! Find the men's room and wait it out!

On his way, he bumped into a portly man dressed in a black cassock. Judd saw a spear of light shoot from the man's eyes to a strand of beads on the floor. Judd picked them up. The man bobbed his head and said, "Most generous."

As Judd pivoted his pinched feet, the woman appeared behind him. Her radiant eyes fixed on his.

"What was it you said, 'Men want what they cannot have'?"

He grinned. "Yet believe they can't live without it."

"You interest me," she said, aroused by his deep voice.

"I do that."

He was reveling in his character now. Oscar worthy.

"I'm Kira," she served her hand. Cool porcelain.

"Sterling." He found his body tilting forward as he clasped her palm. Her magnetism had the undertow of a tsunami.

Kira tapped his badge. "Foster Jolley Foundation."

"On the Board."

"Oh, and what is the Foundation's interest here?"

"I'm actually doing my own reconnaissance, probing laboratories that explore mystical states."

"Ahh …" She hooked her arm around his. "Well, allow me to guide your probe to my lab."

This is it, Judd thought. Now to find out what they know about the Godhead Spot.

"Foster, Foster, Foster …" Kira repeated softly as they walked.

When they approached the Neurokey booth she let go Judd's arm to greet a gaunt, bearded man in a charcoal trench coat. She kissed his cheek.

"Heard your talk was standing room only."

"A herd of nerds," replied the man.

"Theo, this is Mr. Sterling with the Foster Jolley Foundation. I was about to ask him about the work of Foster's sons."

Judd saw a hose of energy coil from her torso around the bearded man's waist like a boa.

Ah …" Theroux took in the taller man. "Sterling, a name of high quality. Where have I seen you before?" Exceptionally long fingers curled around Judd's hand. The man's palm sticky, as if every pore a suction cup.

He's the long-legged stork I saw in the Jolleys' driveway, Theroux recalled. And there was a photo of him in the Defense Department's underground command center.

Feeling his true identity somehow exposed, Judd retracted his hand.

"Mr. Sterling, Mr. Sterling," Tully appeared. "If I may interrupt, I need to apologize for my rash reaction. It was uncalled for. Perhaps I could make it up to you with a special psychometric demonstration?"

Judd nodded to Kira and the man. "You'll excuse me."

Kira touched his sleeve. "Oh, do come back. We have much to share."

Judd felt no desire to see Tully's demo. He needed to ditch the shoes and hole himself up until the hallucinations passed.

"I've seen him before." Theroux said.

Before Kira could ask where, the lab tech who conducted the EEG rushed up, flapping photo paper in his hand. "Kira, Kira." He pointed to a series of lines on the readout. "Have you ever seen wave patterns like this?"

"What about them?"

"They're cursive!"

"What?" Kira took the sheet in her hand. "Whose is this?"

The tech pointed across the exhibition hall. "That tall guy who was just here."

Theroux watched Judd disappear among the guests. He rubbed his thumb and fingers together. I'll have to look in on you Mr. Sterling, now that I have your signature in my vibrary.

# 37
# Shangri-Lab

The Neurokey Laboratory, a three-story, corten steel structure with copper-tinted windows, sat on a treed lot in Arlington, Virginia. Behind its glass front doors stood an expectant Victor King, the CEO. He was dressed in a dark gray suit coat with an eggplant-purple, open-colored shirt.

Marsha met Victor when they were students at Stanford. She didn't like him then, and her feelings had deteriorated since. Yet here he stood, the exam-cheating grad student who tried to copy one of Foster's optical designs, opening a huge door for her. Rather than comment on his receding hairline and expanded waistline, she got straight to the point.

"Who killed Ezra?"

"Good to see you too, Marsha." He let the door swing shut behind them. "Your inflammatory eulogy precedes you."

"You know who did it."

"I'm sure many entertained the thought. Ezra had a big mouth. Your endearing tribute left that part out. Hell, you could hear his cock-a-doodle-doo voice on Mars for Christ's sake: 'Hey everybody! We found the Godhead Spot!' And everybody knew who he meant by 'we.' I get calls from other labs: 'Victor, did they really find it?'"

"The only reason I agreed to meet was to look you in the eye when you said you had nothing to do with his murder."

"Stop with this murder nonsense." Victor let out a long exhale. "Ezra died of a fucking heart attack."

"They took his files!"

"Where'd you hear that?" Victor stiffened his spine, unable to hide his shock at the news.

"His *files*, Victor!"

"You're suggesting, what? I did it?"

"You tell me."

"And your home, that was me too? Who do you think I am?"

"A man who would do *anything* to steal my sons' findings."

"Can I get you *anything*?"

"How about the truth!"

"The truth …"

"Bone on bone."

"How about I give you a tour of the ranch while you crucify me?"

Victor led Marsha across the lobby to a waist-high dais with a schematic map of the building, each section labeled with its area of research: IMAGING, NEUROMODULA-TION, PARKINSON'S, SLEEP, MEMORY, STROKE.

Marsha asked, "Your lab cosponsored the conference and selected the presenters, right?"

"Yeah?"

"So how'd Theodore Theroux get an invite?"

"Oh, The *The*." Victor's eyebrows rose. "Kira's idea. Give the fringe element a voice. You know, a whiff of junk science.

He evidently stuffed the room to capacity. Go figure. The man makes Dracula look appealing."

Victor didn't mention how, according to Kira, Theroux had tracked down Oakley Jolley's whereabouts with his psychic sight.

Shit! He thought. The guy could be spying on us right now!

Marsha followed him down a wide hall that ended at double doors where a uniformed security guard stood, big as a standing bear. On his nametag: BURMAN. He passed a key card over a security pad next to the wide doors. A locking mechanism clunked.

"How are your sons, by the way?" Victor asked.

"How should I know? The Feds confiscated all means of communication. They strong-armed the Dean of the University to remove me, without pay. Can't have a teacher linked to a domestic terrorist cell now can we? They even read my mail for code words."

"Dreadful. And your daughter?"

"Living in a bubble of show tunes and ..." She stopped as they entered a palatial laboratory.

"Welcome to Shangri-Lab," Victor said.

Marsha scanned the immense space, unable to stifle her awe at the number of sparkling workstations, from micromanipulators to tonography machines on anti-vibrational tables.

"Is that an ..."

"ERTZ pulser, fresh off the line."

Glassed-in side rooms housed more diagnostic equipment.

"I couldn't tell you what half the instruments do. I mostly write checks."

Which wasn't true. Victor may not know the technical aspects of each station and device, but he was intimately involved with the results of the neurologic research.

He could see Marsha was impressed with his domain.

"Fundraising must be hot to keep this place cooking," Marsha said.

"A never-ending battle. But thanks to Alzheimer's and Kira's grant writing we keep the lights on."

His indebtedness to brain disease made Marsha squirm. She shrugged it off and trailed him to a door requiring his thumbprint to open.

"Now, for why I asked you to come."

Victor flicked on the overheads. They illuminated an empty room big as a basketball court with a row of clerestory windows along the west wall.

"Picture this as your sons' new playground. A facility all their own, supported with whatever top-of-the-line equipment and professional assistance they desire."

"I see where this is going."

"Let's bring it all here, Marsha. Put it under one roof. A lab of co-lab-oration. Your sons carry on their phenomenal work with no interference, and together we share the winnings and the glory."

"Under one roof? You mean right under the thumb of the Pentagon?"

Victor blanched, wondering how she could have known.

"How ...?"

"They drove me here."

"We've been in discussions, I'll admit."

Hearing crickets, Marsha reached for her phone. She hoped it wasn't Judd having an aneurysm.

"Hang on," she said. It was a text from Arnie with a photo. Marsha's eyes narrowed. "Oh my God." She shoved the phone in Victor's face. "Are you part of this?"

"What is it?" He squinted.

"Special Forces just rolled into Marigold."

Victor's nostrils dilated. "Your sons are not safe. Now, I can bring them back. But I need certain assurances."

"Did Ezra refuse your offer?"

"Forget about Ezra. This is about …"

"Answer me!"

Victor set his hand on Marsha's shoulder.

"We need to be careful here, Marsha, to protect it."

She recoiled. "Don't touch me!"

Victor let go and hardened his voice. "Certainly a discovery of this magnitude requires powerful relationships. It's far too precious to leave to the whims of teenagers."

"Oh, so I should hand them over to a puppet of the devil?"

"Think Marsha. Think what happens if it gets into the wrong heads."

# 38

# Parlor Games

To Judd's relief, there were few people funneling through Reagan National Airport security at that late hour. Even still, it was a dizzy, nerve-jangling ordeal given the waves of energy he saw crisscrossing between travelers and TSA agents. Some were amoeba-like, others firm as spears, from silvery blue to fire-engine red. He kept his head down throughout, shielding his eyes from the surreal spectacle.

Relax. Deep breaths.

Clearly, this was madness leaking in.

Deep breaths now! Bubble of calm, bubble of calm.

As Judd waited at the Delta gate to board the 12:10 a.m. back to Minneapolis, he blinked and squinted his eyes.

Whatever this is, it's got to stop.

He moved his pupils left and right. Eyes are cameras, too, he thought. So do that cinematic technique—rack focus. He shifted his attention from far to near objects. From the exterior lights illuminating the runway to the businessman falling asleep in the next row of seats, his neck tipping back and back as if watching a rollercoaster inch up its track.

Judd kept up the exercise—far to near, near to far. In a short time he figured out how to reframe his sight for normal perception, then expand the aperture to see the strange sub-visible rays extending from people.

Open up the field, he directed himself. Okay, now dial it back. Again ... go wide ... and return. Once more. Yes! He rejoiced under his breath. I can regulate my perception! Wabumba-rumba!

As Judd strolled down the jetway, someone called his name. Marsha looked grim.

"Like you, I need to get back."

She decided not to tell him about Victor and his shady association with the Pentagon, or the task force storming Marigold. At least not until she knew more.

The flight was only half full. They took empty seats at the rear.

"So how'd your meeting go?" Judd asked.

"The Devil made a tempting offer. Who knows, could be a way to bring the boys home safe and sound. Even get my teaching job back."

"I'm hearing a 'but.'"

"Chains attached. More like implanted."

The engines revved to a roar. The plane sped down the runway and lifted into the night sky.

"And you?" she asked. "How'd it go at the exhibition?"

"What is telekinesis?"

"Moving objects with your mind. Why? Is that what they were doing? Spoon bending?"

"One booth hyped it."

"Parlor games. And Kira King?"

"I met her only briefly. By that time I was seeing wobbly strands and rays springing out of people. It got so crazy-making I split."

"Rays? You mean like auras?"

"I guess."

"Are you seeing them now?"

"No. But I can."

Marsha wanted to know more. Once they were at cruising altitude, she hypnotized Judd. He projected his memory on the tray table. First came a big banner in neon-blue block letters: NEUROKEY. *Opening the Doors to Ageless Wellness.* A man in a lab coat led him to a demonstration table.

"You let them put electrodes on your head?" Marsha said.

"Something to do until Kira showed. Then I got bored. Okay, there, right there! See that?"

Marsha couldn't make it out at first.

"Those fiber-like things shooting out of people. Are they like pheromones?"

"Those are *energy cords*!" Marsha exclaimed. "Oh my God!"

"What's that?"

"A dynamic associated with the psychic field. We send cords of energy to connect, and in some cases to manipulate or drain another person's vitality. These are the first I've seen!"

"And there! See how some are ripply and others like laser beams?"

"Extraordinary," she said.

"And here I thought I was going insane."

The flight attendant came by, saw the projection on the tray table, and did a double take.

Marsha smiled up at her. "He brought his own movie."

# 39

# To See More of You

Theroux was about to bi-locate "Sterling," when some-one knocked on the door of his hotel suite at the InterContinental.

"It's me love." Kira King smiled on the threshold. "Wanting to see more of you."

Kira had invited Theroux to a dinner party she was hosting for potential Neurokey funders. He bowed out. Now here she stood, holding a bottle of Bollinger in her hand, her face aglow.

Apprehensive, Theroux said, "If you're thinking what I think you're thinking"—his unbroken vow of chastity was fifteen years and counting.

Kira knew his story. It aroused the conqueror in her. Wasting no time, she set the bottle on a table, flung off her cocoon coat, and undid the sash of his silk pants.

He pulled her hand away. "Now-now," he said.

"Oh, Theo, there is only now." She smelled of gardenias.

His heart pounded in his second chakra as spiritual integrity collided with sexual desire. Coming on to him was the ultimate straight man's fantasy. Kira's beauty, a blushing rose of sensuality—all for him. But he had his purity to maintain. Its three pillars: 1) eliminate carnal cravings, 2) eat only eyeless foods, and 3) insist the wicked change for the better without judging them.

"Mmm," she crooned. "It would be sooo good."

Without a doubt, it would be. A part of him ached for it. It wanted to suckle every sinuous cell of Kira's body—her moist, full lips, her velvet flesh. He thought of how he'd starved himself of physical pleasure for far too long. How he could later justify a sexual fling as selective celibacy. But it would mean caving into Kira's irresistible allure. And this encounter was all about power.

"Maybe another time," he said.

"Playing with you." Kira winked. "Testing your resolve."

"Oh." Theroux re-tied his sash, a bit thrown by her tease.

She took the bottle of Champagne to the kitchenette counter and delicately removed the foil.

"So busy at the exhibition, I neglected to shower you with praise," she said. "So, here I am."

He watched as she eased out the cork, like she'd opened a thousand.

"Praise for … ?"

"Wish it was more chilled," Kira said, as she poured the Champagne in two plastic cups and handed one to Theroux. "Praise for your ESP demonstration. Chief Hayes was awed. I believe his words were, 'beyond belief.' I confess, I take partial credit for recommending you." She lifted her glass. "Here's to you, Theo."

Normally he'd decline an offer of alcohol, but given the moment, he met Kira's eyes and took a sip. The wine was delicious.

"I expected to hear back from Hayes. Did they catch the young man?" Theroux asked, knowing Oakley Jolley evaded capture.

"You were spot on. He was at that mall all right but got away." She topped off his glass. "What do you think of him?"

"Who?" Theroux was savoring the bubbly.

"Hayes." Kira slipped out of her heels and moved to the couch.

Theroux felt inclined to warn Kira about dealing with Chief Hayes. How the man was a master controller. But he held back, believing she'd find out for herself in due time.

"In a word, domineering," Theroux said, as he sat beside her. "Must have legions of underlings to do his bidding."

"For sure, that." She set the bottle on the coffee table and lifted her glass. "And here's to our lasting friendship."

"May it be so," he said, and drank, the Champagne quickly going to his head.

In a flash Kira was on him, pressing a succulent kiss on his lips.

Theroux found himself kissing her back, his groin ablaze.

"No. Hey! NO!" He nudged her away and stood, spilling his drink.

"Oh, sorry, love. You're so captivating, I can't help myself."

"Listen, I appreciate the … "

"It's okay. It's okay. I-I really should be going," Kira said, struggling to offset the slam of rejection. She adjusted her collar. "But before I do, there's a question I've been meaning to ask."

"Yes?"

"You met Foster Jolley's sons at their lab in Minnesota? So, what do you think? Are they legit?"

Where is she taking this? Theroux crossed to the window to conceal the prong in his pants. He looked out at the lights of the Capitol Building, its dome a giant, gleaming bosom.

Kira stood. "I mean there's all this talk about them finding an uplink to God in our brains. Is it for real, or is it their mother's hype?"

Theroux faced her. "Is *that* why you came here? To seduce me into telling you about their work?"

"Oh no, my darling," Kira moved to him with a forced grin. "Like I said, I came to toast your tremendous psychic skill. You are the most remarkable man I've ever met. And I figured you'd want to be in on such a reality-shaking discovery." She slipped on her shoes. "Guess I assumed wrong."

She's spoken to Hayes, Theroux surmised. Or her father. One or both of them told her my demands for bi-locating the Jolley twins.

"And how does your father like being a gofer for the Pentagon?" he asked.

"Victor?" Kira didn't flinch. She downed the rest of her glass and set it on the counter.

"Yes, the man with an outcome for a name."

"He's an all-American capitalist. He'd nose-dive into quicksand to seal a deal." She picked her coat off the floor, blew Theroux a kiss. "Do call me. Soon. We'll set a date."

He followed her to the door. "Goodnight."

"That was close," Theroux muttered, as he emptied the Champagne in the sink. He exhaled relief and inhaled a boost of achievement. The enchantress had challenged his self-restraint and he held strong.

Kira waited at the elevator, rattled. The impossible just happened. Never before had a man rejected her advances.

And she failed to gather any information about the twins. Not only that, the fundraising dinner she hosted came up empty.

So what now? What will it take to corral those Jolley boys? She punched the DOWN arrow again and again.

Him calling her father a gofer stuck like gum in her hair.

While Theroux showered, he re-assessed his connection with Kira. When she first introduced herself at a talk he gave in Los Angeles, he saw her as an access door into Neurokey, the Virginia brain lab she represented.

That was a year ago. I was shopping, my motives opportunistic. But her lab may still lead to something. Best not cut the cord just yet.

As he toweled off, the bathroom mirror reflected the lesions sketching his skin like hash marks. At least sixty scored his torso, legs, and arms. Occasionally one would wake him up. If he scratched, it would burn mean. The salve he concocted reduced the swelling and soothed the itch but left a discoloration. The consequences of his out-of-body excursions kept him from playing a casual voyeur. He had to choose his targets wisely. He also couldn't ignore the rise of dark impulses, an escalating side effect after each successive trip.

Is it worth it? Should I stop? No one more: Sterling. If that's really his name.

# 40

## Straight-Line Wind

After landing at Lindbergh Airport in Minneapolis, Judd drove through slanting snow flurries to the Wilder house. Although it had been days since the botched abduction, his return spiked a chill as he circled the block. Seeing no vans or suspicious cars parked along the street, he pulled into the driveway. Still, as he keyed the back door, he sensed a foreboding. He flicked the light switch. In the kitchen he found cupboards and drawers pulled, the Sub-zero wide open, and the floor littered with thawing meat. He heard murmurs from another room.

Normally he'd panic. But he was too pissed to be cautious. Having to move out was one thing. Dealing with the upheaval set him off. Flight lost out to fight. He plucked a boning knife from a wooden block on the counter and urged his sleep-deprived body into the great room.

"Cops are on their way!" he lied.

It looked like a straight-line wind swept through—chairs upended, unread first editions on the floor, the Flemish tapestry askew. Nobody there. The voices came from a black-and-white movie on the jumbo screen—*12 Angry Men.*

What, the burglars watched TV while they waited for me?

The cold breeze buffeting his hair blew through the open front door. Its side lights glazed with icy fern patterns, the Persian entry rug flocked with snow.

Judd slammed the door and surveyed the damage.

Whoever ransacked the place must have left some time ago.

He blew off calling 911. It would only add another complaint to the stack of grievances called in by the get-a-life neighbor next door.

Judd could barely keep his eyes open. He went to his bedroom and set the alarm for 7:00 a.m.

I'll put the house back in order after I get some rest.

As he kicked off his shoes, he felt eyes watching.

He was not alone.

In the corner a silhouette stood, undulating like dark smoke.

"What!" Judd launched off the bed. "Come on!" He rushed at the corner, slashing the air with the boning knife.

The shape vanished.

Seeing things again.

He flopped back on the bed.

Not my father. That's a relief.

Judd shut his eyes, knife in hand, blade up.

He had to admit, it'd been a good run. Big house on the lake, close to everything. Free rent for a year and a half.

I saved a bunch of money and hosted some fun gatherings until that playwright trapezed the Fonteneau chandelier to the floor. I should be grateful. Always knew the time would come. That's why I wanted to partner with the Jolleys' and market their Death Sight Scanner. Even stole their binder to pitch the Wilders. A dream investment. Make everybody rich.

Won't happen now. They're hunted criminals.

What's next, dinner theater?

# 41

## Comes Down to Poor Parenting

"**K**eep your coats on. This won't take long." Arnie welcomed townsfolk into the Marigold café. Roslyn and Flannery moved about the tables, pouring coffee. Some looked anxious, others appeared agitated, frowning "what now?" faces. Joe Pye entered, saying, "This better be worth getting up 'fore dawn."

Arnie stepped behind the counter and waved his hands. "Thank you all for coming."

The jabber got louder. He caught Roslyn's eye. She stuck two fingers in her mouth. Her decibel-deafening whistle silenced the room.

"I'll get right to it. A military task force is here to hunt down the Jolley twins. They'll claim the boys were making bombs. They'll say the two planned a terrorist attack that backfired and blew up their place. Don't believe a word of it."

"Then who did it?" Ollie Olson asked.

"Not so fast. Those kids got the telltale signs," Bob Zeebart said, "Coupla anti-socialite loners."

"You could say that about my husband out ice fishing," Olive Dunn said.

"Why, I seen 'em set cowpats on fire and fling 'em like Frisbees," another added.

Jan Karlsson raised his hand. "Remember when they hacked the tornado siren and made it wail a Conga beat?"

"The boys played practical jokes, agreed," Arnie said. "But I hope you can put those aside."

"Betcha it was a meth lab," Joe said. "Always is." Which got everyone yammering again.

"Comes down to poor parenting!" Henna Pino shouted, as Marsha walked in through the kitchen looking weary from the late flight.

The room fell silent. Most hadn't seen her in town since Foster vanished. Some took her absence to mean she was too good for them.

Marsha addressed the hard stares. "My sons have been diligently exploring the human brain. Their research led to an astounding breakthrough."

Sheriff Buck came in coughing.

"Don't mind me." He gestured for Marsha to continue.

"We believe the government, among others, is out to quash it."

"Bunch of bull," Joe said.

"Let her finish," Arnie said.

"What kind of breakthrough?" Millie raised her hand.

"Wait a minute," someone asked. "Are we safe?"

"They're not after you." Buck said.

"You mean these soldiers are not here to protect us? Christ on a cracker, we're Americans!"

"So where are your sons?" Henna asked.

"They ran. We don't know where."

"They wouldn't run if they were innocent!" Zeebart shouted, a roadmap of veins reddened his cheeks.

"Let me get this straight," Henna said, "You're saying soldiers are free to rummage through our homes looking for these lab rats?"

"What if they find homemade bombs?" came a voice from a back booth.

"Then they planted them." Marsha said. "The only thing hidden here is the truth."

"What kind of breakthrough?" Millie said.

"I hope those little shits get caught and put away!" Zeebart said.

"Amen to that," someone added. Others grunted approval.

Henna stood and pointed at Marsha. "She can stop all this nonsense. She knows where they are and can turn them in."

"Yeah, turn them in!"

Many joined the chant: "Turn them in! Turn them in!"

"Stop that right now!" Buck clapped his hands.

"Leave Marsha alone!" Olive said. "Anyone here know what it takes to be a single mom?"

The room quieted.

"What kind of breakthrough?" Millie asked.

"Anybody see 'em, call me." Zeebart fired an imaginary rifle as he shouldered his way to the door. "I'll take it from there." He bumped a table and spilled a cup of hot coffee on Joy Moore.

"Sonofabitch!" she screamed.

Arnie looked at Marsha, shaking his head. The message was not getting through.

"One last time," Arnie said. "The— boys—were—not— making—bombs. Pass it on."

People began leaving.

Buck beat them to the door. "Try to be good hosts, best you can. I don't mean you gotta bend over backward. The soldiers can make their own coffee. All I'm saying is be respectful."

"Long as they are," Lars Lundeen, who runs the Farm and Feed Gas Mart, hammered the counter. "But what if they're not?"

# 42
# Selling God

Victor King trundled to the far corner of the exhibition hall where workmen were striking the Neurokey booth. Seeing him approach, Kira closed a phone call.

"Get anything from your dinner meeting?" Victor asked.

"Some interest from a Saudi group. I'll follow up in a couple days."

"That's it? Shit, I just let three techs go. We're bleeding money!"

"No!" Kira turned to two men rolling up a banner. "That goes in the gray case!"

"You wanted to see me?" Victor said.

"I'll jump to the headlines: your dude is using us like slaves."

"What dude?"

"Inman Hayes and the Department of Defense contract he's wagging in your face. It's a ploy. He wants us to do their grunt work and lure the Jolley boys out of hiding and then ..."

"Fine. I have no problem being a rich slave. That contract gives us five years on cruise control, and with those twins ..."

"And what if it's hot air?"

"Can you imagine having the exclusive ability to open a neuropathway to the Almighty? How much we could charge per head? It's a Viagra rocket to Paradise!"

"Selling God is not the issue," Kira said. "Since our lab hasn't found anything resembling such a portal, we're dependent on one thing: we need the boys, *alive*. So ask yourself, why do they treat them like bomb-making terrorists? If Hayes and his goons want them alive, they sure have a deadly way of showing it."

"You been listening to that sorcerer friend of yours."

"That sorcerer located one of the brothers a thousand miles from here."

"Yeah, and the kid slipped away. Makes me wonder if The The warned him."

Kira filed that thought, then summed it up. "Hayes doesn't care about us finding a neuropathway to God. It's bait. He wants to obliterate them."

"That's a switch," Victor said. "What made you a believer all of a sudden?"

"Nothing's changed. But just because I don't believe in God doesn't mean we can't tap higher powers in our brains. And like you, I believe there's money to be made where there's money to be made."

Victor lowered his azure Rapinto shades, glared at his daughter.

"So what are you selling me?"

"Screw the Defense contract. Okay, keep it. But I know a way we can bring the boys into our hands *alive*. I just need to find the right Foster Jolley."

# 43
## STK

Like most of Minnesota's no-nonsense architecture, the Prairie County Law Enforcement Office was a squat, beige, flat-roofed building. It sat on the corner of Water Tower Road and Highway 12, five miles north of Marigold. The office oversaw the Tonka Township and employed the sheriff, two officers, and two administrators.

Arnie was with Sheriff Buck when the Special Ops Commander stomped in and said, "Good god, how can you people live in this ice box?"

"No place for the lazy man," Buck said.

"You hibernate in a silo all winter? I mean I get the quiet country living bit, but this ..." he pointed outside.

"It's always colder somewhere else," Arnie said.

"Like where, Pluto?"

"I'm Sheriff Thorne. Folks call me Buck. This is Arnie, the mayor of Marigold."

"Interim Mayor," Arnie corrected, and reached out his hand.

"Mantz, *Commander* Mantz, Special Ops." He ignored Arnie attempt at a handshake.

The Commander had a chesty stance that invaded another's space. Buck noticed a slight twitch in the man's left eye as if snapping a wink as he spoke.

Mantz spelled out his orders—sweep the town for the Jolleys and their bomb-making materials.

"Bomb materials." The same baloney Buck heard when ATF agents cordoned off the place. He took it in without dispute.

"Anybody in this cow town harboring the fugitives, or concealing knowledge of their whereabouts, will be arrested," Mantz declared.

"Nobody's hiding those hooligans," Buck said. "If they didn't hate them before, they sure as hell hate 'em now."

"Any resistance, we lock down the town."

"Whoa up there." Buck said. "This isn't some city where you need to impose martial law. Look around. This is farm land with law-abiding folks. There's no late night bar in Marigold 'cept the bowling alley, now closed for renovation. But you already know that 'cause you're bivouacked there. And nobody's out after nine unless it's a dire emergency."

Mantz wasn't listening.

"We'll set up a meeting at your town hall to inform everyone."

"No-no, we'll put the word out. Best they hear it from us." Buck didn't mention the FYI gathering that morning at the café.

"Be sure to tell them it's for their own safety and national security," Mantz said. "We start knocking on doors first thing tomorrow."

"Look," Arnie said. "I can save you a lot of time and effort. I know the boys, and they're not here."

"Where are they?"

"Don't know that, but not here."

"Where do you live?"

Arnie gave his address. Mantz peeled back the cuff of his overcoat, checked the liquid crystal Navmax watch strapped to his wrist.

"Be there in one hour. As for you, Sheriff, leave the special work to the Special Forces. Stand in our way and you yokels will suffer such excruciating pain it'll make Hell feel like a tanning booth. And for God's sake, pin these on your APB dartboard."

Mantz slapped a manila folder on Buck's desk and left.

Buck scratched his head. He had no clout when it came to the military. His job was to handle the day-to-day of the township—pull over drunk drivers, clear roadkill, settle domestic disputes, and chair AA meetings. But his face always reddened when bullied.

"I'm familiar with his kind," he said. "Still, snide remarks and that imperial attitude burn my blood. Makes you wonder how the Marigold folks will feel about storm troopers digging through their brassieres and underwear."

Arnie thought of the twins' lab equipment stowed in his barn and his promise to keep it secret.

"Since they'll be searching my place, I better get a move on," he said.

Buck opened the manila envelope Mantz had dropped on his desk. He laid out three eight-by-tens. Two were high school yearbook photos of Oakley and Chester. The third was a snapshot of Judd Russell in the Jolleys' driveway.

"That's …" Baffled, Arnie picked up the picture. It was taken overhead. Judd was walking from the boys' lab holding something white tucked in his coat.

"IMMINENT THREAT" was typed at the bottom of each photo, followed by a crosshairs symbol and the letters STK.

"What's STK stand for?" he asked Buck.

"Shoot To Kill."

# 44

# Greedy for the Godhead

I'll manage, Judd told himself. People more imbalanced and mentally challenged function in the world every day. There's head injuries, bipolar disorder, and all kinds of psychological impairments. Maybe the antidote is some meds or that feedback machine Marsha spoke about. I can wear a hat or ski cap with a metal band to block the movies. I got solutions here!

It took most of the day and, other than the kitchen, Judd had the Wilder's' house back in order. He apologized to his talent agency for being unreachable, joking that he lost his mind. They said he missed out on a national voice-over.

"Lucky Charms cereal came out with a new marbit."

He looked up the latest theater auditions online. He'd read for any theater at this point, however small. Only not dinner theater or The Time Travel Acting Company where he played the lead in *Lost in Florida*, about Cabeza de Vaca's ill-fated 1527 landing depicted present-day. It bombed opening night. Scorched-earth reviews, except for one he submitted under an assumed name that praised his performance.

As Judd read through the Illusion Theater's list of upcoming plays, an odd mishmash of voices assaulted his mind: *Trust in the Lord with free shipping do you suffer from erectile dysfunction? Look at me when I'm talking to you!*

It's nothing. You're exhausted. Take a nap.

*We have to put her down you think you've got it oh, you think you got it from sea to shining check out the bazooms on America Runs on Dunkin your son was caught shoplifting ...*

A word soup. Like his mind was spinning a radio dial from station to station.

"Stop it!" Judd clapped his ears. What now!? Short-circuiting neurons?

He lay on the sofa and closed his eyes. But a never-ending swarm of voices made napping impossible.

*Side effects include we don't have the money so be good for goodness don't lie to me that's gross when Congress reconvenes what were you thinking?*

All the talk he heard over the years from jingles and sound bites to insults flooded his mind in a chattering froth.

*Where's your homework get cash now and deliver us from evil...*

He covered his ears and shouted, "Shut up!" As if his brain had a mouth.

On his way to the wine cellar, he remembered asking Marsha as they deboarded the plane, "What do you do when you can't trust your own mind?" To which she answered, "A wise professor told me when you find yourself lost in a labyrinth, don't look back for the way you came. Keep moving forward. It may lead through thorns and wastelands, but trying to put your life back is a dead end."

So which way is forward? Enough of this shit! This is freaking insane! Time to ingest some serious drugs!

Judd rushed outside for fresh air and food at the co-op. Nobody around. Sparse cars. He strolled down the middle of snow-banked streets, coatless in ten-degree air, taking tugs from a bottle of Burgundy. He tried humming a tune, but it didn't drown out the torrent of babble in his ears.

Judd ditched the empty bottle behind a tree.

What did Oakley say? "Let it unfold." How do I do that?

Letting go was a muscle Judd had never exercised before. But he figured it was worth a try. So, instead of struggling to shut off the banter, he gave it away.

"Take it," he said out loud. "Take all of it."

The change came instantly. The tornadic whirl of words unspooled. They pattered across his eardrums and dispersed like grains of sand in the wind.

There! I had it all wrong! My head is trying to release everything it ever heard!

Not everything, merely the first wave. But as Judd walked on, the decibel level diminished like an outgoing tide. It reminded him of the scant mutterings of a theater audience as the lights dim.

Wabumba! I don't have to commit myself to a psych ward! I can handle whatever comes. He pumped a fist in the air. Bring it on, brain!

By the time he returned to the house with a bag of groceries, the voices in his head had softened to a distant fizz. Although weary, he felt triumphant once again. The previous night at the airport he took charge of his wild visions. Today he found a way to subdue madness by letting the ear ache of words fly free.

But a block from the house an uneasiness slowed his gait. Entering the back door, he sensed a foreign presence.

Not again.

He was about to make a run for it when he heard—"Door was open."

A figure in a thick overcoat and Cossack hat stood at the kitchen window.

Judd nearly dropped the bag.

"Nice place you have here." Theodore Theroux faced him. Long black beard, pony-tailed hair. Forty maybe, hard to pin.

"Remember me, Sterling?" He removed his hat. "Or is it Judd, Judd Russell?"

"Get outta here." Judd avoided the man's eyes, like shining pools of oil.

"We met in DC," the stranger said.

Right, that Rasputin dude Kira King clung to.

"Look, whatever you're after, I can't help you." Judd set the groceries on the granite island. "I don't know where the Jolleys are. You're wasting your time. So go. Now. Get out!"

Theroux didn't move.

"I knew their dad."

"Yippee, you and half the planet."

"I was there at his peak, at his peak. Like riding the tail of a shooting star."

The man's cadence unnerved Judd. How he repeated words the same way some preachers put their audience in a suggestible trance.

"Now Foster's sons, yes, the sons, have taken on his work. And according to some, to some, the sons of Foster Jolley have superseded his findings. A miraculous achievement from what I gather, and here, *here* of all places, flyover land, the charmless pancake house of America."

"Yeah, well those boys made a mess of me."

"How's that?"

"Never mind."

"Have you any idea who's chasing the Godhead Spot?" Theroux said. "The Department of Defense, to name one. And other obscure factions, no less determined. Have you met Cardinal Barberi, the rogue robe? He was at the exhibition."

Judd flashed on the man who dropped his prayer beads.

"Of all people," Theroux continued. "A man of the cloth who denounces every discovery related to enlightenment. If he found the key to Heaven's door, he'd seize it for himself to spite the Vatican. Funny how people change when they're shown a treasure map. In this case, all greedy for the Godhead."

Judd opened his vision and saw a dart of energy shoot at him from the man's torso. He dodged it with a side-step, matador-style.

"Ask me if I care. No don't, don't waste your breath. Judd walked to the mudroom and opened the back door for the man to leave. "Me, I'm looking to get some ordinary back in my life. You want the Godhead Spot you came to the wrong spot."

"It may not be just one."

*It may not be just one.*

Judd revoiced the man's words as he sat in the café kitchen two hours later, projecting his encounter on the kitchen supply room wall as Marsha and Roslyn looked on.

"Yeah, whatever," I told him. "You found me, you can find them. And he's saying": *I'm not looking for the twins. Too many others sniffing their trail. No, I'm looking for what they found and how they found it.*

"There, see that? He tried to stick a cord to me. Like a tentacle. I shout: 'Outta here, before I call the cops!'"

Roslyn gasped. Marsha told her what Judd played back on their flight home, but seeing the energy cord made her jump.

The dark man put on his Cossack hat.

"He says," *I'll go, but you may see me another time. I have your vibe on speed dial."*

Marsha pulled Judd out of trance. He set his head on the prep table and groaned.

"What a creep!" Roslyn said.

"I met him at the exhibition with that woman, Kira King. She coiled around him like a snake," Judd muttered.

"Who is he?" Roslyn asked.

"His name's Theodore Theroux," Marsha said. "The The for short. A self-proclaimed mystic. Heir to billions. Travels the globe seeking altered states of consciousness. He's dabbled in dark magic, the nether worlds, Mardukanism, you name it."

"Mardukanism?"

"People who claim to have come from Marduk, the planet between Mars and Jupiter that disintegrated and became the asteroid belt. Don't ask me how I know that." Marsha threw up her hands. "Anyway, The The's been on the periphery of neuroscientific developments for years. Visited our place. Wanted to pick Foster's brain, literally. Foster called him 'a suck assassin.'"

"Suck assassin," Roslyn mumbled.

"Months ago he came here to see the boys' work. Ezra warned them not to show him anything."

"What'd he mean about having my vibe on speed dial?" Judd said.

"Some say he can look in on people from long distance."

"Oh great, stalked by a psychic psychopath."

# 45

# The Crown

The hypnotic trance left Judd nauseous. He staggered off to the restroom. Flannery sat in a booth, bobbing to a musical on her headphones, while Marsha and Roslyn moved about the café kitchen making grilled cheese sandwiches.

"So all these people are after some link to God in Judd's brain?" Roslyn asked.

"In all our brains." Marsha sliced a brick of cheddar into thin strips.

"After seeing what comes out of his head, I don't want it," Roslyn said as she spread butter on bread. "Hope you don't mind me asking, but do you believe in God?"

"I've never been religious," Marsha said. "As for the existence of a supreme being, I'll say this: nothing comes from nothing. Consciousness is not born from unconsciousness. Red onion?"

"Oh yeah." Roslyn went to the stove top, flicked two fingertips of water on the flat-top griddle. It spat back.

"And you?" Marsha asked. "Do you believe there's a Great Spirit?"

Roslyn paused, then said, "I believe in kindness."

"Hmm. And that speaks to *your* great spirit."

"Thanks, but I don't always act on it." Roslyn placed the sandwiches on the griddle. "The creepy guy, 'The The,' he told Judd it may be more than one spot?"

"That was Ezra's theory—not a single node but a whole corona of them, like a crown of jewels. Each with a transcendent function."

"A crown, you mean like royalty?"

"Makes you wonder if the ones placed on the heads of kings and queens, inlaid with diamonds, rubies, and emeralds, are a symbolic reflection of actual gems inside our heads."

Roslyn imagined such a crown radiating a spectrum of colors. "Ah-lama," she uttered. "How glorious."

"Truly, if true. Imagine what that would flower in us," Marsha said.

Melted cheese oozed out the sides of the grilling bread.

"So what happened?" Roslyn flipped over the sandwiches with a spatula. "Why can't we …?"

"Who knows. Maybe we misused it and they all closed up. Or we aren't evolved enough."

"And we're ready for our crowns to open now?"

"What do you think?" Marsha said.

"Not even close."

They heard the back door shut.

"Somethin' smells tasty." Arnie clapped snow off his gloved hands and came into the kitchen. "Hey-hey, got some news."

"You missed Judd's horror movie," Roslyn said.

"He's here?" Arnie glanced around the café. "Where?"

"The restroom, last I saw."

"Did you tell him about the soldiers?"

There was a rap on the front window.

Arne bent over to look out the pass-through. He saw Commander Mantz standing outside, a grimace on his face.

"Oh, here we go. Speak of the . . ."

Mantz banged on the window again. His lecture on homegrown terrorism at the high school didn't raise a ripple. All he heard back were some seniors spouting hate-laced remarks about the twins. Before leaving, the school principal told him where to find the boys' mother.

Mantz's breath fogged the window. He pointed toward the door.

"Great, another kind of grilling," Marsha said. "You'll excuse me. I'm taking my lunch upstairs."

Arnie stopped her.

"The soldiers can't see Judd."

"Why not?" Roslyn said.

"I'll explain later. Delay them while I get him out of the head."

"Hey Flan, we need you," Roslyn said.

Flannery popped her earbuds.

"Yeah, what?"

Arnie stood outside the restroom calling Judd's name as Roslyn cracked open the front door.

"We're closed."

"Not to us." Mantz shoved his way in, followed by a soldier. "I'm looking for Marsha Jolley. Heard she's staying here."

"Wait up. I'll get her," Roslyn said. Passing Flannery on her way upstairs, she half-whispered, "You're on, kid."

The girl sprung from the booth and blocked the men's advance, singing: "Everybody loves a winner, so nobody loved me. Lady Peaceful. Lady Happy. That's what I long to be ..."

Mantz and the soldier gave side-long glances as Flannery climbed onto the counter. She strutted and high-kicked her legs as she finished the verse of "Maybe This Time," from *Cabaret.*

"Well, all the odds are in my favor ... something's bound to begin. It's gotta happen ... happen sometime ... maybe this time I'll win."

"Can I help you?" Marsha strode in from the back as Flannery curtsied a deep bow.

"I'm Commander Mantz, Homeland Security. You the fugitive boys' mother?"

"I am, and you're wasting your time."

Mantz ordered the soldier to check out the apartments upstairs and the back rooms.

"Your sons are ..."

"My sons are the victims of a government plot to frame them as white supremacist bombers."

"Where are they?"

Marsha smiled to Flannery as Roslyn helped the girl off the counter.

"Talk woman!"

"Okay, and I'll speak your lingo. Your intel is bogus. It's fubar. Have you told your unit they're on a fool's errand? No? In that case I'll tell them. I'll have everyone in Marigold tell them, I'll go on CNN."

Mantz thrust a finger at Marsha's face.

"Let me make this cold and crystal clear. You oppose our operation, we burn your eye blink of a village to ash."

Marsha didn't flinch. "Tell me, Commander, are you seeing anyone about your pain?"

Mantz's eyes flared, a growl rattled in his throat.

The soldier clomped down the stairs. He eyeballed Roslyn in the kitchen.

"Hey there." He sniffed the grilled cheese. "Mmm."

"Anything?" Mantz said.

The soldier shook his head. "Negativo."

Arnie stomped in from the back. "Look who's here. Hey, Commander. I waited for you to come search my property."

Mantz ignored Arnie. He glanced at the bulletin board: cords of wood for sale, a lost cat named Mouser, a good-as-new baby crib. Then he and the soldier went out the front door. Arnie followed them into billowing snow.

"Well, I wouldn't go to my place now. In fact, if I were you, I'd prepare your troops. You feel that whip in the wind?" Arnie nodded to the northwest. "That there's an Alberta Clipper packing a motherlode."

Fetch the dog strolled up, sniffing pantlegs.

"Get away from me, mutt!" Mantz gave the dog a swift kick on the backside.

Roslyn watched from the window. "Maybe it's me but I doubt there's a single gemstone in that man's crown."

Arnie carried Fetch into the café where dogs aren't allowed.

"I'm taking him out back to my truck."

Arnie returned followed by Judd, who teetered on rubber legs like a drunken Gumby.

"Why did you have to hide me?" Judd said.

"Hang on." Arnie poured himself a cup of coffee. He waited for Flannery to take her sandwich to a booth and plug music in her ears. Then he and the others sat at the prep table where he spread out three photos.

"That Commander slapped these on Buck's desk."

One was a snapshot of Judd walking to his car from the Jolleys' lab.

"Me? How'd they get that?" Judd asked.

"Drone. Spies. Doesn't matter. Buck said you're a person of interest. But it's more than that. Look here." Arnie pointed to the letters at the bottom of each picture: STK. Stands for Shoot To Kill."

"I'm out of here." Judd stumbled, knee-knocked over a stool.

"Have you looked outside? It's brewing up a blizzard."

"Besides, you don't look good at all," Marsha said.

Roslyn turned to Marsha.

"It's okay if he takes my couch."

# 46

## Chester

After breakfast at the Grand Canyon dining hall, Chester would go to the main lodge's computer and search for sightings of his father. He'd check in with the ranger, then hike trails the rest of the day. He wasn't worried about showing his face. Most visitors were too busy popping pictures of the scenery with their smartphones and long lens cameras.

On his fifth day he found a cave off a trail. It was only ten feet deep but it gave him a place to sleep under the silent starlight with no one looking on.

That evening, while watching a orangey-gold spoked sunset, he wondered what would happen when he found his father.

Will he recognize me? It's been four years. Who knows what he's been through? He may not remember anything. That's okay. I'll tell him about our brain work. I'll read the paper we wrote with Ezra and show him our brain maps. He'll be blown away.

Chester pulled an unlabeled folder out of his backpack. Inside were diagrams of the five nodes he and Oakley discovered.

Each a colored disk, pictured from different angles with millimeter measurements in brackets.

As he leafed through the folder, he heard Ezra commanding him, "Never let those maps out of your sight!"

"Not gonna happen," he answered back.

Other pages documented their trial-and-error journey—the dates they discovered the nodes; the long hours trying various means to open them; the gems and tones that failed; the ones that succeeded. There was the "Thermostat node" that governs the temperature of the body, and the "Antennae node" that senses a threat in advance. A third node, opened in Oakley's brain, they tentatively called, "The Puzzler," because nothing came of it. Oakley thought it was a false door. Chester believed it would reveal its true nature when the time was right. Along with the two newly found nodes were the seven others that sprung open in Judd Russell's brain.

No idea what they do.

"Ha!" Chester laughed out loud. Like to see what's happening to that actor now.

# 47

# Dark Night in a Whiteout

Snow strafed the apartment window, jarring the sash. The bones of the building creaked and groaned. Judd tossed on Roslyn's couch unable to find his way into sleep. He picked up *The Isness* paperback Marsha left and read the introduction:

*I am a neuro-archeologist. I invented a spectral lens that reveals unseen aspects of the human brain. One day I scanned mine. I was not hunting for anything in particular, merely wandering over furrows of my cerebrum, when a wave of exultant energy rippled my body. I didn't tap or stimulate a lobe. The feeling came by mere attention. The next day I sought that sensation again. It eluded me for several days. Frustrated, I stopped the search. That night I woke from deep sleep cast in a prism of lights. I was frightened. What have I stirred up?*

*The answer: The Isness. A vast, ineffable dimension of subatomic mist.*

*Up to then I'd been living a spiritually dehydrated life. Like a bubbling spring the Isness quenched my arid soul.*

*Come and let the Isness quench yours as well.*

Foster Jolley

Judd leafed through the pages, reading excerpts at random.

*Within the Isness, the meaning of life is ever-changing. This may vex people. I suspect it is the reason the Isness has been avoided. It is too formless a state of being.*

Soon the words swirled into a tightening knot. The walls of Roslyn's apartment tilted in the stuffy air. Judd's brain felt hot and raw, as if sunburned.

*Could be I'm coming down with the flu or food poisoning.*

A gust of wind hammered the exterior wall as if pleading to come inside and get out of itself. Judd set the book aside and lay back on the couch. He could hear Roslyn in her bedroom tap-tap typing on her laptop. He felt about to retch when out of nowhere, a dark, roiling mass slid across the ceiling. He watched it morph into a green-eyed snake with frothy fangs, a darting tongue. Its expanding jaws filled the space.

Then it lunged.

Judd shot off the couch. He rushed to the bathroom to splash cold water on his face. The water was wax. The mirror turned black. Then the room.

*What the hell? Am I inside it? Inside THE SNAKE!*

Everything began to sway. As he reached out his hands to steady himself, he recalled Marsha say, "Don't look back for the way you came. Look for a way forward."

But Judd's legs were glued to each other. Standing in a slurry of slime, all he could do was hop, slip, and drop. The snake's dizzying, side-winding tunnel nauseated him. The sticky glue secreted from its inner walls smelled like tar. In the distance a rattle sounded like a ticking bomb. He yelled for help but no sound left his mouth.

Judd thought he knew despair. Bleak days working for his father. The times of defeat and depression after he set out on his own. But swallowed by this giant reptile drained him of all hope.

As the snake slithered, the darkness thinned. Something appeared before him. Columns, he first thought, until one bumped him and swung like a pendulum. Effigies, in human shape. And so many, from child to adult. Faceless, they hung like carcasses in a slaughterhouse.

Judd didn't need to ask. Suspended before him were the times he stopped his truth, stuffed his feelings, or turned coldly away. All the instances he judged another or hardened a lie, hid a weakness, or shut off the world. Here they hung, tethered in limbo, locked out of the life-flow like stagnant pools detached from the current of a river.

Touching the mummies discharged crackling wires of static electricity. They shook and broke apart in bursts of brittle dust. With each burst, Judd heaved a loaded sigh. And with each sigh, his legs flexed. He could walk, stiff, with rusted joints. The smell of urine spiked the air as he set off toward the rattle's incessant clacking.

A thin veil of hot water whisked through him like the jetting spray of a car wash. Instead of a cleansing shower, it burned like acid and peeled off his face. Only, it wasn't his real face. It was a mask.

Walls of water swept through him. They melted mask after mask—one he wore to fit in, one to look superior, another to conceal inner flaws. The last wave was a mere mist. It revealed a face contorted with sorrow.

Judd bowled over and wept.

The tunnel swayed. He forced himself to continue on. Soon he came to a charred landscape under a shiny steel sky. Dove feathers littered the ground. The rattle was so near now, it shook his limbs. And with it another sound, a choomp … choomp.

A man stooped before him in a slick, gray poncho, digging with a stubby shovel. "Useless life!" he shouted, his feet in tin buckets. He jabbed the blade in the earth and flung clods of dirt and chips of white bones in the air. They rained down his backside and slid between his feet, where he scooped them up again. "All of it! All of it!" The old man had Judd's eyes. He shook the shovelhead at the sky and raved, "All is vanity!"

Roslyn heard someone rail, "All is vanity! What does man gain by all the toil at which he toils under the sun?"

She sat up.

It's Judd. He sounds deranged. What was I thinking? That does it! He'll never sleep here again!

She didn't know he was quoting Ecclesiastes.

"… in much wisdom is much vexation, and he who increases knowledge increases sorrow!"

Hesitant, she cracked the bedroom door. Judd lay sprawled on the round throw rug, his eyelids pinched, his face smeared with tears and sweat.

"Judd?" She nudged his shoulder with her bare toes.

His glassy eyes didn't recognize her.

Roslyn knelt. She felt his forehead. "You're on fire." His whole body shuddered as if driven over a cattle grate.

"Let me go! I got to get to the last rattle!"

He made no sense. Roslyn rushed across the hall and woke Marsha.

"It's Judd."

"He's delirious," Marsha said upon entering.

Roslyn soaked a washcloth in cold water and spread it across Judd's forehead. "Smell that?" she said. "He peed himself."

"Oh, Jeez …"

"We should get him to a clinic," Roslyn said.

"Can't. It's a whiteout. We're snowed in."

They agreed to leave him on the rug and take turns looking in during the night.

Judd's sleep was fitful. He babbled out loud. At one point in the early hours, Roslyn heard him let out a long, agonized wail.

"It's me, Roslyn," she said. "You okay?"

He whispered something.

"What'd you say?" She bent closer.

"There's nothing left but isn't."

# 48

# The Last Ice Fishing Shack

The task force got a late start due to the heavy snowfall. It took hours for county plows to clear the streets. Some drifts high as windowsills. The soldiers searched Marigold in pairs among a chorus of snowblowers freeing up driveways and residents shoveling their walks.

"Sorry for the inconvenience," the soldiers repeated as they trudged from door to door. "We need to ask a few questions while we search your home."

"You won't find what you're looking for here," came the common response.

"When was the last time you saw the Jolley brothers? What do you know about them? Did they hide anything on the premises?"

The unanimous "no" responses did not deter them from rummaging through every drawer and closet. Although prepared for a disruption, the soldiers' hard-nosed attitude made folks feel violated. For some, it stirred up more animosity for the twins. "Those fiendish punks!"

They heard Arnie and Marsha's version. But stories become exaggerated when passed from one person to another and the perception of a place becomes forever stained by events untrue.

Gladys, a zippy hummingbird, made use of the house call. Walking the soldiers to the door she insisted, "Before you go, you nice lads will kindly help me dismantle the nativity scene in the front yard. I need it boxed and stored in the garage. Much appreciated. Oh, be sure to wrap the manger in its canvas shawl. It goes on the top shelf above the pitchfork."

After a tip from Lars Lundeen, owner of Farm and Feed Gas Mart, Commander Mantz sent one of his men to check the ice fishing shacks on Loon Lake. The soldier snowshoed out on the mile-long body of water left by a retreating glacier ages ago. Although the ice was thick and safe to walk on, the dump of snow made it an iron man endurance test.

More than a dozen fishing shanties of various sizes and materials dotted the frozen surface.

"Hello?" The soldier knocked on the plywood building, painted rust red with a chipper, canary-yellow door.

"Who's there?" a gravelly voice shouted back.

"Corporal Webster."

"Not buying."

"Department of Homeland Security."

"Ha! In that case, welcome to the Office of Counterintelligence."

The door cracked and a grizzled face peered out with startled eyes at the sight of the helmeted Black soldier outfitted in a hooded, snow-white camouflage uniform.

"I have permission to search the interior of your ..."

The man shrugged, "My fish house?"

"Affirmative."

The fisherman opened the door wide. He had sagging jowls, bushy gray eyebrows, and tufts of hair coming out his ears long enough to comb.

The soldier took one step inside and met a fart cloud that made him gasp.

"Search all you want. But you can't make me budge my hole one inch."

Raised in Louisiana, Corporal Webster knew nothing about ice fishing, but figured it was territorial, and this a prime spot. He unhitched his snowshoes, waved the door back and forth to fan the stench and stepped inside.

The shack was the size of a walk-in closet, surprisingly well-appointed, with knotty pine walls. Obviously, Oakley and Chester weren't there. Webster scanned the space anyway, noting a power auger propped in a corner, a tackle box full of shiny lures, some green, some glittery gold. Next to the man's stool was a Styrofoam cup roiling with maggots.

"We're looking for two young men."

Seeing the soldier's eyes drift to the cooler, the man lifted the lid. Inside lay two fish.

"No young men in there unless you mean the Walleye brothers."

Webster held up two photos.

"Names Oakley and Chester Jolley."

"Those rascals. There a reward of some kind?"

"Your personal safety, sir. Reward enough?"

The fisherman thought it over before saying, "You might try Goose."

"Goose?"

"Da' lake north a'here."

"Thanks."

"You betcha."

While searching the Moore farmhouse, one of the soldiers found himself cornered in the dining room with Lester.

"Ah, behold the rocket's red glare militia clad in duty-calls Kevlar vest and rigorously lashed Charlie company combat boots complete with caissons go rolling tactical gear strapped to Chicago shoulders and armed semper vigilans with the latest fast action fog of war ballistic blaster of ill omen and forever the fight 'neath the flap of tattered battle flags to conquer we must when our cause is just and gee willikers how weaponry has tipped the battlefield since the Second Amendment became the law of the land."

"The right to bear arms," the solider cut in.

"Precisely, young man, and the arms they bore consisted of muzzle-loaded muskets and flintlock pistols coveted by settlers hatcheting out frontier homesteads amidst painted tribes and feisty bears while the civil guard mustered miles out of hasty reach as well as proper pull chain ball cock plumbing for that matter and stand at attention all humankind and with bugle blare salute those dauntless lavatorial innovators as well as the hygienic fashioning of thin rolls of ready-to-use tissue to tidy up our hindmost fenestrated areas."

"Done here," came the call of another soldier, entering the dining room from the hall. "All clear."

Seeing them to the door, Lester gave one of his homemade farewells, "Nice guys finish what you wish for."

With the task force scouring the town, Marsha and Roslyn fretted about Judd. What if they find him?

Still delirious, he was in no condition to go anywhere. So they kept him on the rug and tugged it under Roslyn's bed. Every half hour they'd check on him, jostle the rug part way out to ladle broth in his mouth and wipe tears and sweat from his face. He'd stammer indecipherables and doze off.

The last ice fishing shack on Goose Lake was a peeling, chipboard box with attached trailer tires. So far, slogging across two lakes in deep snow produced nothing but painful leg cramps for the lone, exhausted Corporal Webster. As he trundled toward the hut, he heard orchestral music emanate from within.

He pounded on the wall.

"Corporal Webster, Homeland Security! Open up!"

The door creaked on its hinges. A rotund fisherman in muck boots peered out, lifted a finger to his lips, "Shhh," and opened the door without asking the soldier's intentions.

The first thing Webster saw was the glint of monofilament line angling through a blue hole in the ice. As in other fishing huts, the line was attached to a short, graphite fishing rod secured to a small, self-standing apparatus with a flag on the end. What was different were two audio speakers next to the hole playing music from a battery-powered CD player.

Webster looked at the speakers, then back at the man.

"An experiment in sonics." The fisherman cupped his hand toward the soldier's ear. "Seein' if it woos 'em."

Webster's sore legs gyrated.

"You look about to keel over. Here." The man slid an upside-down five-gallon bucket across the ice. "Kick off those snowshoes. Give those dogs a respite."

Webster sat and rubbed his calves. The music helped him settle.

"Name's McCollough, folks call me Mack."

Webster nodded and glanced down at the motionless line in the hole.

"It's a discovery process," Mack explained. "Tried some Rachmaninoff and a Vivaldi concerto. This particular score is from a movie called *Mission*, conducted by the Italian composer, Morricone."

Committed to his errand, Webster unfolded photos of Oakley and Chester.

"Seen these two recently?"

Mack squinted at the faces. He patted his quilted vest, found his readers in a pocket. Before he could mount them to his ears the flag on the rod holder wagged. The line hummed. He dropped the eyeglasses, reached around the soldier and snatched the rod. It juddered in his bare hands.

"Oh, boy, hooked an Olympian." Mack let the line out a bit before giving it a jerk. "We got us a Northern running on my spoon. Here, give it a go." He gestured for the soldier to take his place.

"Me?" Webster stuffed the photos in his pocket and took the rod in his hands. He looked at Mack, then at the bend in the rod.

"That's it," Mack said.

It felt like a live wire. "Good God ..." Webster's eyes swelled.

"Oh yeah, you got the lightning in ya now."

Webster held on tight. A sunbright smile lit up his face.

# 49
# Aren't You Cold?

With most of his money in a gym bag at Yolanda's apartment, and the rest spent on food, Oakley was near broke. It was a week since he and Chester fled Marigold. He was tired of running, but not tired enough to turn himself in.

With law enforcement hunting him down, he slept by day, rotating between benches in the Sculpture Garden and Loring Park. When he found a secluded bench behind what he thought was the State Capitol Building, he made it home base. No passers-by, the only sound a steady shursh of traffic on the nearby highway.

At night Oakley walked to the main library thirty minutes before closing. He checked to see if Chester had left a message or if he'd been caught. Since they didn't trust phones, they decided to communicate by leaving a one-star review of their father's *The Isness* book on the Numinous Bookstore website.

He scrolled down the page and found the review he had posted earlier:

```
Heef! The book's a snore. Author deserted
family. Sons framed. Mother canned. Home-
town turned upside down.
```

Nothing from Chester.

On his way back to his home base, a young man and woman approached him. They introduced themselves as outreach workers.

"Aren't you cold?" the woman asked.

They carried green shoulder bags stuffed with handouts—toothbrushes, toothpaste, socks, shampoo, condoms.

"I'm fine." Oakley took a toothbrush without raising his eyes for fear he'd be recognized.

They glanced at each other.

"You sure? It's nine degrees. Aren't your hands freezing?"

Oakley realized that not being wrapped in a thick winter coat made him stand out.

"You must be hot-blooded," the man said.

"Yeah, hot-blooded," Oakley said.

The woman reached into her pocket. "Sorry, no beds available, but here's some tokens for the bus. The drivers are cool. Let them know you're riding all night."

The man handed him a card. "If you need some coin, you can give blood at the Plasma Center."

Up until then, Oakley never thought about the homeless. Out of sight, out of mind. But now, being on the street, he noticed them everywhere. Cast-offs at the transit station, huddled in skyways, drifting between shadows. Young people like him wandering around with shifty, peripheral eyes. He didn't want to know what they must do for food and warmth.

At least I have an internal heater.

Still, Oakley had to accept that his world had shrunk. Catching his stubble-bearded reflection in a store window, his head hooded in a Goodwill sweatshirt, he wondered which bus would take him to the Plasma Center.

# 50
# You Soat!

Chester lost track of days. Had it been a week? He wasn't sure, but he needed to contact his brother. After his midmorning blueberry waffles swimming in maple syrup, he walked to the Grand Canyon Lodge and sat in the lobby until the computer was free. When he saw the one-star review of his father's book that began with Oakley's "Heef!" he grinned. But his delight soured when he read that the university fired his mother.

No way! Students loved her! She was a fixture there! He pounded the keyboard. A line of gibberish skittered across the book review box on the website.

"How long you gonna be?" A tourist hovered over his shoulder.

Chester didn't look at the man's face, but felt his spare tire gut rub the back of the chair. It reminded him of those snakes that unhinge their jaws to swallow large mammals whole.

Dude musta ate a hog.

"Gimme a minute." Chester raised a finger and started to retype a one-star reply to Oakley but stopped midway. The tourist hadn't moved.

Chester looked up at the middle-aged man's eyes, shaded by a caramel fedora. He wore an unzipped jacket with a big red W emblem stitched to it. A Nikon camera dangled from a strap around his neck.

"Can I get some privacy here?"

The man shuffled his feet but didn't budge.

Chester wanted to turtle his head into his chest. Instead, he shut down the web site, pushed the chair back against the man, got up and stood nearby.

As the tourist took the chair and began typing on the keyboard, Chester breathed down his neck.

"Hey, back off young man," the tourist said.

"Now you know how it feels."

The tourist lifted a fist. "Wanna to see how *this* feels?"

A sudden fury fired Chester's blood. He grabbed the man's camera strap from behind his neck and gave it a swift yank. The camera flipped. Its long lens jammed against the tourist's Adam's apple.

"How's that feel, you lard ass bastard?"

Sputtering profanities, the tourist fought to loosen the strap. Chester held firm. The man flailed his arms and yelped for breath.

"What are you doing?!" A woman shouted and began taking photos of them with her phone.

"Just playing around." Chester let go the strap, strutted out the doors of the lodge and ran flat out.

Doopid! He berated himself. She got a picture of you!

Back at the cave he decided to lay low for the day.

What the hell got into you? That lard ass that's what.

Chester's pent-up anger had turned the tourist into the faceless monsters who obliterated his home and lab, and canned his mom.

"Fuckin' oinkers." Chester fumed. "You think you can stop me?" He tore open a bag of corn chips. "I'm going to track you down and break your brains! No, I'm going to strangle you with your bloated intestines!"

Around twilight he felt a presence at the mouth of the cave. It appeared like a smear in the air before extruding into form.

What the …? Chester cringed. It took a moment to place the face, the beard, the shiny, black marble eyes.

It's that ghoulish dude, all touchy with his hands and demanding to see our lab work.

Chester picked up a rock and hurled it at the specter.

The The dodged it.

He pitched another rock, hollering, "Get outta here you soat!"

Theroux disappeared.

"… soat! … soat! …" echoed off the canyon walls.

Chester clamped his hand to his mouth.

# 51
# Combat Ready

It didn't take long for fighting to break out the next morning at Arnie's self-storage facility. He alerted the renters that Commander Mantz's men would search every unit. Although Mantz promised that his team would be respectful, Arnie encouraged the renters to be there. Many showed up, tense and wary, as the doors lifted.

Respectful it wasn't. The soldiers ripped open boxes, spilled contents on the floors—photo albums, archaic farm tools, a stuffed broad-winged hawk mounted to look in-flight—and hurled them outside for a better look. Junk to some, invaluable keepsakes to others, scattered haphazardly in the snow.

Yelling and shoving began when a soldier dumped a carton of old vinyl records on the floor of unit number 3. After another soldier cracked a stack of flow blue china outside number 5, Lars Lundeen punched him in the mouth. The skirmish snowballed into Harvey Clyster's unit. He lugged a soldier out clamped in a head-lock. More fists flew, jackets ripped, noses cracked. Tufts of goose down feathers floated in the still air. Those trying to break it up were cold-cocked or thrown to the hard ground. Joy Moore charged out of unit number 10 swinging a rusty scythe and shouting, "Just you try to touch my stuff you shitheads!" Shots rocked the air. Unhinged, Arnie roared at Mantz, "Control your men!" By the time Sheriff Buck arrived the soldiers had gone, leaving people bruised and bloodied. Having to put things back was the final abuse.

Around noon Arnie looked in on Judd who lay slumped on the couch with half-lidded eyes.

"Looks like you still got a pulse," Arnie said, a red tissue sticking out one nostril.

"What happened to you?"

"Soldiers rifled through every unit at my facility. Fights broke out. Anyway, here." Arnie handed Judd a saucer-size blueberry muffin in a cloth napkin.

"Thanks," Judd muttered. "I'm still pretty weak. Don't know how much help I can be with the remodel today."

"It's tomorrow, Judd. You lost a day and a half."

"You're joking."

"You rest." Arnie left.

Judd nibbled the muffin. Although depleted, he felt a fragile joy; the relief of surviving a frightful night. He reflected on his wretched trek to the end of the snake. How he had to shed his past, the heartless silences, the masks he wore, the futile grudges. There was little left of the old Judd Russell except the beating of his heart. He was the air he was breathing. He was the muffin he was eating.

Regarding Arnie, Marsha, and Roslyn, he realized that being safe is not about protection. In fact, protection is an illusion. Acceptance from those who understand what you're going through, that's the real refuge.

Now Judd wanted to do something for them.

Later that afternoon, a soldier knocked on the café window. He'd been drinking, which was obvious to Tomás, who told him the café was closed. The soldier said he needed to use the restroom. Roslyn was stocking shelves when the man strutted past.

"Hey there sweetcakes, 'member me?"

"What are you doing here?" Roslyn said.

He stuck an arm against a shelf, fencing her in.

"Let me give you a hand with that."

"No-no, don't need help, please, go."

"What's the hurry?" He pressed in closer, the taint of tobacco and alcohol on his breath. "Hey, we're here to help."

"You're drunk." She drew back out of his reach.

"No, I'm Randy. Must get pretty lonely out here in Siberi-oh. But I can warm you up." He stroked her shoulder.

Roslyn shoved him away with a bag of corn flour. "You do *not* want to mess with me." She slipped past him into the kitchen.

"Oh, I won't mess. I'll be clean. Even tidy up," he snickered and shuffled toward her. Tomás intervened.

"You're in my way, little man," Randy said.

"We want no trouble," Tomás said.

"Nooo trouble." In a flash, the soldier thrust the heel of his hand into Tomás's chin, hurtling him to the floor. "No trouble at all."

"Tomás!" Roslyn crouched over him only to be jerked up by her wrist.

"Nobody gets in my way. Wow, you got some eyes." Randy pulled her to him. "Now, where were we?"

She wrestled to break free. But he held on. She snatched a mustard squeeze bottle off the counter and squirted it in his face.

"Jeezus!" He let her go to wipe his eyes. "Now you lick it off!"

Judd heard a shout as he plodded down the stairs. The first thing he saw was Tomás moaning on the floor, gripping his jaw. In the dining room a soldier had Roslyn pinned against the counter and was hiking up her skirt.

"Hey!" Judd shouted.

The soldier spun on his heels toward the voice, his face drooling a yellow paste. "Who the hell …?"

Roslyn squirmed out of the man's grip. "Judd, get out of here!" She squirted another jet of mustard at the man.

The soldier batted it away. "Judd, huh?" He rubbed his eyes. "Hey, you're that dude!" He spread his feet, combat ready, and unsnapped a sidearm from his belt. "Well I'll be. Must be my good luck day and your bad luck day."

Seeing the gun, Judd lifted a table by its legs as a shield. A condiment caddy slid off and spilled on the floor.

The soldier leveled the weapon at Judd's head. His left eye blinked a dollop of mustard.

"Nooo!" Roslyn screamed.

Impelled by a primal force he never felt before, Judd charged. Roslyn lifted a napkin dispenser and hurled it at the soldier. He ducked and fired blindly. A bullet whizzed past Judd's head. He kept charging, knocking over chairs, legs pounding. He slammed the table into the soldier and drove him back until he crashed through the front window. Hitting the sidewalk, the man jerked in wild spasms, shooting rounds into blue sky. Blood leaked into the snow around his head where shards of glass had sliced his scalp.

Judd crumpled to his knees, spent.

Roslyn vaulted over the windowsill. "He's having a seizure!" Kneeling, she disarmed the soldier, then cupped her hand under his head. The blood and mustard congealed into a sticky orange goo on her fingers. After his contortions eased, she wiped her fingers on her apron, and went inside.

"Get up!" she yelled at Judd. "They'll be after you!" She retrieved her coat. "Put this on and go to the river park. I'll come when it's safe."

Calls went out.

Police and volunteer firemen carried the semiconscious soldier off in a stretcher. Roslyn and Tomás swept up the glass.

Hearing Tomás mutter something, Roslyn asked, "Are you okay?"

"No, but I'm reminded of a quote: "*En este mundo traidor, nada es verdad ni mentira; todo as según el color del cristal con que se mira.*"

"What's it mean?" Roslyn said.

"From a Spanish poet, de Campoamor. It means, in this traitorous world nothing is true or false. Everything is colored by the prism you look through. In other words, where the soldier sees a battlefield, me, I see a cornfield. My son, a soccer field."

# 52
# Roslyn and Judd

Judd lay on a bench by the river as twilight surrendered to night. The temperature was falling fast. But instead of cold, he felt a mix of revulsion at the soldier's attack and surprise at his daring reaction.

A scuff of boots broke the silence. Someone called his name.

"Hey. It's me." Roslyn stood over him.

"You okay?" he asked.

"Pretty shaken up."

"Want to talk about it?"

"Rather not. You?"

"Same." Judd sat up. "There's a lot less light pollution than in the city. More starry out here."

Roslyn glanced at the sky. "You were really sick," she said.

"I was." Judd slid over and tapped the bench.

Roslyn sat beside him. "And your brain? You're not going to beam pictures out your head on me are you?"

"I'll warn you first," he grinned.

"You know that joke, I forget the comic's name, how he used to think the brain was the most important organ of the body until he realized where that thought came from."

Judd chuckled.

Roslyn pointed to the sky. "There's Orion."

"The hunter."

"Do you know how to find his dog? You follow the line of his belt over to the left and there's Sirius, the dog and brightest star."

"Oh yeah, I see it," Judd said.

They looked on silently until Roslyn chimed in. "I've been meaning to apologize for being so ... so repelled by you."

"Hey, no need, I get it. I'm a freak show. If anybody should apologize it's me. You been nothing but helpful. You let me sleep on your couch, nursed me through the snake pit of hell." He turned to her. "How can I make it up to *you*?"

"Serious?"

"Sirius," he pointed at the star. "No, really."

Roslyn thought about it.

"We can always use help in the café washing dishes. But you can't be anywhere near here. They're probably hunting for you as we speak."

"I was planning to clean up some things in North Dakota. Guess now's as good a time to go as ever."

Judd wanted to see his mother. He also needed to pay back all the twenty dollar bills he'd pocketed from the church's collection plate. At least $1,000, by his count. Rather than send it, he could hand it over in person.

He stood stiffly. "Tell you what. When it's safe to come back, I'll help you out at the cafe."

"Are you okay driving there?"

"I think so. Just need to get my stuff."

"I better go first. Make sure the coast is clear of soldiers." Roslyn pressed her finger to her lips. "Shh."

While cautiously crossing Main Street, they heard pounding. Arnie and Tomás were nailing sheets of plywood over the hole of what was the café's front window. No one else out. Roslyn and Judd took the alley to the back door. Neither noticed the dark cargo van.

"Say, I saw skis in your apartment. Do you cross-country?" Judd asked.

"When I have time. Pretty much never," Roslyn said.

"Maybe when this is all over?"

"I'd like that. And thanks for ... you know." Roslyn gave Judd a hug.

"Wabumba. That was sweet."

"Your wow shout?"

"Uh-huh. You got one?"

"Yes, but I need a reason."

Judd leaned down and pressed a soft kiss on Roslyn's cheek.

"Ah-lama," she said.

He smiled.

"You should take some food along for the—"

She didn't get all of it out. Three shapes rushed them. They knocked Roslyn to the ground, grabbed Judd's arms, and slipped a ski mask over his head backward. It was sticky and saturated with chemical. He struggled to pull it off but grew faint within seconds.

Struggling to her feet, Roslyn ran after the men as they hustled Judd away. She hollered for help. The van kicked up chunks of frozen snow, swerved out of the alley, and was gone.

"No!" she howled.

Groaning, Judd rose from brain fog into blind darkness. He spat threads from the ski mask duct-taped to his face. He couldn't see or move. His wrists and ankles were zip-tied to what felt like a plastic patio chair. He could tell he was naked when somebody shuffling past buffeted the hair on his legs. His mouth was dry. His tongue felt like he'd been licking stucco.

"Morning," a man with a thick throat said. "Time to wake up and smell mortal fear. You may have eluded us once, but there are no icy roads here."

Three of them, Judd figured, by the sound of their footsteps.

"We'll keep this simple." A woman's voice, caustic, younger than the thick throat. "Simple, simple. You tell us where the boys are, we let you go, or ..."

"I can't help you. I don't know where ..."

"*Orrr* ... we give you a radical manicure ..."

Judd felt the weight of a fist on his right hand and something hard clamp onto his index fingernail.

"What are you doing?" he said. But he knew.

The wrench bit down, jerked back and forth for purchase, then yanked.

"GAHHH!" he wailed, every nerve ending white-hot fire.

"... and force it out of you."

The shock took Judd's breath away. His exposed fingertip throbbed with rage where the nail was gone.

"H-hey!" he panted. "I don't have a clue! They screwed me over! I want to find them too!"

The channel lock pliers clasped onto his thumb nail.

"Honest, I'm telling you all I know!" Judd sought a haven where he wouldn't feel the pain to come.

He didn't find one. He reeled and blacked out.

When he came to, the acoustics had changed. He heard the woman talking, presumably on a phone. She sounded pissed, demanding payment.

"What's it gonna be, beanstalk?" Thick Throat talking again, like he had an oyster of phlegm lodged in his larnyx. "You seein' the light now?"

"You can wedge toothpicks in my eyelids and make me watch reruns of *The Bachelor,* it won't change nothing 'cause I got nothing, I know nothing, swear to God!"

"Swear all you want, and tell us where to find those assholes and we'll let you go."

"What is it about 'I know nothing' you can't understand?"

The space quieted. But Judd could hear the woman and Thick Throat arguing in clipped whispers about what to do with him. Given the pain he endured, she figured he was telling the truth. So they needed to work out where to dispose of his body.

"Listen!" Judd howled. "I can't see you. I don't know your names. You can walk away and no one's the wiser."

"I got an idea," she said.

"Let's give it one last go," Thick Throat said. "Hey!" he hollered, "Bring me the bolt cutters."

Bolt cutters?

The side door of the van slid open and shut. Judd heard a tool scrape along concrete. The sound rippled gooseflesh up his arms.

"Jesus *Christ!*" he shrieked.

"Sorry, no Jesus here."

"Look at the size of those feet!" The third one exclaimed. "And this one here, it's all scars."

"If this doesn't do the trick …" Thick Throat again.

The cold, steel blades of a bolt cutter slid into position around Judd's little toe. He tried to twist his foot away.

"Hey, I'll give you all my passwords, my bank account numbers …"

"Hold it down tight, bro. Right there. Yeah, that's good."

"Wait, guys, get this into your thick heads, I don't know shit!"

"Okay, okay, you gonna help us? You gonna spill the beans, beanstalk? Huh? Last chance. Yes? No?"

"If I knew anything, *any-thing*, believe me, I'd tell you!"

"That's a no. Three … two … one …"

There was a 'chonk' as the bolt cutters bit through the bone.

The last thing Judd felt were hot tears scorching his cheeks before he plummeted through depths of burning oil.

"He'll be a popsicle in an hour," the driver muttered as she steered the cargo van into the Prairie County landfill, climbed the bulldozed road to the end, and killed the lights. Two of the abductors jumped from the van in the subzero night, their breath puffs of white smoke. Out the rear doors they grunted and muscled Judd's nude body by his ankles and armpits. They tumbled it onto the frozen trash and wheeled away in a burst of acceleration.

Flakes of snow soft as moth wings fell on shredded bags of food scraps, a busted Styrofoam cooler, a sock monkey missing one eye, and Judd's blank face. Soon the falling snow filled the nooks and shrouded it smooth as dunes.

A flare of pain jolted Judd out of numb sleep. He sat upright, lifted his hands. His inflamed fingertips drummed an incessant beat, black with dried blood. Sucking air, he looked around. An eerie, alien landscape surrounded him in the somber, predawn light. Small purple clouds scudded across the eastern sky.

"What is this place?"

He struggled to stand, soaking wet from melted snow. Something stung his left foot. He looked down at the grotesque stump where his little toe used to be.

"No! It's gone!"

Bits of memory flashed—getting jumped, hooded, sedated, strapped to a chair. A man and a woman grilling him while another administered the torture.

No wonder my throat's so raw, it's from railing in pain.

As sunrise stretched its rays, the snow-covered trash became a field of glistening ice crystals.

It's a landfill. The thugs dumped me here to freeze to death.

"Oh my God, the twins!"

For the first time he felt grateful to them. If Chester and Oakley hadn't activated his thermostat node, he'd have frozen to death.

Seeing he was naked, Judd lifted a broken beer cooler off the pile by his feet. He held it to his groin as he stutter-stepped down the hillside between mounds of trash.

At the entrance gate a security guard in a bulbous winter coat hunkered by the scale. He held a padlock and fumed about the chain being cut.

"Idiots. They don't need to bust in here. It'll all be coming to them soon enough. Just you wait and see. Goddamn glacier of garbage gonna swallow the swing set."

Seeing Judd, he straightened. "Ah! You scared the screamin' shit outta me!" Judd could almost read the words written in the vapor of his breath. "Where'd you come out of?"

After a moment, Judd replied softly, "Death's door."

The man stared at Judd's blackened thumb gripping the cooler.

"You stay right there," he said, then turned his attention to an approaching Waste Management truck.

Judd limped down to the main road. A few cars sped past, blowing his scruffy hair around. The frigid air amplified the roar of their engines.

A red eighteen-wheeler blew out of nowhere, grinding its brakes. The driver blasted the horn.

"Hey, what you doin' out there? Get in man before your junk snaps off."

"Going to Marigold?" Judd asked, wincing as he climbed into the cab.

"No. Heading south. Le Sueur."

"Do you have a phone or some way to reach the sheriff in Marigold?"

The driver nodded, adding, "Man, what'd you say to her anyway?"

# 53

# The Enchantress

While Theodore Theroux boarded his private plane in New Haven, Connecticut, Kira called. He had just given a talk on "Exo-spirituality" as part of Yale University's *Outer Islands* program, a series featuring speakers with diverse metaphysical viewpoints. It was his last East Coast engagement.

"Theo, were you peeking in on me?"

Not Kira's honey voice, this was curt. The best Theroux could tell from the image on his phone, she was walking, a breeze ruffling her mahogany hair.

Theroux hadn't been in Kira's physical presence since she came on to him at the InterContinental Hotel. He had to admit, her sensuous appeal nearly aroused him to breach the chasity of his messianic quest.

"No," he said. Actually, he had looked in on her, but not recently.

"Oh, sorry. I felt your presence. Anyway, it's been crazy here, and I've been meaning to reconnect. I *miss* you."

Now the allure. She's working me. Oh, so sly.

"And while I have you on the line, I'm wondering if you would apply your amazing psychic powers for another look-see. You still have the brothers in your vibrary?" She grinned saying the word.

Kira wanted to film a Foster Jolley impostor to lure the twins out of hiding. But casting proved difficult. His likeness needed to be indisputable, or the trick would backfire. She'd keep up the search. But in the meantime, she worried that Inman Hayes and his goons would find and kill the boys. So she decided to try another approach. Make an end run around the Pentagon and find them with The The's help.

"I never heard back from Hayes," Theroux said.

"Oh, he's out of the country," she lied. "But we don't need him. How would you feel about partnering with *moi*? You bilocate the boys, and I see about bringing them to Neurokey. I know you want their goods, at least you intimated as much without saying it."

So *that's* her play. Do I tell her about Chester in a cave at the Grand Canyon and where homeless Oakley sleeps during the day in Minneapolis?

Kira heard silence. "Will you think about it?"

Theroux didn't care if the boys were dead or alive. Still, he wasn't ready to hand them off. He wanted what Hayes promised: access to their tools and methods. Kira was right about that.

"I'll take a look and get back to you," he lied.

"You precious man!" She ended the call with, "We can go on this adventure together, all in, all the way."

Partner with that enchantress? "No way will she sucker me into her vortex," Theroux muttered to himself. She didn't mention Judd Russell. He was still alive when I saw him last.

Well, barely. If he was dead, I wouldn't have been be able to bi-locate him outside that warehouse.

Theroux recalled spooking two masked men as they struggled to load Judd's limp and naked body into a vehicle. Seeing his specter, one guy yelped, "Ghost!" lost his grip, and dropped Judd on his head.

They didn't look like seasoned professionals from the Defense Department. Yet it wouldn't be beneath Hayes to hire freelance grunts off-book to do his bidding.

# 54

# The Orange

Tucked under blankets in the backseat of Sheriff Buck's police cruiser, Judd rode to the barricaded town. Parched and frail, he looked like a skeletal wreck.

The tension in Marigold had escalated since his abduction. The residents united in their resentment of the occupation. As for the soldiers, the grinding cold and futile search sunk morale.

"How long have I been gone?" Judd asked.

"Two nights. A lot's changed. Whole town's on lockdown. There's a 7:00 p.m. curfew. They put video cameras on power poles. I guess the good news is they're not letting any strangers into town like the ones who nabbed you. Or the media for that matter. Only a few stories in the press, but not much. The military occupation of a small rural community must not be newsworthy."

The soldier at the barricade moved the stanchions blocking the road and waved the sheriff through with a swat of his gloved hand.

"So, you say it was the same gang that tried to nab you before?"

"Pretty sure. Exept there was a woman with them this time. She seemed to carry some sway in what was to be done with me."

"A woman, huh."

"Where we going?" Judd asked.

"Arnie's farm. Stay down." Buck clamped up the rest of the way.

Behind the barn, the sheriff led Judd to a shed-roofed cinderblock structure.

"Best you hole up in the underground bunker for a while, out of sight."

Buck gave the door a swift kick. Crusted snow broke off. He grabbed the frosted metal handle and rattled it open.

"You can hang on to the blankets for now. Someone will be along with clothes." Buck hit the light switch for Judd to see his way down the concrete steps.

Judd thanked the sheriff, who waited for him to reach floor level before closing the door with a clank.

Sitting on a canvas cot, Judd took in the surroundings. Arnie kept the bunker clean. It had a space heater, a mini-fridge, jugs of water, a portable toilet, camp stove, and enough canned food to feed someone for a week.

Judd nodded out only to hear one of his abductors yell in a panic, "A ghost!" waking him up.

He uncapped a container and chugged the water with relish. He felt a tickle around his temples and an odd giddiness. He didn't want to sit any longer, he wanted to move.

Clothed only in a wool blanket, he climbed the stairs and shouldered the bunker door open. The sun at his back, he ambled down to the lake. The air was delicious, as if newborn. He passed a small wooden structure near the bank—a sauna, gray strips of wood stacked next to its door.

He looked across the lake of wind-ribbed snow dotted with fishing huts and inhaled the brightening day. A feeling of elation softened the pain of his fingers and missing toe. He didn't try to pinpoint the reason. It didn't matter. What mattered was letting it prevail.

"Judd?"

It was Roslyn, carrying a cardboard box.

"Ahh! Just the person I hoped to see!" he said.

Though Judd looked pale as paper, Roslyn saw a welcoming spark in his eyes.

"When I heard they found you, I couldn't believe it. We thought you were ..." Roslyn wanted to hug him, tell him how she feared for his life, but held back. "Have you been out here this whole time?"

"No, I was in the bunker."

They stared at each other for a moment without speaking.

"I brought you some food." She held up the box.

"You're an angel."

"My body's not as hot-blooded as yours, so could we ..."

Roslyn had been in the tornado bunker before. She knew where to plug in the space heater. As she set the box of food on a fold-up table, she saw Judd's burnt-looking finger and thumb.

"We need to get you bandaged."

"I lost a toe as well."

"Oh, God!" She gasped at the sight.

"Hurts like hell, but I can now tell people the phantom limb myth is for real."

Roslyn's nurse training kicked in. She reached to a shelf and pulled down a tackle box with a red cross on its side.

"Agh!" Judd winced as she gently swabbed the dried blood off with an antiseptic cloth.

"I'll be careful."

They were quiet while Roslyn tended to his wounds.

"I thought of you," Judd broke the stillness.

"Yeah? As your nails were being ripped off?"

"No, how I promised to help you out in the café."

"Not with these fingers. You'll scare the customers."

"I'll wear latex gloves."

Roslyn gingerly cleaned the wound left of his little toe. "There." She popped open the lid of a container and began applying butterfly bandages. "So are you still going to North Dakota?"

"I will at some point, but right now I need to catch my breath."

Watching Roslyn at work, Judd marveled at her hands, and human hands in general—such magical feelers and tools of creation. How they touch and caress, strum guitars, knead bread.

"Artists at the end of our arms," he whispered.

"What'd you say?"

"Hands … they're extraordinary!"

"Especially when they have fingernails. All done."

Roslyn put back the first-aid box.

Judd wiggled his bandaged fingers.

"Thanks."

"When was the last time you ate?"

He shook his head.

"You must be starving." Roslyn pulled a large navel orange out of the carton and set on the table. Judd locked his eyes on it as if seeing one for the first time.

"Oh … my … look at you," he said. "You're so *orange*!"

Roslyn saw him oddly admiring the fruit.

"I'll peel it for you."

He palmed the orange and held it up like a lantern.

"It's luminous."

"Let me ..." She took it.

He kept staring as she skinned the rind.

"Here," she handed him a wedge.

"Mmm, it tastes ... wah-bumba ... like a thousand sweet kisses."

Must be the trauma, Roslyn thought. She didn't know Judd's perception was heightening.

As Roslyn broke off another section of the orange, Judd saw the drumming of her heart send a warm, loving ray of energy toward him. His heart responded in kind.

The two rays fused. The bunker lit up. Pastel-colored filaments encircled their bodies as if weaving a cocoon.

Although Roslyn couldn't see the rays, she felt the exchange, looked into Judd's eyes and smiled. "What did you just do?"

"What did *you* just do?"

# 55
# Us against Them

The bunker door screeched open.

"It's me." Arnie descended the stairs carrying a paper bag and a pair of ski boots. Seeing Judd, he shook his head. "Blow me over with a feather, ain't you a sight! Here. Hope these fit."

Judd did a double take. "Those are mine."

"Broke into your car." Arnie cracked a smile. "Didn't want to hear any more whining about tight shoes."

"I better get back." Roslyn touched Judd's arm. "You rest."

Arnie held up the bag. "Brought you some overalls, unless you want to go round naked from now on."

"You look tired, Arnie," Judd said.

"Since your skirmish with that soldier, it's us against them. Folks stopped answering their doors. The café's now off limits to the task force, including Mantz. So there's that. Hope you're not going anywhere. I could use some help with the remodel. And thanks to you, we'll need to install a new front window for the café."

"Count me in. By the way, been meaning to ask you when you're going to tell Marsha about your feelings for her?"

"What?"

"The other day I saw your heart cord leap out to her."

Arnie looked away. He fidgeted with the overalls, pretending not to hear.

"You can adjust the straps," he said, handing them to Judd. "And, and there's a shaving razor on the shelf. We'll find a better place for you than Roslyn's couch."

"Bunker's all right for now. Beats a landfill."

Marsha and Roslyn stopped by around sundown with a plate of hot food. Recalling his abduction, Judd said, "It was like one of those movie scenes that's so overdone it's cliché. They had an urgency, as if on deadline. I overheard one on the phone, demanding to get paid."

"Want to go back and re-run it?" Marsha asked.

"Go through that trauma, again? No. I'd rather forget it."

"Understood."

"Call me a coward but I got to confess, if I knew where your son's were, I would've told'em. Any news?"

"No, and I'm worried. But enough's enough. I gave in. Victor King at Neurokey is writing up an agreement. Call it a swap. He claims he can arrange to stop the manhunt, the APB, BOLO, whatever they call it, in exchange for the boys working at his lab. Why are you smiling?"

"Mother bear."

"What?"

"Your caring. It's so deep."

"Caring, hell, I want them back so I can strangle them."

# 56

# The Price of Love

Two days later, Judd began helping out at the Marigold Café. With its picture window boarded up, and being off limits to the soldiers, the café was safe for him to work without being spotted. In fact, a smattering of non-regulars came to get a glimpse of the hero who rescued Roslyn from sexual assault.

Arnie would drive Judd to town where he'd assist Tomás in the kitchen for the morning rush. As cook for more than a year, Tomás Maderos added a few Mexican meals to the traditional "farm fresh" menu, including huevos rancheros, carne asada omelettes, and muskellunge tacos. Since many Minnesotans lacked a palate for hot salsa and spicy food, Tomás was careful not to overwhelm them. He brought out new dishes gradually, striking the rejects.

Judd's primary duties included stocking the supply room and washing dishes, a striped apron belted round his waist. Roslyn took orders until the morning rush dispersed, then she homeschooled Flannery. The girl had no playmates. Since her brothers became wanted fugitives, she was off limits.

Marsha wrangled with her home insurance broker who refused to acknowledge her claim, saying: "We don't have a policy that covers terrorist acts, or botched science experiments." She then met with her husband's attorney in Minneapolis about a contractual dispute with his publisher. Foster had agreed to write a sequel to *The Isness* and failed to deliver. The publisher filed a lawsuit to return the large advance, the money spent.

Unknown to Judd, the next day his brain cells began to change. He seemed outright merry, which enlivened the glum ambience of the café with the front window covered up. Tomás picked up Judd's upbeat mood. When Judd became fixated on the red sheen of a tomato, Tomás recited a poem in Spanish.

"Pablo Neruda," he said, then translated: "The street filled with tomatoes, midday summer, light is halved like a tomato; its juice runs through the streets ..."

That afternoon Judd helped Arnie remodel his place. Roslyn visited the farm later. The two were becoming inseparable.

No longer in a hurry to return to the actor's life, Judd called his talent agency to say he was on vacation. They told him Zach Kitchener came through on his promise to make up for the aborted *Waiting for Godot on Ice.*

"He wants to cast you in a TV series pilot, *The Price of Love,*" said the agent. "Here's the summary: A clever, product-placement-driven soap opera where, instead of cutting to commercial breaks, the ads are seamlessly inserted into the scenes."

Judd would play Dr. Perry Stallsis, a clinical psychologist on staff at Hyde Hospital. The talent agency emailed a scene for Judd to read, along with a shooting schedule for him to appear at a studio in Los Angeles.

## 36.  INT. DR. STALLSIS OFFICE, HYDE HOSPITAL - DAY

DR. STALLSIS sits across from patient, KAY SADIA.

> STALLSIS
> How long have you been feeling homicidal?

> KAY
> Ever since Bertram left me for that witch, Angina. I want to kill him. Nobody dumps me like trash. Nobody. I may have parts that aren't recyclable, but I'm not all trash.

> STALLSIS
> Rejection hurts. So naturally, you feel cheapened, marked down.

> KAY
> I bought a gun.

> STALLSIS
> Of course you did … but you hesitate using it.

> KAY
> Death is too kind. I need him to suffer.

> STALLSIS
> And suffer he will, once he smells you wearing Lavalanche.

*STALLSIS lifts a small vial from a glass cabinet, offers it to KAY who reads the label.*

*CLOSE UP OF LAVALANCHE LABEL.*

STALLSIS (VO)

It's an avalanche of molten hotness. An aroma of unstoppable desire condensed in a weaponized perfume. One whiff and your feelings of abandonment vanish. He'll come begging. He'll be so relentless, you'll need a restraining order.

*Kay pumps the vial. A spurt of vapor drifts past her nose.*

KAY

Ohhh ... how can I thank you, Doctor.

STALLSIS

Now for only $29.95 at Walgreens. Hurry while the sale lasts.

Two weeks ago, Judd would have paid to be in the TV pilot—his headstart to stardom. But he declined. His appetite for portraying other people had lost its spark. Besides, it would take him away from Roslyn.

# 57
# He's Changed

Three days after Judd started working in the café, visible changes began, not with him at first, but with the regulars. Having served breakfast for two years, Roslyn could predict what people would order. But that morning, instead of the usual eggs, sausage, and home fries, Erling tried the muskellunge taco with hot salsa. A seemingly minor shift, but for Erling, seismic. Normally a tightwad, Ollie Olson gave her a tip. Typically late, Tomás arrived early. And the winter blues Roslyn often felt didn't happen.

She noticed the overall tone lighten up when Judd was there. Marsha attributed it to a feeling of solidarity in reaction to the task force. But Roslyn saw how folks lingered. They sat with Judd as he ate breakfast, shared their stories, many quite intimate. Something about being near him. Roslyn felt it too—a magnetism.

"He's changed," she told Marsha. "His whole attitude. He's less impressed with himself. And there's a honey-colored glow around his head."

The aura became more evident the next day when Roslyn drove her rusted, green Ford F-150 out to Arnie's place.

Because Judd's body self-adjusted to the cold, Arnie set up work tables in the barn, giving them more elbow room than in the house. For Roslyn, the barn was her old school. It's where Arnie taught her to work with gas-powered equipment from chainsaws to skid loaders.

Arnie took the food she brought and left them alone. He didn't want to be in the way of a romance warming on low heat.

The two made plans to eat, ski, and take a sauna.

They brought towels, laid wood, got the fire started, and went off skiing. Although unspoken, they knew where this time together would lead.

"You've heard how the Eskimo have fifty words for snow," she said as they glided across the lake.

"Thought that was a myth."

"This is called Osaknuq. Big, fluffy flakes. My favorite kind."

"Assak …?"

"O-s-a-k-n-u-q. Osaknuq."

They circled the lake and skied back to shore.

The wood-burning sauna was only big enough for two. It hadn't been used since Arnie's wife left him for the city lights many years ago.

Roslyn lit the candles. Judd stoked the fire.

"Osaknuq," he said.

"I made it up," she admitted. "Sounded good."

"You got me," he laughed.

Once the rocks were hot, he splashed on water. The room sizzled with steam. They sat across from each other, knees to knees. In no time the air turned tropical. Perspiration beaded from pores.

In the dim candlelight, a subtle radiance appeared around Judd's head. Roslyn's eyes widened.

"You're looking at me funny."

"Oh, sorry, it's …" She made a circle with her hand. "… you're beaming, and I mean really, really beaming."

"Well, you've seen me desperate, crazed, sick, even downright cruel. High time I showed you a good side." He took her hand. "You bring it out."

He saw a wave of energy extend from her heart. He leaned forward and pressed a kiss on her wet cheek, then on her lips. She let her towel slip to the bench. Her body glistened in a sheen of wetness.

Roslyn had never surrendered to the luxury of her sensuality. She'd been on a couple dates that led to cowboy sex—a giddy-up fit of huffing in her ear that ended in a bucking thrust and rodeo over. As for Judd, no one was ever good enough. His love life was sporadic, at times hurried, clumsy.

This was tender, rushless, and loving. He palmed her plush, round breasts, the nipples aroused and moist. They spread the towels on the cedar floor for cushion and caressed, relishing each other's touch. The only sound the soft patter and suction of lips on slippery flesh. She helped him find her, purring "Ah-lama," as their slick, sopping bodies fused in the hot mist.

"Ah-lama." Roslyn didn't want it to stop.

Later that night above the café, Roslyn told Marsha about the light around Judd. Marsha took it as an illusion, a symptom of Roslyn's infatuation.

The next morning Judd appeared even more luminous. Roslyn urged Marsha to go to Arnie's barn that afternoon after the café closed. When Marsha saw Judd's brilliant aura, she stiffened, awestruck.

"Good of you to come," he said. "I was planning to stop by and see you two later. Something's happening."

"No kidding. Your aura is brighter than I've ever seen," Marsha said.

"Yeah. Arnie couldn't take his eyes off me. And there's something else. Kind of hard to describe. Simply put, there's more of me now, more presence, for lack of a better word. It's as if I've been frozen solid all my life and now spring has come. It's thawing my shell."

"Through your crown?" Marsha asked.

"All over," Judd said.

"How does it feel?" Roslyn asked.

Judd thought about how to put it into words. "Like a freeing up of all constraints. Like sunshine pouring out from inside."

He took Roslyn's hand. It tingled, electric.

"Is this the Isness Foster spoke about?" he asked.

"No," Marsha said. "He described it as a shower of living essence. But it never manifested like this. Not from *within*."

Marsha couldn't help but wonder if her sons' spiteful intentions accidently sprung open the Godhead Spot, or Ezra's fabled "Crown of Lights."

"I know what you're thinking," Judd said. "But, no, it's not God, Marsha. It's more of me, more of my own soul. I've been wandering, detached from it all my life, and now I'm coming home."

Speechless, they stared at him. Then Marsha asked, "Can you see where these changes will lead?"

Shutting his eyes, Judd took a moment before responding.

"Here … and more here, and more … "

# 58

# All the Way to Mexico

Chester woke at daybreak to the ripping of a rag. He stood at the mouth of the cave and listened. The silence thick as clay. Across the canyon the light in the east painted the crest rosy pink in slow time. He wondered if traveling all the way to the Grand Canyon to find his father was crazy. Still, he didn't regret coming. The place is like no other. He even fantasized about setting up a lab on the north ridge. But now he smelled a hint of sulfur in the air and a tightening feeling, as if his skin was shrinking. Both warning signs.

He didn't go to the dining hall for waffles. Not with such a menacing force closing in. As he stuffed his backpack, he wondered who recognized him. That tourist he choked in the lodge? The woman snapping pictures? And Theroux, the creepy phantom showing up, what was that about?

Chester heard the swarming beehive of a drone. He peeked outside and saw it swoop above the trail. His heart leaped a beat as he ducked into the shadow of the cave.

Time to find another hideout.

Four armed men in fatigues hustled down the park trail and humped up the escarpment, weapons at the ready. They found the cave, but other than potato chip bags, candy wrappers, and a crushed cola can, it was empty. One of the search team stood outside and called it in.

On the trail, a hundred yards below, Chester stopped at a switchback. He peered over the edge at the meandering Colorado River. Nowhere to go but down.

At the floor of the canyon, he had an idea—hike the riverbank and follow the current.

Of course! The river runs all the way to Mexico, right? Nobody will be looking for me in Mexico. And it's cheap to live there I hear.

He didn't know the Mexican border was more than 400 miles away by water.

He scampered along the bank, his pack bouncing on his back. At a bend in the river, he caught his breath, his lungs heaving. Before him, the river slid along, smooth and teal blue. He had an out now. Freedom. High above, the morning light undressed the strata of the canyon ledge by ledge.

Chester thought of the Spanish classes he took his freshman and sophomore years.

It'll all come back to me when I'm around the language in Mexico, eating my fill of burritos!

A stray lesson bubbled up, the vocal exercise of trilling double R words— *"Irre con irre barrile, irre con irre cigarros, alla en el ferrocarril, rapidos corren los carros."*

He repeated the line, its meaning lost on him. Riffling his tongue, the chant became a happy companion as he rambled along the rocky shore. He felt bold and confident about his escape plan until he heard the helicopter. It tilted in the sky, a shock of sunlight splashed off its dome.

Chester broke into a sprint, repeating out loud: *"Rapidos … rapidos corren los carros!"*

The helicopter descended behind him, a giant demon-eyed dragonfly, serrating the water. The tornadic thwop of its rotor blades roared low through the canyon. As he jostled around boulders, the brain maps he hoped to show his father sprung out his backpack in a flock of flapping white sheets. If he looked over his shoulder, he would have seen boots on the landing skid and the barrel of a rifle poking out the chopper door.

A bullet chipped the rock face inches above his head.

The helicopter lifted, swept its shadow across him and angled around.

He heard tramping sounds and voices bouncing off the stone walls behind him.

He ran for his life.

When the river bank hit a dead end, he looked for a way up. But there were no trails, and the cliffs too sheer to climb.

No getting around it, the river was Chester's only way out. He watched it glide past.

Would it be smooth like this farther down? Would there be rapids and boulders and waterfalls?

He gaped at the water. He didn't want to die.

Not now.

He wanted to eat a big jelly donut. He wanted to experience sex. He wanted to try motocross dirt bike racing, go paragliding. The list went on.

There it was again, the torrid blades of the helicopter pummeling his ears.

"It's no adventure if there's no fear," he said and dove into the river.

He didn't hear the rifle crack or feel the swift current carry him along.

Blood plumed around his lifeless body. It stained the sheets of brain maps red as they floated by.

# 59
## The 100ᵗʰ Monkey

After the Marigold café took down its television back in October due to conflict over watching CNN or FOX, Ollie Olson started reading newspaper articles aloud to his booth buddies. His choice of stories was simple—make them either hoot or cringe.

"Here's one." He read about a sinkhole that swallowed a gas station in Florida. "Cars, pumps, and all. Filled 'er up."

In time the regulars wanted to hear the odd piece Ollie chose. He'd stand at the end of the counter, ruffle the paper in his hands, situate his glasses comfortably on the bridge of his nose, and say, "Got one." Mouths closed, service stopped, even the kitchen silenced as Ollie shared a wild, and at times, wincing story.

As Judd's aura grew brighter, the stories Ollie read became more uplifting. Like the Kansas prison warden who ordered a special dinner for the inmates. The caterer included barbequed ribs and beef brisket, baked beans, potato salad, with peach cobbler and yammer pie. "Even threw in the burnt ends."

There were accounts of spontaneous savant-like skills, among them a Chilean miner who woke up a concert pianist, and people having sudden moments of remorse or humility, turning themselves in for decades-old crimes, offering their law practice or dental work gratis to the poor.

In Marigold, long-standing quarrels and resentments came to peaceful resolutions. Joe Pye returned the Weedwacker he borrowed from Harvey Clyster. A daughter, eight years estranged from her parents, showed up to make amends.

A lot of good news went unread, such as the group in Idaho who incinerated hundreds of assault weapons, and the global ban on hunting whales.

Roslyn was the first to claim that Judd's metamorphosis created the remarkable changes in people.

"It's here and jumping continents," she said. "Like the 100th Monkey Effect I learned about in anthropology."

"Oh, stop. You're saying he's like a beacon?" Marsha asked.

"What's the 100th Monkey?" Flannery asked.

"Years ago on a Japanese island," Roslyn said, "scientists studying the monkeys fed them raw sweet potatoes in the sand. One day they watched a young monkey wash a potato in a stream to make it more palatable. Other monkeys noticed and washed their potatoes as well. Then the practice jumped. Monkey colonies on other islands started washing potatoes. One theory claimed that when an activity reaches a certain field of awareness, the knowledge passes over land and water, from mind to mind."

"Balooge!"

But Judd's condition wasn't mimicry like the Monkey Effect. These were lightning flashes of inspiration, touching one person but not en masse, like a single leaf gyrating on a tree while other leaves remain unmoved.

Could the boys have opened Judd's crown? Marsha worried his transformation would repeat what deified her husband

and incited "save-me, heal-me" followers to foam around him. Unlike Foster, Judd didn't need attention or adulation. Marsha wondered if his transformation was more complete than Foster's. Did caring and humility come to the forefront because his Life Review cleared the path?

Another difference—her husband never emanated such vivifying light.

# 60
# The Defrost Effect

There seemed no logical reason why Judd's beacon resonated with one person and skipped another. Those deeply
touched had varying reactions. Besides epiphanies, heartfelt
acts of kindness, and bursts of uncanny creativity, a common
symptom was the heightening of emotions, both suppressed
and spontaneous.

Along with seizures of giddiness, others experienced the
opposite—implosions of self-sabotage and brutal rage. Overlooked among Ollie's surprising stories, and Roslyn's sunny-
side point of view, were reports of polarizing behavior—people
snapping for no reason, mass shootings, run amok stabbings,
and random bombings.

Judd likened his change to a spring thaw. "Much like the
sun melts winter's ice, the deeper connection of my soul dis-
solves the armor that imprisoned me."

But the boost of Judd's soul light created a splintering
Defrost Effect. Responses depended on a person's degree of
solidity. The more open and flexible, the better chance for
a life-lift. For those locked in their beliefs and their need to
control, the Effect drove them to rampage.

Such was the case with Commander Mantz. Although he adapted to the Minnesota cold, the occupation took a toll on his team. He lost three soldiers—one to pneumonia, another to a cracked pelvis from a slip on the ice, and Randy, who was hospitalized. Finding nothing resembling the twins or their tools, the remaining members of the task force called it "a bullshit WMD hunt."

Low morale notwithstanding, for Mantz the Defrost Effect magnified a crack in his rock-hard psyche. His moods swung from overt hostility to catatonia.

Returning from vacation, Del Johnson, the bowling alley owner, became enraged at the snow soldiers tracked in that pooled on the lanes and raised the grain of the wood. Resenting the accusation, Mantz lost his temper and beat the man unconscious before being wrestled off. There were also nights in the bowling alley when his eyes, reflected in the glass cabinet of trophies, looked blank as dead moons. Then the time another soldier found him in the back office, a revolver on his lap.

One night, Mantz went out. No one saw him leave. Wind-blown grains of ice peppered his face as he wandered aimless, hearing disembodied voices. Crossing the frozen river, he stopped and hollered, "You ball sack licking scum!"—reliving an argument with his ex-wife's boyfriend. He waited for the feeling to pass. It didn't. In no time the cold burned his lungs. A slow paralysis moved in. His lips turned blue. His body became so hot he feared it would combust. He couldn't undress fast enough. He flung his coat, boots, shirt. Still overheated, he tore off his trousers. His fingers became stiff, distant things. He groaned until an impenetrable wave of darkness engulfed him.

When Mantz didn't appear for morning muster, a search party went out.

Buck called Arnie. "They don't know where he went. The snow filled any tracks he might have left so …"

That's all Buck needed to say. Arnie found Fetch sleeping in his barn and drove to the bowling alley. In the parking lot he kneeled eye to eye with the dog and said, "Fetch, we're looking for a missing man." He scruffed the dog's back, collecting a few bristly hairs. "Okay if I join in? You know, like the last time."

Fetch sniffed the air. The wind blew out of the northwest, streaked with horizontal flurries.

Arnie got back behind the wheel of his truck. He rubbed the hairs he'd gathered from Fetch between his palms, closed his eyes, and centered his full attention on the heart of the dog.

"Okay, Fetch, let me in."

The dog's legs came alive first. He could feel their loping stride in his shoulders. Arnie's nostrils flared and his sense of smell heightened. Diesel fumes mixed with the odor of onions and sausage wafted from the bowling alley.

"Remember that man who kicked you outside the café?" Arnie said, looking out the dog's eyes. "Let's find him."

Fetch lifted his head and whiffed the air. Picking up a scent, he broke into a trot south.

In the middle of the river, Fetch found the Commander sitting in his skivvies, eyes open, unseeing, bone hard.

So riveted by the sight, Arnie didn't hear the police car door slam. Buck knocked on the driver-side window of his truck .

Arnie jerked and barked, "Arr-urf!"

Mantz's death ended the occupation. Barricades came down. The soldiers loaded their gear into trucks and vans. They meant to depart quietly, but their exit didn't go unnoticed.

People came out of stores and homes to wave as the caravan moved down Main Street and out of town. Some blew farewell kisses with their middle fingers.

Flannery stood outside the café serenading the soldiers from *Les Miserables.* "I dreamed a dream ..."

# 61

# The CQ

Commander Mantz wasn't the only meltdown from the Defrost Effect. Around the world, acts of extreme violence and suicide crashed records.

"It's Judd," Roslyn said. "He's causing both extremes."

Marsha remained skeptical.

The notion made Roslyn look at people differently. She wondered what would happen when the Defrost Effect hits Henna Pino? Or Bob Zeebart? Or the whole country? Does the hardness of the heart determine your fate, or can you still choose to change your ways?

On the positive side, Cardinal Barberi was inundated with candidates for sainthood. Advocates submitted names of righteous and reverent Americans to their priests. Churches notified the Vatican. The Pontifical Commission contacted Barberi to look into "these matters."

Barberi kept a spreadsheet of claimants. He emailed a Canonization Questionnaire—the CQ—his list of questions for applicants.

He reviewed every response. If answers failed to meet the criteria, he replied with a kindly worded rejection:

*These are certainly favorable signs, and your late uncle Windom sounds like he was an exemplary, God-fearing man. But simply providing selfless humanitarian acts does not in itself qualify.*

Barberi had three boxes in the CQ. If all checked and clearly explained, he'd schedule a phone interview.

1) Did the person live a holy, virtuous life? If so, describe.
2) Did the person die a heroic martyr? If so, describe.
3) Did the person perform miracles while alive or post-mortem? If so, describe.

The candidate needed a minimum of two miracles. These included incurable healings, supernatural acts, resurrections, and God-induced deeds. All miracles required verification. There were countless frauds and exaggerated accounts, easy for Barberi to debunk.

The most important factor separating the wheat from the chaff was that the candidate must be dead. Two referrals were so impressive, Barberi felt compelled to meet with witnesses for the full story. One described a martyr, a high school student killed in a school shooting after kneeling before the gunman, shielding fellow students, and praying for his soul. Another was a healer from Atlanta who could swim inside a dying person's body as if it was clear water. "With the energy of the Christ Force," he could shrink tumors, remove blood clots, and unblock arteries.

Barberi also kept a chart of living, "in the running" saints to watch. The number of these potential candidates for sainthood had recently exploded from forty-seven to more than 2,000 names. Such a flood of goodwill ramping up coast to coast moved Barberi deeply.

One of them stood out from the others because exuberant witness accounts described the man as physically "luminous."

This he had to see.

# 62

# The Sun Man

Being so tall, Judd stuck out in a crowd. But now, emanating such scintillating light, people couldn't take their eyes off him. Each day his aura grew in brilliance, a hypnotic sight, impossible to ignore. The light was more than a halo or a golden dinner plate behind a saint's head in an icon painting. This was a lustrous, egg-shaped radiance around his entire body.

His luminosity became so evident, café regulars took selfies with him and told others. Word spread through social media.

"Here we go!" Ollie Olson folded back the newspaper and read an article entitled, 'The Bio-Luminescent Dishwasher.' "Working in a café in a small farm town twenty-five miles west of Minneapolis, Minnesota … "

The photograph didn't show Judd's face clearly because his brilliance blushed out the resolution as if overexposed.

The curious came to town to catch a glimpse. They wedged themselves among café regulars and watched Judd's every move as he washed pots and pans in the kitchen. Some wanted to see a savior, needy, gushing, bowing and bathing him in preciousness. Petty flaw-pickers looked for specks of impurity and condemned him a fraud, his glow due to an unnamed radioactive skin affliction. "Something in the dish soap," one conjectured. The Mayo Clinic inquired about running tests. Judd declined. Lars Lundeen proposed turning him into a Ripley's Believe It or Not! act.

"Call him *The Sun Man*. Tell everybody he's like a solar eclipse; you'll need sunglasses to see him. Trot him around the country, state fairs and stuff. Kick back and count the profits."

"Better yet, a reality TV show!" another suggested.

"Not in my café," Arnie said.

Judd took the attention with humility.

"Can you walk on water?" a reporter with the *Star Tribune* asked.

"Yes! When the ice is thick enough."

"Are you the Messiah?" a visitor asked.

"No, I am not. Unless, by messiah, you mean the indivisible unity of all beings from atoms to stars."

Some unconsciously sent energy cords to attach to him, which he graciously deflected. But the more it happened the more annoying it became, like swatting away mosquitoes.

"Can you levitate?" another reporter asked.

"No need. I'm tall enough to see over people's heads."

Confronted in the alley behind the café, a local visitor begged, "I'm lost. Please, tell me what I need to do?"

"Attend to basic tasks," Judd said. "To start with, see that your pots and pans are washed clean."

When he was asked about any changes in his perception of the world, he said, "Colors are richer, much more vibrant."

"How about people? Do they appear different?"

"In a way they look like walking lockers. The kind of metal lockers you see in schools and fire stations. Some have doors welded shut. Some are latched, others open a crack. Only a few are doorless, showing their innermost valuables."

Another stranger asked Judd if he had a remedy for depression.

"Everyone is different. In general, I'd say movement."

"Calisthenics?"

"Skipping." Judd grinned.

"Did you say *skipping*?"

"And wonder. Without hope you sicken a lifespan. Without wonder you kill eternity."

# 63
# A The The Problem

Kira King sat in the wealth corner of her mezzanine office at Neurokey. The minimalist decor had ecru-painted walls, potted pink orchids, and eco-friendly furniture carefully arranged for optimum chi by a Feng Shui practitioner. On her kidney-shaped desk were three eight-by-tens of Foster Jolley taken during his book tour, two full face, one profile.

"I'm ready." She gestured to her assistant. "Bring in the first one."

Kira didn't tell her father she was filming a Foster impostor. She had tried to win him over by pitching the idea of a news report on national TV that would say: 'In other news, the mystery surrounding the whereabouts of Foster Jolley can now be put to rest. For the last four years the neuro-evangelist and author of the best seller, *The Isness,* has been living in seclusion …' then it cuts to video of our stand-in."

Victor thought it too risky.

"Expose the lie, we lose everything."

"It's marketing," Kira countered.

"No, it's a lie."

"There's a difference?"

Since Kira hadn't heard back from Theroux about her proposal to collaborate, she focused her energy on the Foster fraud. Having found six look-alikes, she set up a casting session.

"Way too short," she told her assistant after rejecting the first candidate. "Foster's six foot. Send the next one and make sure they all sign the nondisclosure agreement."

A veteran actor stepped in. He handed Kira his headshot with an extensive theater bio on the back. She looked at the pictures of Foster, then the man. His height, eye color, and age were spot on. His satiny brown hair was gelled back and flavored the space with vanilla.

He can grow a goatee, Kira noted. And we can dye and rework the hair.

She handed him a sheet of paper with a few sentences on it.

"I want to see my sons!" he read.

"Say it again, warmer."

The challenge was not simply matching the facial features but also the voice. Based on recorded interviews, Foster spoke in a mellow tone with a slight lisp. She didn't want to dub in a voice if she could help it.

"I want to see my sons."

Kira read the next line: "They're calling the boys domestic terrorists."

"Don't believe that for a second."

Kira was about to have the man repeat the line when Victor stormed in. Seeing the actor he stopped cold.

"F-Foster?"

The man glanced at the page in his hand, then at Victor. "I want to see my sons."

"What the hell?" Victor glared at the man. "You're not …"

"I don't see this on my page," the actor said.

"I'm right in the middle of casting Foster," Kira said.

"I thought we agreed to shelve that." Victor squeezed around Kira's chair to her computer. "Doesn't matter. You need to see something. Didn't you get my email?"

"Is he in this?" the actor asked, unsure if he was still auditioning.

"No, he's not," Kira told the actor, then swung around to her father. "What are you doing?"

"Bring up the link I sent," Victor said.

What now? Kira thought. Her father was becoming more manic by the hour.

"Oh... kayyyyy ..."

The actor held up the page of script. "Am I still ...?"

"No!" Victor hollered.

"Hang on," Kira told the actor. She opened her father's email and clicked the video of an illuminated man moving about a commercial kitchen. "What am I looking at?"

"Just what it says: The Sun Man," Victor said. "Name's Judd Russell. Check out the name of the town."

Kira read the type at the bottom of the screen: MARI-GOLD, MINNESOTA.

"They did it!" Victor reached over Kira's shoulder, paused the video, and pointed at Judd's radiant face. "Look at him! The Jolley brothers must have tapped his brain!"

Kira sprang to her feet, still locked on the image.

"It's that tall guy. I *met* him!" She remembered his deep voice.

"Where?"

"At the exhibit. He came to our booth. Went by a different name, but that's him all right. He's the one with the odd EEG."

"Listen," Victor was hyperventilating, "put his brain under our lenses and we've got it all!"

True, Kira thought. Who needs the Jolleys? This guy's head is the key.

"Whoa!" The actor yelled.

"Shut up!" Victor batted the air between them.

"Sorry, thought I saw a ghost!" the actor huffed.

Kira felt a sudden chill. "A ghost? Where?"

"Over there." He pointed to the wealth corner behind Kira. Kira spun around.

"It's gone, now," the actor said.

"Oh, shit! He's been watching!"

"Who?" Victor looked around. "Is this part of your audition?"

"We're done," she told the actor. "Thanks for coming."

"Yeah, get the hell out!" Victor said. "You're nobody here."

"Nobody? How dare you insult me. *Me!*" The actor flung the script at Victor. "I have read for Harold Prince, for Zelda Fichandler!"

Kira and Victor didn't hear him slam the door. Victor wiped his forehead with a handkerchief.

"Listen," he said, "I've been trying to reach Inman Hayes all morning."

"No! You keep that man out of this. He'll have the guy shot."

"But we need his help. Kira, this is the break ..."

"Wait. Leave it to me. I'll clear my calendar and fly out there." She tapped the computer screen. "He knows me. He was *attracted* to me."

"Shocking."

"Only one thing ..."

"What?"

"We may have a The The problem."

# 64
## The Juddites

In no time Judd's celebrity mushroomed. Sheriff Buck's limited staff couldn't handle the pilgrimage of "Juddites" overrunning Marigold. Press vans clogging the snow-plowed roads, added to the onslaught.

"And this is the middle of winter," said Buck. "What happens come high summer?"

He recalled the last roadside attraction in the township—the crop circle in Vance and Luverne's soybean field. That was something. Vance charged people $100 each to traipse across his land. The aerial photo showed a design that looked like a harp on wheels. Not that you could make it out from the ground, just a bunch of pancaked plants. But the number of crop circle visitors was a fraction compared to those converging on the town.

The front of the café became a shrine to Judd. On the plywood-covered window someone painted a big, flaming sun on two legs. Christmas wreathes, crucifixes, prayer flags, and friendship bracelets hung from nails and push-pins. Bundles of frozen flowers sat on the sidewalk among candles, Virgin Mary figurines, and obscure handmade art objects. People spray-painted CALL ME phone numbers and personal pleas on top of others. "John 3:16" was stenciled over "Pray for my sister Ida," and "Drove nonstop from Juneau."

Braving the frigid air, the Juddites appeared hours before the café opened. Under their coats some dressed in honor of Judd, mimicking his kitchen duty clothes—short-sleeve white shirt, striped apron, latex gloves. Some chanted, "Open up!" Others sang, "Mister Sun, Sun, Mister Golden Sun, please shine down on me."

Inside, Roslyn, Buck, and Arnie told Judd the novelty had become a fiasco.

Judd agreed. "It appears I've changed from a person of interest to an interesting person. Too interesting. They seem to think I'm a Jesus. Which I'm definitely not."

"We don't know what's next for you, Judd," Arnie said, shading his eyes.

"I will be who I will be as I am," Judd said.

"Fine," said Buck. "But folks are goin', 'What's worse, the soldiers or hordes of strangers and media pouring in?'"

"And we're worried they'll rip you to shreds." Roslyn added.

People began pounding on the plywood. A woman hollered, "I want your baby!" Good thing Buck had brought in more police to maintain peace and guard the front and back doors of the café.

"My God, listen to them!" Roslyn said.

"If we don't do somethin' fast," Buck pointed at the front door, "we're gonna need the National Guard."

"We think it best you leave for a spell," Arnie said. "Let things settle."

"What if I stay out at your place?"

"In time they'll find you. Buck?"

Buck coughed and said, "I got a hunting cabin up north. It's remote. That's something, at least for now."

"And I'll drive you," Roslyn said.

"When do we leave?" Judd asked.

"Soon as possible," Arnie said. "Give you a day or two to pack food and things."

"I apologize for being such a problem. You've been so good to me. I don't know how I could ever make it up."

The outside shouts and hammering quieted.

"What happened?" Arnie said.

Peeking through the door, Tomás saw the crowd part for a white stretch limo. The driver opened the side door. Cardinal Barberi stepped out, dressed in scarlet vestments and biretta cap.

"I won't be long," he told the driver.

The words, "luminous as the sun" and "the second coming" piqued the Cardinal's interest. When he read that this man came from the same town as the notorious Jolley brothers, he made Marigold, Minnesota his first stop.

"Make a path!" the driver said.

The corpulent Cardinal gesticulated blessings to the people and crab-walked to the café entrance, saying to himself, "Time to debunk."

Tomás watched the man approach. A knock followed.

"The café's closed," he said.

"I am Cardinal Barberi, here to meet the Sun Man."

The gathering murmured his name.

"It's a cardinal?" Tomás called back.

Judd's first thought was the bird, and for good reason, the cardinals he fed at Arnie's farm ate seed out of his hand.

"Says the Pope sent him," Tomás added.

"Judd?" Roslyn said.

"Let him in." Judd sat on a stool. His aura, reflected on the stainless-steel prep table, brightened the space like a Klieg light.

The officers Buck posted struggled to block fanatics trying to squeeze in the front door.

One woman pressed her blue ribbon, red velvet bundt cake into Barberi's hands. "See that he gets this."

Barberi entered smiling. "*Buongiorno.*" He gave a slight bow of his head to Roslyn behind the counter, who pointed to the kitchen.

The cardinal saw the Sun Man and stutter-stepped. The startling light around Judd swelled and subsided in brilliance with the ebb and flow of his soul.

Barberi shaded his eyes from the glare and carefully set the cake on the table.

"I am Cardinal Barberi."

"And who are you inside?" Judd asked.

Barberi didn't answer. He blinked and blinked in petrified awe while his spindly legs quivered.

"Some people seek something to believe in," Judd said. "Others are sightseers. Which are you, a seeker or a sightseer?"

"I am a servant of the living God."

"A servant." Judd thought a moment. "And does your living God have a God to serve and worship?"

"I do not understand. God is the one and only God."

"I see. And does your God want?"

"Want what?"

Judd spoke slower. "No, my question is, does your God want? Does your God desire?"

"No. God is omnipotent, omniscient, and omnipresent."

"Then there's neither want nor no want, is there?" Judd said. "Everything to be, nothing to seek."

The Cardinal began to perspire. "May I take off my coat?"

Judd nodded. Barberi forgot about the coat, too busy sorting out Judd's words.

"And does your living God change?" Judd asked.

"Change?"

"Yes. Does your God *change*?"

Barberi's eyebrows pinched. "No, he's eternal, he's …"

Judd stood.

Taking in the Sun Man's six-foot-seven inch height, Barberi's heart flared. He never imagined seeing such a being of light.

Shouts and pounding started up again.

Arnie came into the kitchen. "Time to go."

"I'm ready," Judd said.

"Go? I just arrived," Barberi said. "Oh, please stay," he pleaded and followed them out the back door.

Tomás waved for the police car that blocked the alley to move.

Judd got into Arnie's truck, covered himself in a packing blanket, and sunk low in the seat as they wheeled away.

Barberi took off his cap and held it to his chest.

"Are you a disciple of his?"

"No," Tomás said. "I'm the cook."

Arnie's pickup turned the corner and disappeared.

The cardinal noticed steam rising off the footprints Judd left in the snow.

"Do you know the writer, Homero Aridjis?" Tomás asked.

"I do not," Barberi said.

"Homero wrote: 'Once he has met up with himself, a man may be the angel he has sought throughout the world.'"

The crowd swarmed Barberi as he came out the front door. His driver tried to push them back.

"What did he tell you?" one called out.

Barberi didn't answer. The Sun Man's question, "Does your God change?" lingered in his mind.

"Is he the incarnate?" another hollered.

The cardinal told the driver to get his luggage. "And collect the cake from the kitchen."

People pushed in close. Barberi raised a palm. Expectant, they shut their mouths.

"Is there a bed and breakfast in town?"

# 65

# The Basilica

To Oakley's surprise, the colossal building in Minneapolis he thought was the State Capitol because of its huge dome, turned out to be the Basilica of Saint Mary. It didn't change the bench he chose to sleep on during the day, isolated from public eyes. It was also only a few blocks from a soup kitchen.

One afternoon he woke to the grunt of a side door. A man in coveralls stepped out of the church and lit a cigarette. He noticed Oakley, stubbed out the cigarette and went back inside. A minute later, a different man came out. Oakley noticed a shiny golden crucifix hanging outside his overcoat. The man waved a kind hand, strolled over, and asked how Oakley kept from freezing.

"I run hot."

"So it is."

The man introduced himself as Father Lawson Hall and invited Oakley inside.

The nave looked like a hollowed-out marble mountain. Its sky-high ceiling, majestic arches, and stained glass made Oakley feel small, yet elevated by the immensity. There were sculptures of biblical figures and foreign letters engraved in slabs of white stone.

Passing rows and rows of pews, Oakley remarked, "Wow, you could sleep a lot of homeless here."

"Helping to end homelessness is one of our primary missions," the priest said. "You saw the bronze Homeless Jesus bench out front?"

Oakley shook his head and turned down a side aisle.

"Must be buried under snow. I couldn't help thinking of it when I saw you on that bench in the lunch park."

Oakley walked on, Father Hall at his shoulder. He saw the smoker, a custodian, standing on a ladder dusting a polished stone structure that looked like a mini mausoleum.

"It's a confessional," the priest explained. "We believe in absolving sins through confession."

Yeah-yeah, Oakley knew about that. "Do you do exorcisms?" He opened a side door. The phone booth-sized room had been sprayed with a strong disinfectant. "Yow," Oakley wagged a hand past his nose. "That last sin musta stunk to high heaven."

The priest smiled. But overhearing it, the custodian squinched his nose like he smelled a turd. Oakley felt the man's derision and moved on to the next booth, and a third.

"How many do you do?" Oakley asked.

"Many."

"You must hear some horror stories."

"If left unspoken, sins fester."

Oakley watched the custodian climb down the ladder, still glaring at him.

"How about yourself?" Father Hall asked. "Do you carry any guilt or shame you'd like to unburden?"

"Huh?"

"Anything you want to get off your chest?"
Do I ever. "Don't I have to be Catholic?"
"There are exceptions."
"And everything I say in there stays private?"
"Your mouth to God's ears."
Oakley stepped into the confessional and sat.
"Buckle up, God."

# 66

# Now This

Annoyed by Victor King's relentless hounding, Inman Hayes stopped taking his calls. But Victor's latest text message alerted him to a sensational story coming out of Minnesota.

Hayes opened the safe in his Pentagon office and pulled out the box labeled *Operation Mind Control.* He dumped the contents on his walnut desk, pushed aside Ezra Katz's materials, and found a sleeve of photos in the Spitball Committee folder.

There it was, a drone shot of Judd Russell in the Jolleys' driveway with something white tucked in his coat. Even though the video on Hayes's computer looked like a walking lightbulb, the name and description had to be the man he had terminated.

"He's *alive?*" Hayes reached for the Soviet F-1 hand grenade on his desk. A souvenir he brought back from a kill zone during a paramilitary operation when he was twenty-four. The dud became such a lucky charm he had it gold-plated.

"No-no, they swore they took him out!"

Hayes thought he was nearing the finish line. Now this.

As he mulled it over, his mind began to unravel. He heard what sounded like roaches scurrying and chattering in the walls.

"Shut up!" he barked. He squeezed and unsqueezed the grenade like a stress ball. Report papers and photographs lifted off his desk by invisible strings. Some slapped his face. He swatted back at them.

"Stop that!"

The paneled walls bulged. Three sets of enormous eyes emerged—his tribunal of hooded Judges.

"All right, all right, my task force failed," Hayes acknowledged. "Who'd think Mantz would go berserk. The man's got a plate in his head. He's fucking Achilles! But I demolished their lab, didn't I? *And* their home for Christ's sake! I burned down the hangar with all their shit. Got one dead on the Colorado River. All that's left is to flush out the other brat, incinerate the files, and the doing is done. So don't start in on me!"

Someone knocked on his door.

The roaches stopped scratching. The fluttering papers gathered and returned where they lay in piles on his desk. The owl eyes of the tribunal closed their lids as they receded into the wood.

"Not now!" Hayes shouted at the door. He set the photo of Judd next to the Sun Man's image on his computer. "Looks like they activated the dude's pleroma or something." He brought the photo up to his eyes. "The fuck I gotta do, take you out face-to-face?"

# 67
# Chief's Gone Bonk

Confined to Arnie's place, Judd felt like an outcast. He wondered if he could create a dimmer switch to soften the brightness of his aura. That way he wouldn't appear from another galaxy. After all, he adapted to the severe changes in his perception. He adjusted his vision for the energy cords. He released millions and millions of words his ears had heard. He made it out of the snake and survived a brutal torture. He could even slow the speed of his projections under Marsha's hypnosis.

What's more painful? To be a freakish spectacle in the eyes of the world, or incarcerated in a solid, lightless body?

Word spread that Judd no longer washed dishes at the café, to the relief of many townsfolk. Some figured things would return to normal.

Buck and Arnie told everyone Judd's light went away.

"It's a rare genetic condition called Saint Elmo's Fever," Arnie said. "Passed as surprisingly fast as it showed up."

A few took it as a loss.

"Will there be a relapse?" Harvey Clyster asked.

"I've got jumper cables I can clip to his ears," Lars suggested.

Others felt relieved. "Who wants to be around that?" Joe Pye said. "Makes us all look dull as pigeons."

Another quipped, "Musta been a case of premature illumination."

"So now will you get rid of that godless shrine?" Henna Pino quacked.

Stray Juddites still gathered outside the café hoping to see the Sun Man.

Instead, what they saw was a waxy, black, Apache helicopter circle the town. Inside, Inman Hayes sat across from two snipers he persuaded out of retirement. They wore unassuming civilian winterwear, their eyes fixed on Hayes. Something was not right with the Chief. He was spouting long-buried secrets, names and sites of black ops. His face distorted, as if pinched in a vice.

"What's got into him?" the bearded sniper murmured.

"Hell if I know," the other said.

"Were you there when we firebombed that godforsaken village in Yemen?" Hayes murmured.

The snipers glanced at each other. They knew Hayes spoke in spirals, fuzzying his real motives. But he'd never call out past exploits—classified ones at that. Yet secrets come with expiration dates. The ones he concealed in the name of the flag were long past due.

"What a waste. Never should've gone down." Hayes thumbed his grenade. "They were *innocents!*"

The folks outside the café watched the chopper descend. One looked up with dread. "What now?" Another yelled, "It could be *him!*"

Among the crowd stood Cardinal Barberi. He'd been in town two nights, sleeping in Lars Lundeen's Airstream trailer. He didn't believe the talk that Judd's light came from an illness. Though he didn't know where they hid him, he made a daily pilgrimage to the café in case he returned.

"We're here," the pilot informed the men.

"Nicaragua?" Inman fisted his grenade.

"What's the matter, sir?" The bearded sniper stuffed the photo of their target, Judd Russell, in his coat pocket.

"Were you on that mission?" Hayes asked.

Landing at the intersection of Main and Maple Streets, the helicopter whipped a cyclone of snow. The pilot cut the engine. When the rotor blades came to rest, onlookers moved in.

"Or was it that unsanctioned one, Operation Red Tide?" The door slid open. Hayes didn't budge. He slouched, lips pursed, shaking his head. A tear welled up. "What I done?"

"Chief? Hey? Good to the last op, right?"

"What did I …" The gold grenade slipped from his hand and plunked on the floor. The snipers jumped and watched it roll around.

"The fuck," the bearded one grunted.

The other snapped his fingers in Hayes's face.

"Hey. We doing this?"

Hayes moaned. He undid his safety harness, stood wobbly, and looked out at the town. Instead of actual people, he saw bodies in flames. He saw bloated dead floating in rainy gullies. He saw innocent women and children blown apart.

"No! Oh, god no …" He collapsed to his knees and yelled at the crowd. "I'm sooo sorry!"

"What the hell's happening!" the pilot hollered back.

"Chief's gone bonk!"

Hayes covered his eyes. He could not stop sniffling and wailing. "Please forgibee!"

The people gaped. "You seeing what I'm seeing?" a Juddite asked.

Although Cardinal Barberi had spoken to Hayes on the phone, he didn't connect him to this broken man.

"Chief, hey, come on, get up!" the bearded sniper demanded.

"This is embarrassing," the other said under his breath.

"What do we do?"

"Call it in."

"Call in to who? He's *the fucking who!*"

Hayes clutched his chest. "No, no more *horribles!* Stop showing me that!" His head tilted forward as if wilting to gravity. Then he toppled down to the street and lay motionless on his back, arms and legs splayed out. A snow angel at dead stop.

The snipers clambered out of the helicopter. They hefted the chief's slack body back inside. His eyeballs were white, as if staring at his brain.

"Check his pulse."

"Not gettin' nothin.'"

The bearded sniper shouted at the pilot, "Go! Go!"

"No, wait! Their phones!" The other man hopped out. He stepped toward the gathering, palms up, a sudden pleasant expression on his face.

"It's all right everybody. We're paramilitary doing a remote training exercise."

Barberi asked, "Is that man all right?"

"He's fine. An actor. Yeah, ya' see this was an act. How'd he do? Was he … convincing?"

"Convincing?" said a Juddite. "He spatchcocked!"

"For those who snapped photos," the sniper said, "if you don't mind, I'd like to have a look. See if you got any keepers."

Three people handed over cellphones.

"Why here?" one asked.

The sniper ignored the question. The engine wound up.

"Thanks." He pocketed the phones and hustled back to the helicopter.

"What a colossal disaster!" the pilot spat.

"Hey!" A man in a striped apron and rubber gloves ran at the chopper as the door slammed shut. "You took my phone, asshole!"

People backed away, shielding their eyes from the pelting snow spun by the blades.

If Roslyn had seen Hayes's meltdown, she'd call it another example of the Defrost Effect.

# 68

# The Future Has Not Been Written

Oakley jolted upright on the park bench, his antenna blaring an alarm. He rubbed his eyes.

Somebody's coming.

He looked about. No one in sight. The sky a ceiling of low clouds. Midafternoon, he figured by the light. He stood and stretched his legs.

Minutes later a police cruiser pulled up in front of the Basilica.

Someone identified me. Someone *talked*.

Up until then the bench felt so safe he didn't consider devising an escape plan. When another black-and-white appeared with roof lights flashing, Oakley set off, trailing a square of cardboard to cover his tracks in the snow. He ran behind the Basilica and climbed into the second of two dumpsters. It was empty but the smell of fermented garbage made his stomach pretzel. He squatted in a corner and listened in the dark. The hollow metal shell was so silent, he thought the drumbeat of his heart was the stomp of boots.

Time passed. His fear gave way to anger.

Who betrayed me? Had to be the priest. But he acted like he believed my story. Said he would "look into the matter." No! It's that smoker, the custodian, that soat. Shit. They're going to kill me, or worse.

A voice inside him responded, "Don't you have some *say*?" It sounded older than him.

"Not with a bull's eye on my back."

"There is no destiny. The future has not been written. You still have choices."

What choices? I can either hide out, homeless, give blood at the Plasma Center, or turn myself in and get killed so horribly I'll be in pain long after I die.

"Do they want you, or do they want what you know?"

They want what Chester and I know. And what we stashed in Arnie's barn.

"What would they do if it no longer exists?"

Good question. They'd still kill us. Wait, no, that's it! Oakley punched the air. I'll destroy everything and *film it!* Give them nothing to use! Yes! I'll explain who I am, what Chester and I discovered, how we've been framed, hunted as dangerous criminals. I'll sledgehammer the instruments on camera and post the video.

"How do you get to the barn?"

I'll find those street outreach people, borrow their phone, and call my mom or Arnie to come get me.

"The Feds could be tracking them."

Okay, then … then I'll walk. It's like, what, twenty miles? If I leave tonight, I can be there by morning.

Oakley listened for the police. He cracked the lid of the dumpster and peered out. Dead quiet. Light snow falling. He could still sense the force field of a threat but didn't want to wait a second longer. He had a plan. As he clambered out of the dumpster the lid slipped from his hand and shut with a loud bang.

The police rushed toward the noise. They saw Oakley and gave chase.

Oakley didn't go far before twisting his ankle. He hobbled a few steps and held up, his arms raised in surrender. Two cops charged him. They pounded his head and torso with riot sticks. A third stood watch.

Father Hall noticed police cars and went outside. The bench where Oakley slept was empty. He heard welps and thrashing in the parking lot. Seeing the assault, he pleaded for the police to stop.

"He's a terrorist!" one yelled.

Another raised his hand. "Step away, Father!"

"No, I will *not!*" He wedged between them, waving his arms. "That's enough, for God's sake!"

He knelt down and covered Oakley. Using his body as a shield, he took several hits.

The cops backed off.

Oakley lay like a broken doll, his face a dripping, red mop.

"He resisted arrest," a cop said.

Father Hall glared at him and groaned, "Don't just stand there, call an ambulance!"

# 69

## Victor's Lost It

After countless unanswered calls to Inman Hayes, Victor King tried phoning others in the Defense Department to reach the man. Recorded voices handed him over to other recorded voices numerous times before a live person told him Hayes was gone.

"Like gone out …?"

"Like dead and gone."

The DOD person could not find anything resembling a pending contract with him or Neurokey.

*The shithead played me! Been playing me all along!*

Victor counted on a Niagara of cash. He not only lost his funding from the Pentagon, he lost his dream of the Jolley twins turning his lab into "Godhead Headquarters." And he doubted Kira could seduce this Sun Man into donating his brain to science.

"Tell me you found something!" Victor yelled at the lab techs. He stumbled across the shiny floor, taking stiff pulls from a bottle of Grey Goose. "It's in there!" He finger-poked the skull of a scientist. "Find it!"

"We're looking, Mr. King."

"Well look *again* goddammit! If hick teenagers can find it, why the hell can't you? I'll tell you why, because your head's up your flabby ass!"

Victor's face flared strawberry red. He set the bottle down and lifted a Landau Imager off a tech's desk.

"Do you know how much this $60,000 scope costs? Answer me, you dolt!" He held it over his head and slammed it to the floor. A broken shard shot back and nicked his forehead. Victor didn't notice. He took another slug of vodka and moved to the next station.

"Don't throw that face at me!" he shouted at a cowering assistant. A seam of blood slid down his cheek. "Stupid, stupid idiots!" He set the bottle down and picked up a stool. "You're as rotten as the government!"

He hoisted the stool to his shoulder and pitched it like a shotput. People ducked. The glass door of a cabinet exploded. He reached for another stool, heaved it at a touch-screen Zylon monitor and roared, "Haaayes! You maggot mouth!"

Hunkered under a table, an assistant called security in a whisper, "Main Lab and hurry! It's Mr. King! Yes, Victor. Come right now! He's lost it!"

Victor's jealous rage began years back when Foster Jolley found fame. Later, it swelled to a boil when Ezra declared the Godhead Spot within reach. All it took was Hayes's subterfuge to blow the lid.

"No!" a technician howled. "Not the Ertz Pulser!"

Victor stared at the machine. Wiped blood dripping down his nose. Then snatched the technician by the collar.

"And why not?"

"Because ..."

Victor's eyes grew wide. "Wait, wait ... you found it? You *found* it didn't you?"

The tech shook his head. "No sir."

"Don't lie to me!"

"No, but ..."

"But you're close, right!"

Everyone sprinted for the door.

"Where the hell you going!" Victor drained the bottle, pitched it, and struck a deserter in the back.

Burman, the beefy security guard, hulked in.

"Stop them!" Victor commanded.

"Enough, Mr. King. That's enough!" Burman squared off.

"Out of my way!" Victor swung feebly at the big man.

"Really? You going there?" Burman came back with a right hook that shattered Victor's nose. He teetered to the floor.

"Done?" Burman loomed over him, rubbing his knuckles.

Victor held his broken nose with both hands. "The meaning of life," he burbled as three figures appeared. They cinched straps around his torso and hauled him away. "What are you doing? We're this close to the meaning of *life!* Do you know what that means? 'Cuz if you don't know what that means, then you don't know what it means! You know what I mean?"

# 70

# Dzzoyarzuff

Marsha took the call. She and Flannery sped to Methodist Hospital. Oakley, battered and barely alive, was admitted the previous evening.

The nurse, about to sign them in, was called away. She returned, biting her lip.

"Sorry. It's been a turbulent week of ups and downs. And today looks no different."

Marsha had to ask. "Have there been any abnormal displays of extreme emotion or behavior?"

"Abnormal?" The nurse gave Marsha a 'how'd you know' look. "Don't get me started," she said and led them to the ICU wing. "Let's see, there's the doctor who was relieved from open heart surgery because he couldn't stop bawling into the patient's chest cavity. And the girl who came out of anesthesia singing *Nessun Dorma*. Not to mention the patient who, after hearing her prognosis, speared an intern with an IV stand."

Oakley lay semiconscious and sedated. The doctors had just brought him out of a twelve-hour, medically-induced coma to prevent brain swelling. His puffy blue-black face was barely recognizable. His knobby right eye looked like he was sprouting a second head. Unseen were fractured ribs and missing teeth.

Sensing a presence, Oakley's left eyelid lifted a crack. He saw his mother standing over him. He tried to speak but only uttered a skuzz sound. Marsha set a hand on his shoulder.

"It's okay," she said. "Try not to talk. I'll be right back." She stepped out of the room and shouted, "Who the hell did this!? Who brought him in!?"

"Where'd the priest go?" The nurse looked down the corridor. "Oh, there he is."

A middle-aged man shuffled toward them on crutches, his head bandaged.

"If not for him, your son would be in the morgue," the nurse said.

Father Lawson Hall introduced himself.

"You brought my son in?"

"You must be Marsha, his mother." As the nurse went to find the doctor, Father Hall explained, "I don't know what rage and darkness police encounter every day. But it looked like they took it all out on your son."

"They couldn't simply *arrest* him? I want names and badge numbers. I want a formal inquest! It's 2:00 p.m. Why did it take so long to reach me?"

"The police confiscated his wallet," Hall said. "I submitted an eyewitness account. They questioned me for hours. I called a lawyer, a member of the congregation. She condemned their excessive brutality. Still, they didn't release Oakley's name until late this morning."

Flannery came over. "Mom, he looks real bad. Can I go in and see him, please?"

"All right. Keep your hands behind your back and don't touch anything."

"I'm not four!"

Marsha and Father Hall looked on through the window.

"Your son confessed everything," he said. "And, if needed for his defense, I will share it. But I don't believe the authorities will place him in custody after all this. They'd face a public relations nightmare of legal hurdles and media backlash."

He may be right, Marsha thought. No Federal Marshals or police guarded the room. Not that Oakley was going anywhere.

"He's worried about his brother," Father Hall said. "They set up a way to communicate online. There's been no response."

Flannery looked at the monitors that bleeped and scribbled jagged patterns. She leaned over the edge of the bed.

"Hey. They put you in a coma? What was that like?"

Oakley gave his sister a crooked smile.

"You should see Judd. He turned into a lamp."

Marsha came in, scooted a chair next to the bed. She told Oakley about the agreement with Neurokey. How it required his approval and, presumably, signing it would end the manhunt. He and Chester would have high-paying jobs at a large laboratory with their alleged crimes expunged. However, to make that happen, they needed to relinquish their research and equipment.

Marsha didn't know Chief Hayes was dead, that Victor King was in a mental facility, and that Chester had been murdered.

"Even if you reject the offer, it would be good for us to know where it is."

Oakley shook his head and sputtered, "Dzzoyarzuff."

Marsha leaned closer. "Say again?"

Oakley wheezed. "Dzz ... oy ...ar ... zuff."

"Flan, can I borrow your tablet?" Marsha propped it on the bed next to Oakley's good hand and whispered, "A military unit swept the town. They searched everywhere. You hid it quite well."

He typed: DESTROY IT

"Really?"

Oakley drew in a labored breath, winced and nodded.

"Where is it?"

Oakley punched the letter keys: ARNIE BARN

A phantom figure in the corner of the room read the words on the tablet.

Marsha nodded, "Okay …"

"Mom?"

"Not now, Flan."

Oakley typed: JUDD?

"You lit up his crown and …"

"MOM!" Flannery shouted.

# 71

# One Little Wrinkle

Theroux blinked hard as he returned from bi-locating Oakley in his hospital room. He looked out the aircraft cabin, reorienting himself. The plane sat parked at Flying Cloud Airport, eighteen miles east of Marigold. After some deep breaths, he jotted: ARNIE BARN on a notepad.

His decision to fly to Minnesota came minutes after seeing Kira and Victor King at their Virginia lab wildly excited about a "Sun Man." The man looked to be Judd Russell, the naked guy he saw being loaded into a van. How can it be the same man? Surely, he died.

To prove it, Theroux attempted to bi-locate Judd and encountered nothing but dense fog.

So who's this Sun Man? And why would Oakley's mother and daughter speak his name like he's alive? Is there a second Judd Russell?

"Drop it!" He blurted out loud. "Forget about the dead man and seize the lab equipment!"

*ARNIE BARN.*

After some Googling, and a few phone calls, Theroux brought up an aerial of Arnie Arneson's address. The property was on a lake—with a barn!

"We need a lighter plane," he told Jurgens, his pilot, "to land on a frozen lake. See if you can rent one."

All right, now let's try bi-locating again to make sure, he told himself. If it's the last one you ever do, you need to know who this Sun Man really is.

Theroux stilled his mind and set his attention on Judd Russell's vibratory signature. After a flurry of motion, he saw the same foggy gray void as before. He shifted his attention to the big house on Lake of the Isles. A couple in matching Egyptian cotton bathrobes sat at the granite kitchen island munching flaky croissants and sipping espresso. He dashed room to room. No Judd Russell.

If he's alive, why can't I find him?

Theroux uncapped his vial of salve to spread on his collarbone where the skin had ruptured. The vial was empty.

"Shit!" He pounded the seat. Without the gel the lesion will welt.

Okay, I'll have to deal with it.

"Got a Cessna rental, master," Jurgens said.

"Let's fly," Theroux said.

Arnie's barn. Their instruments will soon be mine!

Just one little wrinkle—that girl in the hospital saw me.

# 72

# Like Jesus Only Dark

It was unlike Flannery to see spirits, and what she saw terrified her. Marsha took her daughter's hand as they left the hospital. The change had come. You'd think it would've happened when her father vanished, or their home bombed, or seeing her brother's battered face. Surely those were traumatic. But it took seeing a ghost at Oakley's bedside to pop the girl's sunny balloon.

Marsha already missed the innocent, bubbly child. Still, it was time Flannery knew evil forces were at work in the world.

"It's going to be okay, sweetheart. Now tell me again what you saw."

"He looked kind of like Jesus, only dark. He had a long face, black hair, and a beard. And his eyes ..."

"His eyes?"

"Scary, really scary mom."

Only one person came to mind—The The. Marsha went cold at the thought of him spying on them. Then it hit her. He's coming!

"We need to get hold of Arnie."

Flannery found Arnie's number on her mom's phone and called.

"Not answering," she said.

"Okay, then call Buck. Tell him get out to Arnie's farm now!"

# 73

## It's Demonstrative

Lars Lundeen stood behind the cash register at his Farm and Feed Gas Mart on the phone with Buck.

"It's your wife," Lars said.

"What about her?"

"You better come quick."

Buck knew something was brewing with Grace that morning at breakfast. She wouldn't stop yapping. He told her to take a yap nap, but that only infuriated her. As he pulled up to the store, he got another call.

"Hi Buck, it's Flannery."

"Hey kid. Can't talk now ... What? ... Arnie's? ... Okay, I'll get out there soon as I can."

Grace stood outside the Farm and Feed Gas Mart, her boots doused with gasoline from the ethanol pump. She was ranting with a ratchety throat, "Nobody's listening!"

"What's going on, honey?"

For Buck, high drama had become an everyday occurrence. Somebody in the township was either snapping or bubbling with gleeful generosity. Joe Pye up and quit his job as a die cutter in Shakopee to teach kids about rocks. His wife threw a cast iron skillet at him. When Bob Zeebart's chickens stopped laying, he sharpened his machete and headed for the coop.

Buck refused to believe Roslyn's "defrost" theory that Judd Russell was a beacon that triggered extreme behavior, positive and negative. Still, he couldn't deny something was happening, and now Grace, raving.

"I told you this morning, but you wouldn't listen," she said. "I was in the backyard and the land spoke to me. It's been talking all this time. Only now I'm hearing it."

"The land?"

"Yes, the land! Can't you hear it crying?"

"No. Why would it be crying, dear?"

"Cause it's hurtin', that's why!" She shook back tears. "It's hurtin' real bad."

Seeing a box of matches in Grace's other hand, Buck tensed up. He'd dealt with his share of panicky people while wearing a badge, but nothing rivaled the shock of seeing his wife in such hysteria. Customers who gathered to watch intensified his stress.

Although Lars shut off the gas pump, Grace still held the nozzle and nervously clicked the handle. Only dribbles came out.

"All the while it's been talking and I wasn't listening," she said. "Like my hearing was constipated. You understand?"

"I guess. But honey …"

"Then *start listening!*"

"I hear ya, I hear ya."

"Not me, dammit, the land! It's whimpering like a pound dog."

Grace dropped the hand pump but remained standing in the puddle of gas. She rattled the box of matches like maracas.

Buck inched toward her. "Gracie please, for God's sake get a grip. Hand me those matches."

"Listen people," she said. "The natives know this, er, knew this. Their ears were tuned to the land. We come along, stack buildings on it. Pour concrete all over." Grace stomped her boots. "Pave it so hard it can't breathe. Well, I say to you, nature will have its day. This land shall heave and rise."

"And setting yourself on fire is gonna change that?"

"It's demonstrative, Buck." She hurled the match box at him. "How else can I call attention to the land's agony?" She turned to those assembled. "This land is as much our body as our body is our body. If we don't start listening, we're lost. We're just goin' round numb as cold cuts."

# 74

# To Be in His Presence

Roslyn came out of the café. As she set a box of food in the back of Judd's car, her phone chimed.

"Roslyn, it's Flannery. Mom wants to talk to you ... Oakley? Not so good. They put him in a coma. Anyway, here's mom."

"We could use your help," Marsha said. "We left the hospital and can't reach Arnie. Could you go out there and search the barn for the boys' equipment? I need you to hide it somewhere else temporarily. We'll be there in half an hour. I'll explain then."

Roslyn wondered why Marsha sounded so desperate. But given the Defrost Effect, everything felt about to explode. It did for her that morning. She raged out of bed with vengeful feelings for her parents. She rarely gave them any thought since they left her on her own. Too busy scrapping out a life. But this time the scar tissue had peeled back. The hurt of abandonment was so overpowering she wanted to punish them, track them both down and inflict permanent bodily damage.

Would that take the wound away?

Looking inward, Roslyn came upon her fourteen-year-old self huddled in a corner. The girl was weighed down with guilt for what she must have done to cause her parents to leave her. Roslyn embraced her younger self. No, she wasn't ready to forgive them, but she understood how some people lack the caring to raise a child.

I can be the mother I didn't have.

She filled another box with bread, eggs, and cheese. Right outside the back door of the café a woman stood.

"Oh!" Roslyn jumped.

"Sorry, didn't mean to frighten you." Kira King wore a white, fur-collared winter coat and blond leathers. "I'm looking for Marsha Jolley. Do you know where I can find her?"

"Not here."

"My name is Kira. I flew in to meet Marsha about an arrangement with her sons. I'm with a large scientific laboratory. We study brains." Kira handed Roslyn a black business card with her name emblazoned in gold.

Something about the woman's vibes unnerved Roslyn. That and the weed killer perfume she oozed.

"Excuse me. I'm ..." She set the box of food in Judd's car.

"I also came to see Judd Russell. And you're Rose-Lynn, his girlfriend, am I right?"

Roslyn stiffened.

"I asked around," Kira said. She gestured to Roslyn's face, "You know, a little lip gloss, say a raspberry mist, and some eye shadow would elevate your—

Roslyn brushed past her toward the café.

"Oh, good let's do go inside. My feet are fur-reezing." Kira followed only to see Roslyn lock the door and head back to the car.

"I know Judd," Kira said. "He was at our exhibition booth in DC. And it's urgent I meet with him. His EEG results were unprecedented."

That almost made sense, Roslyn thought as she climbed behind the wheel. "Sorry, I'm in a hurry."

"Looks like you're leaving town, which I totally get. What a horrid place to be."

"Then leave." Roslyn slammed the door, started the engine. As she drove down the alley she called Marsha. Flannery answered, put it on speaker.

"Do you know a woman named Kira King?"

"Why?"

"She's here. Wants to see you. Something about an arrangement."

"She's there at the café?"

"And wants to see Judd."

"Don't let her. I don't trust that woman," Marsha said.

"Oh great, I think she's following me."

"Oh … can you lose her?"

"Maybe." Roslyn closed the call, stopped at the end of the alley. She grabbed an egg carton from the back seat and hopped from the car.

Kira pulled up behind. She thrust her rental in park and stepped out.

Roslyn opened the cardboard cover and tossed an egg. Surprised, Kira crouched behind the door to shield herself. But Roslyn wasn't trying to hit her. Egg after free-range egg splattered the windshield. Broken shells and yellow yolks slithered down the glass and froze.

Kira raised her middle finger and yelled, "You will die!"

"All do at some point," Roslyn murmured to herself, tossed the empty carton in the SUV and veered onto the road out of town.

Attempting to climb back in her car, Kira slipped and fell flat on the gravel, scraping her chin.

"Shit!"

Seeing her tumble, a man came over. "May I help you up?" he said.

He looked like a buffalo, dressed in a big, black fur coat, head covered in a balaclava. All she could see were two big brown eyes.

"Yes," she said.

Cardinal Barberi took the fallen woman's arm.

"Yuck!" Kira slapped dirty snow off her coat. "That woman—she attacked me. Look at my car!"

Barberi saw the marbled smear of frozen eggs on the windshield.

"Oh, that is …"

"A fucking mess," Kira said. "I can't see a damn thing."

"I don't know cars, but I saw someone yesterday use a credit card to scrape ice off the glass," Barberi said.

Kira reached into the rental, took out her purse, and handed the stranger an American Express card. "Do you mind?"

Barberi poked the card at the glass. "Not working," he said. "This may take some time."

"Oh, what am I thinking, I can turn on the defrost." Kira climbed into the driver's seat.

"Yes, the defroster," he agreed.

Kira lowered the window. "I'm Kira. Kira King."

"Cardinal Alfio Barberi. It is a pleasure to meet you."

Cardinal, right, another crazy local, she thought. Okay. Play the game. He may know Judd Russell's whereabouts.

Then it struck her—Barberi. The name. The man's Italian accent.

"You wouldn't happen to be the same Cardinal Barberi who visited our laboratory in Virginia? My father is Victor King."

"Victor King. Yes. What a coincidence. How is the man?"

Kira wouldn't reveal that her father was strapped to a bed and medicated to the skies in a mental facility. She dodged the question and asked, "Why are you here of all places?"

"To be in his presence."

# 75
# The Suck Assassin

As Judd hand-fed cardinals and chickadees at Arnie's place, he heard the drone of a small aircraft.

A shadow was coming. When the engine noise drew near, the birds flew off.

Arnie was in the house, installing baseboard with a nail gun. He didn't hear the plane. The air compressor drowned out the sound.

Back in the barn, Judd cleared scraps of wood off the worktable. The plan was to clean up odds and ends from the remodel before heading north with Roslyn that afternoon.

The small-engine Cessna landed on the frozen lake. It skirted the fishing shacks and pulled up next to the dock. The pilot shut off the engine. Theroux stepped out and scanned the property. The swelling lesion on his collarbone felt like a riot of army ants. Suffer it, he told himself. Scratching will make it spread and infect.

Approaching the weathered red barn, Theroux noticed a light inside. He peered through its partially open doors, saw Judd's radiance and stopped still, gaping at the luminous figure.

My God. It *is* Judd Russell. No wonder I couldn't bi-locate him. His vibratory rate jacked!

Judd noticed a silhouette backlit by the afternoon sun.

Theroux entered the barn. His long face and lean body, tree-trunked by a wool overcoat, became more distinct with each step.

"I knew you'd find me at some point," Judd's deep voice reverberated. "What you want is not here."

"Really." How strange, Theroux thought. This man could be out in the world, amassing countless followers, yet here he is in the middle of nowhere with a tool belt strapped on his waist.

"You want a conduit to the Godhead. This is not that. And it's not something you can take. Believe me, I know all about stealing."

Theroux crossed the plank floor partway and held up, mesmerized by the glossy rose, coral pink, and turquoise beads bubbling up and down Judd's aura like ethereal circuitry. Twelve starbright beams of light shot from the crown of Judd's head.

"Remarkable," Theroux said. "And so unfair. You, of all people, are not *worthy*! Have you traveled to the ends of the Earth, apprenticed with ascended masters? No. I have whirled with Dervishes. I have endured death-defying shamanic initiations. I have fire-walked with Enzo of Ibarra …"

"Are there rules?" Judd asked. "Spiritual boxes you check off to become who you already are? This is merely who I am in the greater light of my soul. My home soul. Where is yours?"

"*Mine …?*"

Theroux glanced at the piles of lumber and drywall, a rack of garden tools, a loop of rope, looking for a weapon.

Be wary. Judd studied the man.

"As long as you're driven to possess and control, the light of your home soul will remain out of reach."

"Is that so?" Theroux skimmed his palm across a stack of two-by-fours.

"Yes. You'll never embody your home soul if you intend to use it for power."

"Well if I can't have it …" Swiftly, Theroux slid a two-by-four stud off the top of the stack and rammed the end into Judd's solar plexus. He collapsed, a punctured balloon, gasping for breath. Theroux chucked the board. "… then I'll drain it out of you!"

He shed his gloves and seized Judd's head. "Light's out, Sun Man," he spat, as energy cords sprung from his hands and latched onto Judd's crown.

"Hey!" Arnie ran into the barn. He dove at the stranger and tried to wrestle him away.

"Get off me!" Theroux twisted, unable to shake the burly man.

Arnie dug his fingernails into the stranger's neck and unknowingly tore open the raised welt.

Electrified, Theroux wailed. He pulled the claw hammer out of Judd's tool belt, wheeled 'round and bashed Arnie between the eyes. Rocked by the blow, Arnie shuddered for a moment, lost his legs, and hit the barn floor with a heavy thud. Blood and brain fluid leaked out his punctured skull.

"That didn't have to happen!" Theroux stood rickety, panting. "I am not a violent man. The guy grabbed me!" He felt the inflamed lesion on his neck, took a whiff of the fetid pus on his fingertips.

Judd scrabbled on his knees to Arnie's body.

"Oh, God, no!" He moaned at the sight of Arnie's vacant eyes.

"Shit!" Theroux unclicked a phone from his belt and called his pilot. "I'm in the barn, hurry."

"He's gone." Judd said.

"You're coming with me." Theroux booted Judd hard in the groin.

Judd lay balled up on the floor, his brilliance dimming by the second.

Theroux removed a nylon rope from a hook on the wall and tied Judd's wrists together.

"Before we go, you need to tell me where the Jolley boys stashed their equipment."

Judd couldn't speak. Theroux pulled the rope taut. Judd resisted.

"Get up!" Theroux whacked him across the face with the knotted end.

The pilot stood in the doorway fixed on the man lying dead on the floor.

"It was an accident! Never mind him!" Theroux shouted, picking up the hammer. "This one comes with us. Go search for lab instruments. They're hidden somewhere."

Theroux tugged Judd out of the barn. After a few feet, Judd flopped to the snowy ground. Having to drag a dead weight infuriated Theroux. He whipped Judd's arched back again and again.

"Get up now! *Now!*" he howled so loud he didn't hear tires crunch on the driveway.

Roslyn stomped the brakes and jumped out of the car.

"What the hell are you doing!"

The The threw her an exasperated glare.

Roslyn recognized the man from Judd's projection in the café—the suck assassin.

"Let him go!"

Judd was on his knees. His mind in cobwebs. Blood dribbled out his nostrils. His once glorious aura flickered like a guttering candle.

"Judd?" Roslyn turned to Theroux. "What did you do to him!" She noticed the plane parked at the dock and dashed to block Theroux's path.

"Back off!" He waved the hammer at her.

"Arnie!" Roslyn shouted. She reached for her phone only to realize she'd left it in the car.

"False prophets must be crushed!"

"Stop right there!" Roslyn pumped her hands. "I know who you are. If you let him go there won't be any criminal charges, I swear. Just drop the rope and go. Okay? Okay?"

"No-kay."

"Arnie!"

"Get your ass out of my way!"

"Judd, get up!"

The The kept coming, pulling Judd like a stubborn mule through ankle-deep snow.

"Listen," Roslyn backpeddled. "I know what's going on. It's the Defrost Effect."

"The what?"

They passed the corner of the barn.

"You're conflicted, right? You, uh, you're being compelled to do things you normally ..."

"I am not a violent man, but if you don't step the fuck aside ...!"

"I can't let you take him."

"Then I can't let you *live*." He threatened her again with a swat of the hammer in the air.

No time to think, Roslyn looked for something to defend herself. Seeing nothing on the ground, she snapped an icicle from the sauna roof and held it like a four-foot lance. It was slippery, and as she grappled to point it at him, the surprising weight made her stumble and topple on her back.

"I warned you." Theroux tightened his grip on the hammer and raised it high.

"Judd!"

Hearing Roslyn cry out, Judd yanked the rope. It jarred Theroux's grip. He faltered, lost his footing and slammed his shoulder into the sauna wall, dropping the hammer.

Roslyn didn't hesitate. She stood up and speared the icicle into the man's shoulder. It barely pierced his thick overcoat, but the impact staggered him to the ground. When she tried to drive it deeper, the icicle broke off, leaving its tip embedded.

Someone was coming from the barn, hollering. Before Roslyn could scream "Arnie!," Theroux stood, let go the rope, and lunged at her, his teeth bared as if to bite off her face. She swung the icicle wildly, its jagged end slicing a gash across the man's brow.

"Christ!" Theroux crumpled to knees. His hands clutched his face as blood flooded his eyes.

Jurgens appeared.

"I couldn't find anything, master. Hey, you okay?"

The pilot turned to Roslyn. Her eyes on fire.

"You hurt him," he growled.

"He tried to kill me." She aimed the bloody end of the icicle at the pilot.

"Help me, goddammit!" Theroux hailed.

Jurgens lifted Theroux by the waist and hustled him to the plane.

Judd tried to stand, foundered, and sunk back against the sauna wall. Roslyn started to untie the rope from his wrists. He shook her off.

"Arnie," he exhaled. "In the barn. Hurry."

She found Arnie crumpled on the floor. His head in a pool of blood.

"No-no, don't be, don't be ..." Roslyn bent over him, checked for pulse. Feeling nothing, she took his hand in hers and tottered back and forth.

As he boarded the plane, Theroux glanced back. Although smoldering with defeat, he felt a smirk of satisfaction.

I may not be leaving with what I came for. And that's okay. At least I snuffed out another rising messiah.

The propeller whirled. As the plane lifted off the lake, its tires tore the corrugated metal roof off a fishing hut.

Judd watched with blank eyes. His light was gone. The once vivid world had shut its doors. He felt stranded, cramped in a concrete body. He heard Roslyn crying and shuddered as the chill air sunk in.

# 76
# It's Melting

Barberi sat in Kira's rental car, engine idling, the defroster dialed high.

Kira had ceased fuming. Something about this jovial fat man in the passenger seat comforted her. As she tilted the mirror and dabbed makeup to her scraped chin, he told her his service to the Roman Catholic Church was to root out frauds.

"I've become adept at vetting people who claim to be masters of the universe, self-ordained prophets, or divine healers. But my main mission is to refute all neuropathways relating to God."

The Godhead Spot. So that's why he took a tour of our lab. To get ahead of it, Kira thought.

"Well, I don't believe in God," she said.

"That's fine. God doesn't require belief to exist."

A police car sped past. They were so enrapt in conversation they didn't notice.

Kira realized they were at odds. The Cardinal stuck around Marigold to bask in Judd's sunlight. She flew in to capitalize on the man. Stick his head under a microscope and replicate it.

"I mean to say, if there is a God, he, she, it is beyond our comprehension."

"That's fair," Barberi said. But he believed once Kira saw Judd, she'd wake from the spell of her misguided purpose.

"So you go around denouncing ..." she went on.

"Saintly people do exist, thank the Lord. But there are degrees. You have your everyday prayerful, your reverent and virtuous, and the rare ones, the pure, pure vessels. All beautiful people, truly. However, in my many encounters I never met a heavenly sentient being until now."

"Judd Russell?"

"Yes."

"But he's ... I mean, they fiddled with his brain," Kira said. "So he's no pure-pure vessel."

"Does it matter?" Barberi gently curved his fingers around Kira's forearm. "My dear, consider the transfiguration on Mount Tabor. Jesus changed into a dazzling raiment of light. What caused that? The spirit of the place? The song of a wren or warbler? Something touched him there. Now, take Judd. He was touched and *ecce homo!* Behold the man!"

Kira took it in. For someone who exposes impostors to feel such adoration was remarkable.

"A tower he is. I sat with him," Barberi said. "I heard the vibrato of his speech. I bathed in the rays of his being. There is no need to question anymore. No need to pursue the incomprehensible. He is here of all places."

"Yeah, the frozen tundra."

"It's not so bad once you're outfitted." Barberi lifted a boot to show her the traction cleats attached to the soles.

"Do you know where he is?" she asked.

Barberi pointed at the windshield. Broken eggshells slid down.

"Look, it's melting."

Kira offered her credit card. Barberi stepped out and scraped the mush off the glass. She turned on the wiper fluid and then the wipers.

Through the clear windshield she saw a glint in Barberi's eyes and heard him say, "Shall we go find this heavenly being?"

The streaks Barberi saw were not on the windshield. They were tears and black eyeliner raining down Kira's cheeks.

"Yes, let's." She nodded. "Let's go."

# 77

# Candles in Canning Jars

Sheriff Buck leaned against his police cruiser, quaking with anger and grief. "Ten! If only I got here ten minutes sooner."

Even Marsha could no longer be her unflappable self. As she watched Arnie's sheet-covered body carried to an ambulance, she wiped at tears Flannery had never seen her mother shed.

The barn was yellow-taped. Inside Arnie's kitchen, Roslyn sat with Judd while one of the sheriff's officers recorded their stories. Shrunken and gray, Judd shivered in an emergency foil blanket. Roslyn stammered and sobbed, her eyes rubbed red. The man who took her under his wing, the man who taught her self-reliance, was dead.

Within minutes, news of Arnie's death swept through Marigold. People went to neighboring houses so they wouldn't suffer the loss alone.

After the police finished questioning, Buck took Marsha aside.

"Listen, I'm thinking, even though his light's gone, we stick to the plan. Get them out of town for a spell. When word comes out Judd's the reason for Arnie's murder, there's no telling what folks 'll do. Whatcha think?"

"I can't think. I want you to find that man, The The, and kill him."

"How about I do that tomorrow, Marsha? It's getting dark. Let's put Roslyn and Judd on the road. There's no time to waste. The gawkers are coming."

Back inside, Buck handed Roslyn the key to his cabin.

"Now?" Roslyn said. "But he's …" she gestured to the stool where Judd sat hunched over, glassy-eyed, drained of color.

Buck opened his wallet. "You got the map I gave ya?"

"In his car," Roslyn said.

'Here, gas money and some. Now you two need to go before the road jams up with you know who."

Marsha nudged her despondent daughter.

"Come on sweetie, let's see Roslyn and Judd on their way."

"Noooo," Flannery refused.

"We'll be back, Flan." Roslyn gave her a wet-eyed hug. "I promise."

They went outside into the night. Roslyn buckled Judd in the passenger seat of his FJ Cruiser. Marsha held Roslyn a long time before letting her climb behind the wheel.

Seeing the headlights of approaching cars, Buck shouted, "Go on now!"

Roslyn steered the SUV past the sauna and out across the frozen lake. Ice fisherman had placed candles in canning jars beside their shacks. The candles turned the lake into a twinkling field of stars.

# 78

# Walk the Razor

Three black vehicles sat outside Theroux's remote adobe villa in New Mexico, their government plates caked with dust. An agent wearing a blue FBI jacket talked to the caretaker working a broom on the veranda.

Inside, Special Agent Daisy Franks rifled through drawers in Theroux's study. Finding nothing, she stepped into the hall where another federal agent approached.

"Show you something." He beckoned with a finger. She followed him down a terra-cotta tiled hallway. "Except for the caretaker's bedroom, all the rooms are cleaned out. But check this one." He opened a solid steel door and they entered a windowless space empty of furnishings except for a double sink attached to a wall. "Look at all the plug-ins. Eight in the floor and some in the ceiling." He opened up an electrical panel. "And get a load of this breaker box. It's independent of the house. I'm telling you, this setup requires a city of juice, and we aren't talkin' home theater."

"No, we're talking home laboratory." Franks shrugged. "And not for cookin' meth."

She went out to the veranda and asked the other agent, "Anything from the caretaker?"

"Nothing," the agent tapped his temple. "He's real dim upstairs. Says the master was here. Now he's not."

"No shit."

Franks glared at the lean caretaker, fifty maybe, dirty blonde hair and beard slivered with white.

"So all we've got so far is the pilot's canceled phone number," she said.

"That's right. He's smoke."

Franks hiked up the path to the sweat lodge and stepped inside. No one there. The stones cold to the touch.

She flung the leather flap closed and berated herself. Why didn't I trust my instincts the last time I was here. We could have sealed the place, brought him in for questioning. Probably prevented a murder.

She scanned the desert landscape with binoculars, looking for movement among the arroyos and red rock mesas.

"I won't stop, Mister Theroux. You hear me? No place too hidden, no distance too far. If I have to walk the razor I will catch your bony ass."

Franks ambled back down the hill to the adobe house.

"I'm calling in a chopper," she told the agent.

The man followed Franks to her car. "One thing … "

"What's that?"

"I showed the caretaker photos of the missing. I asked if he'd seen any of them here. He locked in on one, like he recognized the guy."

"Who's that?"

The agent fingered through a plastic folder and pulled out a photograph of Chester Jolley.

"This one. I held it to his face and said, 'You've seen this guy here?' He shook his head. 'Not here,' he said. And I swear his eyes welled up."

Franks squinted at the young man's face in the photo.

"That's the bomber guy," she said.

"Yeah, most wanted. Happened to be with the others in the sleeve."

Franks stared at the old man sweeping the ceramic tiles.

"Did you get the caretaker's name?"

"Foster."

# 79

# Arnie's Ashes

An inkling of spring in the air. Forty degrees. A February teaser. It would be another eight weeks before the snow pack retreated from the base of trees, and the smell of the earth filled the air with a flourish of green leaves. Still, the minute-by-minute gain in sunlight each day brought the uplift of winter's impending departure.

With an orange sun squatting on the western horizon, a flock of mourners gathered on Arnie's dock to toss his ashes on the frozen lake. His friends and well- wishers agreed not to wait for April, but to let his ashes melt into the water with the timing of the thaw.

Marsha kept her speech short, her throat raw. "A friend to many. My hero to the end. And as for you on the other side, you're lucky to have him."

After a brief silence, Lester Moore bellowed his "Ode to Arnie."

"In halting heels the fearful refuse to resign these armature bones to the Earth's ready clay as Eternity beckons our spirit to slough off the split depictions of hell's rabid agonies and heaven's polished pavilions and craft a raft out of ineffable vision to ply the curvaceous straits of Mystery's formless enormous."

Feeling that Lester would ramble on without end, Flannery, with a cue from Marsha, started singing from the musical, *Cats*.

"Memory ... all alone in the moonlight ... I can smile at the old days ... I was beautiful then. I remember the time I knew what happiness was ... let the memory live again."

Buoyed by her singing, Lester kept going.

"Arnie, be not charmed by jolly good fellow songs or pause for grieving sirens but set sail to another shore under scattered stars unseen before and stretch the cartography of Death's dominion to a fine and farther hereafter."

The clash of Flannery's singing and Lester's oration didn't last. Soon their voices coalesced into a crazy duet, tickling the hearts and watering everyone's eyes.

As people stepped to the edge of the dock to cast handfuls of Arnie's ashes, a dog limped in among their legs. Fetch went straight to Marsha and nuzzled her shin with his snout. Others ignored him.

Henna Pino tramped up to Marsha. "This is all because of you! You and your two abominations!" She hurled a handful of Arnie's ashes at her face.

Although assaulted, Marsha kept her composure.

Buck escorted Henna away.

Some of the ashes landed on the dock and slipped between a gap in the boards. Fetch pawed at the spot. Flannery went to find out why the dog was barking. She caught sight of a blurry swatch of yellow under the dock where the ice appeared thin.

"Mom, what's that?"

Marsha made out the corners of three large airtight YETI cases and a yellow waterproof canoe bag.

After the others trudged off, Marsha and Flannery lingered for a closer look. It had to be the boys' instruments, their research, the gemstones.

So that's it, Marsha thought. Arnie must have moved them under the ice where Mantz and his unit would never look.

"What are you going to do, Mom?"

Marsha thought about the double-edged fate of discovery. How one person might share its benefits, while another use it for harm.

"What I'm going to do and what I wish to do are different. Oakley wants to destroy them."

"How about we leave them for now?"

"Let's do that. He'll be out of the hospital in a few days. He may have changed his mind."

"And maybe Chester will come back," Flannery added.

Marsha and Flannery joined the others for a reception in the café. They butted tables together, set out platters with bread rolls, slices of turkey and cheddar cheese, mixed fruit bowls, and pots of strong coffee.

Nobody knew if the café would ever re-open without Arnie and Roslyn. With its front window still sheeted over with plywood, it felt like a tomb.

While eating, people shared memories of Arnie. Marsha stood in the kitchen looking out the pass-through at the slumped shoulders and wadded handkerchiefs. She wanted to tuck her body into a fetal ball.

After everyone left, Marsha sat in a booth with Buck. He hoped to persuade her to take up residence at Arnie's place. Instead, he talked about how grateful he was things had settled. No violent eruptions or meltdowns, no happy attacks or "epi-fanies," as he pronounced it.

"Maybe there's something about Judd being a beacon after all. Arnie sure believed it."

He's right, Marsha thought. Things had calmed since Judd's light went out. No more drama. At the same time, Ollie Olson no longer found outrageous, day-brightener newspaper stories to read. She remembered Roslyn saying Judd's illumination created an effect, "like defrosting a freezer. If not prepared for it, your meat goes bad."

Defrost Effect or not," Marsha said, "doesn't change the sad fact how we've all been living in a spiritual ice age."

"People like to blame it all on your sons," Buck said, "but that's not fair. We make our choices."

Marsha didn't respond. She glanced at Flannery, asleep in the next booth. White ear buds dangled around the girl's neck, a Mozart harpsichord concerto faintly audible.

"Chester 'll show up," Buck said. "Wait and see." He coughed, pulled a paper napkin from a dispenser and wiped his mouth. "And nobody can deny their scientific breakthrough, that's for damn sure."

Buck took a slurp of coffee. Still no response from Marsha.

"You know Lars, he wants to put up a sign, 'Welcome to Marigold, Home of the Sun Man.'"

"The Sun Man …" Marsha repeated softly to herself, seemingly adrift.

"Out-of-towner's will line up to take selfies in front of it," Buck added.

"Sun Man … ah!" she gasped, recalling something Judd had said: '*It appears the more light I let out the more it attracts.*' Oh my God!" Marsha's hands sprung off the table, tipping over the napkin dispenser, her blue eyes wide, crystalized with revelation. "That wasn't the end."

"The end of what?" Buck said.

"The magnitude."

"Huh?"

"Stardom."

# 80

# Who Will Judd Be Now?

The Boundary Waters is a vast wilderness in northern Minnesota that borders Canada. Roslyn envisioned herself one day canoeing its myriad glacial lakes, but not in winter, and not this way, holed up in a rustic cabin for unknown duration. The old structure had rough-sawn siding and paint-chipped sills. Looking out its wavy glass windows was like wearing bifocals.

She and Judd had been there four days. Judd in a listless haze, homesick for his home soul. And she a wreck of constant sobs, grief-stricken over Arnie's death.

Who will Judd be now? Roslyn wondered. Would he regress to the self-centered actor, or someone else? Although he seemed to be sleepwalking the first couple days, they did manage to share in chores—chop wood, keep the candles and oil lamps lit, the wood stove hot.

Judd actually seemed better that fifth morning as she left for supplies in town. He was amiable, gave her a grateful hug and a warm kiss on the cheek at the door. Roslyn even thought she saw a slight gleam around his head, but it must have been her wishful imagination.

Taking Buck's advice, she hid Judd's car in a grove of conifers on the far side of the lake. She skied across to the vehicle. It felt good to get out, to take a drive, charge her phone. Marsha said she'd call when the time was right for them to come back. No word as yet.

The town of Ely was a twenty-minute drive from Buck's cabin through thick forest and snow-covered lakes. Miles of screen-saver beauty. Being Roslyn's first time going to town, she noted landmarks along the way.

Find the store. Act pleasant. Don't linger. Buy the basics—bread, eggs, bacon, and cheese, along with some oranges.

The landmarks came in handy on her return. She veered off road right after the topped tree snag and parked the car the same place as before. She kicked up snow to cover the tire tracks. After stuffing the supplies in her backpack, she tromped to the shore and clipped on skis. In the distance, the cabin stood barely visible under the shadow of the forest canopy. A wisp of smoke curled out the chimney.

Fat snowflakes filled the air as she skied across the lake. They reminded her of the pluffy snow the day she and Judd skied the lake behind Arnie's farm. Judd was catching the flakes out of the air and, watching them melt in his hand, said, "What a wonder to have these crystalline designs telling us without words how exquisite life is."

That was when he was becoming a beacon to the world.

Seemed like a long time ago, if it ever really happened. Yet half way across the lake, something shiny caught Roslyn's eye. A dot of light. She squinted. Was it the lamp? The flashlight?

As she skied closer, the brightness increased.

Theroux didn't suck out Judd's Crown of Lights after all! The twelve nodes in his brain only retreated, closing up like sea anemones for protection against attack.

Roslyn's heart leaped. It wasn't the oil lamp or the flashlight. It was Judd walking toward her, his body a radiant bloom so intense it turned the veil of falling snowflakes into an aisle of sequins, shimmering gold.

"Ah-lama!" She beamed.

# Acknowledgements

Heartfelt thanks to Veronica Smith for her unwavering support and feedback throughout the book's creation. Thanks to Jeffrey Smith for his story instincts, guiding wisdom, humor, and the cleaver he wields at every hint of over-writing. I'm also grateful for the brilliant editing and input of Cheryl Isaac—a gift to writers. Thanks to the poets, playwrights, philosophers, and lyricists who I quoted. May readers seek out their work. And thanks to the artist, René Magritte, whose painting inspired the cover of the book.

# About the Author

This is M. St. Croix's third book of fiction. His storytelling ideas come from life experiences as a painter, sculptor, carpenter, actor, playwright, educational TV producer, Earth energy practitioner and world traveler.

www.mstcroix.com